To Do   Noreen

The Vigilante

"Justice Will Be Served"

Enjoy

Ferrier

Ferrier Richardson & Alex Meikle

Happy Reading
Alex Meikle

On a Plate

First published in Great Britain by On A Plate.
This edition was published by On A Plate, Glasgow, Scotland. 2025.

All rights reserved. No part of this publication may be reproduced, stored in a retrieval system, or transmitted in any form or by any means, without the prior permission in writing of the publisher, nor be otherwise circulated in any form of binding or cover other than that in which it is published and without a similar condition including this condition being imposed on the subsequent purchaser.

A CIP catalogue record for this book is available from the British Library.

Cover illustration by Mark Reihill.
Design and typesetting by River Runs Deep, Glasgow.
Printed by Think Solutions, Glasgow.

ISBN 9781068206092

The right of Ferrier Richardson and Alex Meikle to be identified as authors of this work has been asserted in accordance with the Copyright, Designs and Patents Act 1988.

Ferrier Richardson is one of Scotland's finest and best-known Chefs. He has travelled the world extensively representing Scotland for multi-national companies and government departments.

Earlier in his career he was responsible for re-establishing the culinary reputation of both the Rogano and Buttery restaurants alongside the legendary Ken McCulloch. Ferrier was the opening Executive Chef for Glasgow's first Five-star hotel and has owned and operated some of Scotland's finest award-winning restaurants.

Over and above this he still works privately on a worldwide basis, and has a client list that includes Royalty, Presidents, A list celebrities, world class sports stars and ultra-high net worth individuals.

He is the editor and owner of The On A Plate Book series, having just released Glasgow, Edinburgh and Northern Ireland with London and Manchester in the pipeline.

All these books are available from Waterstones in store and online.

Alex Meikle is a thriller writer and was formerly CEO of several third sector social care organisations in Glasgow. He also spent many years working in the addiction services in the city and has just recently retired.

Alex's main interest is writing, and he published his first novel, Deception Road, which is a political thriller set in Glasgow, in 2017. This is the first of four thrillers centred on the career of MI5 officer, Eddie Macintyre. He is also the co-author of Dining Tales celebrating Glasgow's hospitality scene and is a major contributor to the On A Plate series.

"And once the storm is over, you won't remember how you made it through, how you managed to survive. You won't even be sure if the storm is really over. But one thing is certain: when you come out of the storm you won't be the same person who walked in. That's what the storm is all about.

**Haruki Murakami,
Kafka on the Shore, 2005**

PROLOGUE: A DAY IN PRISON

It was the same dream. Always the same dream. Sarah, looking stunning in a dark bikini, lying beside him on the pristine beach, surrounded by verdant tropical forests and the occasional breaker from the azure sea crashing into the beach. Charlie Carty was in heaven. This was the good life all right, a million miles from Glasgow.

It was his day off and in a minute he and Sarah would walk the short distance to the President's compound where his deputy would serve them a sumptuous meal washed down by a bottle of vintage red direct from a French vineyard. He took Sarah's warm hand just about to get up when it all came crashing down, as it always did.

He was brusquely awakened from his tropical idyll by the cell door barging open and McInnes, one of the prison staff, virtually shouting at him:

'All right Charlie. Still Alive?'

He grunted back at him, 'aye.' McInnes moved away, locked the cell, and virtually shouted at the guy in the next cell. The screw wasn't threatening; virtually shouting was McInnes's default mode.

Charlie looked at the display clock beside him, the LED lights blinking 7.05am. He looked around at four grey walls, one of which was adorned with pictures of his family in his chef's whites with various celebrities at one of his restaurants, but they couldn't compensate for the bleakness of his cell. Why did he always have to have that same effen dream of his heyday which just cruelly mocked the reality of where he was now?

Yawning and stretching, he washed himself as best he could at the basin next to the toilet seat, then put on fresh underwear and his prison clothes of a red polo shirt and jeans, switched on breakfast TV to Channel Four's repeats of Fraser which he loved and waited to be called for breakfast.

He could hear his cell getting unlocked again which meant all the numbers throughout the prison had tallied. His flat or landing was first for breakfast today, so he was only a couple of minutes into watching the programme when there was a rap on the door and the shrill cry of 'breakfast'. He opened his door, which McInnes had left unlocked, walked onto the landing and waited until the guys in the cells to the left of him went by and followed them along the landing, down the stairs to the ground floor. In the evenings this was the recreation area, where guys could play cards, pool or watch a movie.

Now, the centre of attention was a large desk in the middle of the Hall which Charlie and the rest of the prisoners on his landing approached from a clockwise direction. At the desk a trusty, called a Fat Passman handed each inmate a breakfast pack of a carton of milk, a small box of cereal, yoghurt and a bread roll. Once Charlie took his pack, he walked back with the others to the stairwell, ascended back up to his landing on the second floor and went to his cell to have his breakfast, Fraser still on the TV.

To an outside observer the whole breakfast procedure seemed brisk, almost hurried. But to the guys and the staff it was performed on autopilot. There were 300 prisoners in this

Hall alone and fifteen staff to supervise and monitor them. There was a lot to do in a short period of time and every man knew his role and slotted into it.

Back in his cell Charlie ate his breakfast quickly. The prison was fully awake now and filled with the energy of 300 confined men and their fifteen keepers. Once he'd finished his breakfast, he switched off the TV and stood in the doorway. After a few minutes an officer came up to him.

'Staff dining hall today, Charlie?'

'Yep,' he agreed.

He followed behind the officer, back down the stairwell. At the bottom he joined a queue of men who were waiting to go through a metal detector; other men started to queue behind him. The line moved rapidly and after he went through the detector, he was patted down by an officer to ensure the machine hadn't missed anything.

Groups of men started assembling at the entrance to the Hall under the careful eye of officers. Charlie, who was 56 and of medium height, stood beside a group of mixed, mostly younger guys though there were some about the same age as him or older. He worked out regularly in the prison gym, keeping his figure in trim and warding off middle-age spread. The big Hall door opened, and the men started exiting, some turning left, others, including Charlie and his group to the right, with the brisk commands of officers in their ears.

It was February and the cool air hit Charlie as he marched along the route to the staff dining hall. The sky was grey and leaden, typical Glasgow weather, with the odd shaft of sunlight as he made his way between the grim, dank Victorian Halls with their dark, hulking facades. This was Barlinnie Prison in Glasgow a truly forbidding place, no matter how long you were stuck here, Charlie reflected.

By the time he reached the cookhouse, most of the other men, besides his group, had dispersed to various workplaces or the gym. All the men who'd left the Hall, about eighty in all, were passmen or trusties who were allowed to work at various activities during the day. Most of the group around Charlie went into the cookhouse, but he and three other younger men, walked further along, with one officer accompanying them, to a newer wing of the building where the staff dining hall was located.

Charlie and the three others walked into the small kitchen area where Aiden McManus, the staff cook, a rotund man of medium height, with a beery fleshy face, and a large drooping moustache greeted them.

'Ok boys,' he said, 'a busy day in front of us, about fifty covers.' He looked at Charlie. 'You up for it, Mr. Carty?'

Charlie flashed a broad grin. 'Sure am, Chef'.

'All right, let's go for it.'

Charlie lit up as he appraised the kitchen. This was his element. Today, there was an all-day health and safety training session for some staff, including senior staff, the Governor among them and Charlie was getting the opportunity to do what he loved best: cooking good food and serving it.

In the nearly four years, Charlie had served in B Hall, the hall for convicted prisoners, he had spent most of it working either in the cookhouse, or here in the kitchen of the staff dining hall. The cookhouse was fine but offered little opportunity for a chef of Charlie's skills and talents to show what he could do. The food in Barlinnie was batch processed, meant to feed 1,500 men daily. Charlie had been able to add some flavour to the soups and other foods and using his beady restaurateur's eye, identified some efficiencies in the way the food was being distributed which earned him brownie points with the assistant governors.

But the staff dining room was where he could show off his talents. Aiden McManus couldn't believe his luck when he heard renowned international chef and local Glasgow boy, Charlie Carty, was coming to B Hall. The prison grapevine always knew in advance who was coming into Barlinnie for a considerable stretch and McManus had lobbied hard with the powers that be to get Carty into the cookhouse and then the staff dining room.

And he hadn't let him down. In the kitchen Charlie could do magic with what were basic ingredients, considerably enhancing the quality of the food to the delight of the staff, including the all-important figure of the Governor. McManus got on well with Charlie and let him have the run of the place. Why not? McManus wanted an easy life. Charlie was a superb manager and effectively mentored the other trustees, particularly the younger chaps who he imparted some good culinary skills to, that would help them considerably on their release. It was a well-run kitchen serving good food to satisfied customers. For McManus what was there not to like.

Today, they were making lasagne and as Charlie got to work instructing the others what to do, occasionally deferring to McManus by saying, 'Is that right boss?' Or 'is that what you want gaffer?' a casual observer would quicky recognise that Charlie Carty was more than Aiden McManus's right-hand man: he effectively ran the kitchen.

It'd been a good day, Charlie reflected as he potted a coloured ball on his third game of pool which set him up to win the game, his third of the evening. He was on a roll today, he thought, as he wasn't always as good as this and there was plenty of pool sharks in the Hall. His opponent gracefully conceded the game just as an officer declared:

'Ten minutes to go.'

He looked at a wall clock and couldn't believe it was twenty past nine already. The day had flown by. All around him men stopped what they were doing and started making their way to their landings. Nine thirty was when all prisoners had to be in their cells for the night, numbers counted, and doors locked.

Charlie climbed the stairs to his cell exchanging good natured banter with guys on the way up to his landing. Once in his cell, he switched on his TV to a drama on BBC1 and sat on his bed waiting for the ten o' clock news; he always liked to keep himself updated on what was happening in the world outside.

He lay back on his bunk bed, the sounds of the TV drama and cell doors clanging shut in the background as the day's events rolled past in his mind. Dinner was a great success; many of the staff on the training event, including the Governor, had complimented him and the official head chef, Aiden, on the food. That was good because, otherwise, Aiden's nose would have been out of joint, and while he wasn't a bad boss, it didn't do to make him resentful or jealous; that could have serious repercussions for Charlie. But he knew, and probably Aden knew as well, that the plaudits were really aimed at Charlie.

The Governor "asked" to see him later that afternoon. So, after supervising the staff in cleaning up the kitchen, including along with Aiden, ensuring the number of knives tallied and were placed back in a box attached to the kitchen wall known as a shadow board (cookhouse and dining hall trusties were the only prisoners allowed to handle knives), Charlie was escorted to the Governor's office.

He was slightly apprehensive as he made his way there, after all he was sure he hadn't done anything wrong; he'd kept his head down, played by the rules, made himself useful and popular to the staff and fellow prisoners. Above all, he hadn't annoyed anyone, especially the top boys. But there was always a worry he'd inadvertently noised somebody up or broken some official or unofficial prison rule.

He needn't have worried. After a few minutes waiting outside, he was led into the Governor's office, the escorting officer beside him as he stood in front of the Governor, a stout but robust bald man in his fifties seated behind his neat desk. He had a good reputation for fairness and speaking frankly. After referring to a file on his desk he looked straight at Charlie and said:

'As you're no doubt very aware, you're approaching the end of your fourth year here at Barlinnie. You would normally have been transferred to a long stay prison some time ago but,' he put his hands up, palms forward, 'there's not a spare place anywhere in the estate. So, I'm giving you the heads-up, Carty, it's been decided to keep you here, but for your final year you'll be transferred to Letham Hall, probably about May.

'Continue doing what you're doing until then. We're very pleased with your progress and the rest of your time here will pass by. Is there anything you want to say?'

A wave of relief broke over Charlie. Prisoners in Letham Hall, which housed long-term prisoners coming to the end of their sentence, were able to leave the prison most days to work as part of the process of becoming attuned to life outside prison. He would have the chance once again to work in a real kitchen and serve real diners. Though it was always good practice in prison not to show your feelings, especially in front of staff, Charlie couldn't help a wide smile alighting upon his face.

'Thank you, sir, thank you very much.'

'You'll get official notice in due course. Unofficially, and I never said this Carty, but I'm glad you're still with us for a while longer. I'll say it again that lasagne at lunch was excellent. You can give the best Italian places in this town a fair run for their money. Ok, dismissed.'

'Sir,' he turned round with the escort, left the Governor's office and spent the rest of the afternoon in the cookhouse, with a renewed vigour, helping to get the dinners out and assisting with loading the "chuck" or dinner waggons that took the evening meals to the halls. As with all the cookhouse trusties, he was later getting back to his hall than other working prisoners, eating his own dinner in the cookhouse and attending to the numerous after dinner chores.

Back in his cell, he was totally awake as he closed his eyes on the bunk, full of energy from the exercise and gym session he'd managed to get after preparing the dinners, listening to the hall settling down for the night.

He could see his release beckoning. A year at Letham Hall, with the prospect of working in a kitchen every day outside Barlinnie. Then, if all went well, transfer to a TFF for six months and after that, liberation. TFF was a Training for Freedom prison where he would be allowed out at weekends to stay with his family.

He'd been sentenced to seven-and-a-half years. If he hadn't been a first offender and pleaded guilty, it would have been a lot longer. He'd now spent four years in Barlinnie, a lot longer than normal for what was meant to be a short-to-medium term prison. But, as the Governor had pointed out, the prison "estate" (their peculiar bureaucratic way of speaking about jails as if they were ordinary houses or country homes) was overcrowded, and he'd avoided transfer to a long-term prison.

That suited him. He'd acclimatised to Barlinnie where he'd spent nearly four months on remand in C Hall before his trial, most of it sharing a cell with a young addict called Mick in his mid-twenties who'd been jailed after trying to rob his local newsagents wearing a pair of his girlfriend's sheer tights making him instantly recognizable to the owner behind the counter.

At first, bristling at the thought of sharing with a "junkie", he'd got to know Mick well and began to understand the traumatic background that had led him to becoming a heroin addict and the sheer desperation that ultimately led him to embark on his pathetic attempt at a robbery.

Charlie took Mick under his wing. The lad was semi-literate and had never worked. Quite early in his remand, Charlie was given a trusty's role, helping with the laundry (as a remand prisoner, he wouldn't be allowed to work in the prison). This wasn't beneath him, because even as a head chef, then a restaurateur, he'd mucked in and performed menial tasks. In the long evenings, after he'd finished his laundry roles, Charlie helped Mick with his reading and writing and was delighted that Mick stayed "clean" inside despite the lure of drugs being available around him.

After his trial, Mick spent eighteen months in B Hall where Charlie was re-acquainted with him (though they didn't share a cell again) and was able to get him a trusty position in the cookhouse. Shortly before Mick's release, using his contacts, Charlie persuaded a fellow restaurant owner to give Mick a job as a KP (kitchen porter), the lowest rung on the kitchen hierarchy

They'd kept in contact (Mick was one of his regular visitors) and the good news was that Mick had been promoted to a chef's assistant, was working hard and had remained clean in the community. Charlie was delighted. At least one good thing had come out of his time in jail.

Being in prison in Glasgow also meant he had regular visits from his two sons Although he still felt ashamed to be seeing them in prison, he looked forward to their visits immensely.

His only regret was that Sarah, his estranged wife, had only visited him twice. She'd left him after he owned up to the "act". It'd been a dreadful time. So much had happened. Then the "act" and the subsequent arrest, publicity, trial and sentence were too much for her. His heart had leaped when he saw her during the visits, but there was a barrier there, the warmth and love had gone, though he was still madly in love with her. Could he ever get her back? Well, cooped up here he certainly couldn't. Now with the tangible prospect of release in Eighteen months, after serving a total of five-and-a-half years with two years deducted for good behaviour, he was determined to try everything he could to salvage their relationship.

'Carty!'

He was abruptly brought out of his reverie by the officer on the landing outside his door checking the numbers for the evening roll call.

'Yes, here,' he shouted out. The officer locked his cell door for the night and moved on.

He looked at one of the family pictures on the wall opposite. There was Calum and Caleb, his two sons. The picture had been taken five years ago before the "act" at one of his restaurants in the city. Calum, already looking his father's double.

At the centre of the picture in the empty restaurant was Charlie in his whites with Sarah beside him, looking gorgeous as ever. He had to avert his eyes from the picture. Oh, how much he wanted to get all of that back. And now, the real prospect of that was on the radar.

Yes, Barlinnie, hadn't been too bad compared to what it could have been. He'd come through the madness of remand and C Hall. Right from the get-go in B Hall, he'd had his own cell, where most prisoners had to share. He'd not been bullied or subjected to any threats or harm which was the lot of quite a few prisoners, especially the more vulnerable.

And he'd ended up with a job in the prison that he loved doing and had done all his life.

But prison was still prison, confined in a grim Victorian hulk of a prison, cooped up with 300 guys around you, with all the smells and sounds that brings. Sure, he didn't have to "slop out", doing his business in a chamber pot which he and the other guys had to empty or 'slop out" into a huge vat every morning and which had been common practice in Scottish prisons until a few years earlier when it had been banned. But his every movement was monitored and there was the almost total absence of privacy, except for these few hours at night and even then, he could be watched through the peephole by staff at any instant, including when he was on the toilet!

What about the "act"? Did Charlie experience any feelings of remorse or regret for the severe act of violence he'd perpetrated on his victim which had earned him a seven-and-a-half-year stretch? He'd explored long and hard into the very depth of his soul on that and...No, no regrets. What that "animal" had done had a catastrophic impact on his family, not least the death of his younger brother which had brought on the passing of his heart-broken mother. Not forgetting, the impact on himself and the strains it'd put on his marriage and his beloved Sarah.

Charlie Carty was resolute, as he had been from the beginning of his sentence. He'd serve his time; the end was in sight, and he would go back outside to pick up the pieces of his life. His attention was diverted by the news starting. He sat up to watch the bulletin. There was no longer "lights out" at Scottish prisons and he could sit up all night watching TV or reading if he wished, as many did in the hall and walked about like zombies during the day. But he was determined to read for a while after the news and then lights out and a good night's sleep. He just hoped that nobody took a "flaky" during the night screaming and shouting in his own hall or the neighbouring ones, requiring the intervention of the medics and staff back up and disturbing his rest.

Above all, he didn't want a recurrence of that bloody dream of Sarah in that bikini on the beach in the tropical paradise. It reminded him too much of what he couldn't have and that was worse than any inmate screaming like a banshee.

ONE

Charlie Carty's path from a humble background to becoming a renowned international chef followed by imprisonment in one of Scotland's most notorious prisons, began with some luck and his ability to capitalise on it.

Born in the early 1960s, he was brought up in a respectable working-class household, the oldest of two brothers. They lived in a semi-detached, council house where Charlie shared a bedroom with his brother Raymond on a quiet street in an area called Hamiltonhill. Next to Hamiltonhill was Possil, an area later to become infamous for drugs and deprivation but for much of Charlie's formative years was a centre of industry dominated by a large foundry where Charlie's father worked in a semi-skilled job as a lathe operator.

His mother worked part-time as a clerkess in a city-centre law firm. Both parents were hard-working and looked after their children well. Charlie and his sibling had a comfortable upbringing. There was the usual domestic ups and downs but also love, affection and plenty of encouragement

Charlie went to a local secondary school, where in those days, a leather strap or belt was liberally dispensed for even minor misdemeanours, but overall, the school wasn't too bad. He kept his head down (as he was to do in Barlinnie), got on well with his teachers, avoided the usual assortment of psychos and bullies and acquired a solid bunch of schoolfriends.

He was good at his subjects but wasn't academically minded. He had no aspirations to stay on beyond 16 - the official leaving age – and certainly no intentions of going to university, which only a tiny amount of school leavers in Scotland went to at that time.

As his sixteenth birthday approached in the mid-1970s, Charlie wasn't sure what he wanted to do which worried his parents. Unemployment was rising steadily at that time; indeed, his father had been made redundant when the foundry closed, taking with it loads of smaller supply firms and plunging Possil into an employment desert. Fortunately, his father found work at a wire making firm in the east-end of the city, though on a lesser wage.

To his parent's despair, Charlie left school to sign on the dole. His father tried to encourage him to attend a local college, but he was determined not to go back to formal education. This led to a growing rift with his parents, particularly his dad. For a few months, Charlie drifted, sleeping late, idling through the day, signing on dutifully once a fortnight at the labour exchange for his meagre Giro and increasingly arguing with his exasperated father.

Then, one day, his cousin, Gerry, who worked as a waiter in a busy hotel in the city centre phoned his house, asking to speak to him. It was late afternoon on a Friday. His mother handed him the phone. Gerry told him there was a panic on in the hotel kitchen. There was a full house that night and one of the KPs – kitchen porters – had phoned in sick and no-one else was available. Could Charlie come in and do a shift? There was no experience required, and Gerry made it seem as if it was a piece of cake: washing dishes, moving plates, pots and pans and so on.

'It's easy money, Charlie,' Gerry declared. 'They'll pay you cash in hand at the end of the shift, and you'll no have to worry about the dole knowing.'

'I'm no sure. Gerry,' Charlie prevaricated.

'Listen,' Gerry insisted, 'I need to know, they're phoning other people, they might get somebody else.'

Charlie was still swithering, when he saw his father walk up the garden path. He always got home early on a Friday, though worked terribly long hours the rest of the week. Charlie dreaded the prospect of another protracted argument about his 'idleness' and 'not getting off his arse to find work!' He made the snap decision:

'All right, give me the address and I'll be there.'

Charlie had no previous experience of cooking or dining. Indeed, he'd hardly been in a restaurant except for a few family occasions at a Rio Stakis or Berni Inn where he'd ate gammon steak while the adults drank Liebfraumilch, and his parents thought they were "toffs" for a night.

In a country awash with game and incredible seafood, the diet of most working people in Scotland was basic. Mince and tatties, stews and fish and chips procured from a local chippy, were the staples washed down by copious amounts of tea or sugary drinks with dreadful dental consequences; both his parents had to have dentures fitted in their forties which was not unusual. Food was fuel. Delicacy, taste, texture, quality was not considered to be of importance.

On the bus the short distance into town, Charlie was growing increasingly alarmed at what he was getting himself into, especially when Gerry had told him the name of the restaurant. La Maison Rose was part of the huge Glasgow Central Hotel, a towering gothic edifice that adjoined Central Station, Glasgow's main railway terminal. Central Hotel had a prestigious history behind it and was one of the few hotels catering for an upmarket clientele in the city. But, despite the fact it was just one shift and as a KP, the lowest rank in the kitchen hierarchy, his parents were impressed. His mother's eyes had lit up.

'Oh my God, that's where all the posh folk go!' while his father nodded approvingly to his wife:

'At least it'll get him from under your feet, if only for a night.'

That was some small compensation, getting his father off his back for a day or two.

He walked up the short steps to the entrance of the hotel, opened the sturdy doors, entered and immediately felt intimidated. There was an aura of opulence about the reception area: wood panelled walls adorned with prints, a plush carpet, upholstered burgundy seats and sofas, where well-dressed, besuited men and women in expensive dresses were seated surrounded by classy looking cases and bags. This was posh all right.

He felt like a tramp in his denim jacket, white T-shirt, faded jeans. He was thankful his mother had made him change his white tattered sandals or gutties for a pair of black, shiny shoes and approached the desk where both reception staff, a man and a woman were dealing with guests signing in. He noticed how deferential, obsequious even, both staff were with the guests. Finally, after what seemed an eternity, his nerves taughtened, the affluent looking couple dealing with the man, left escorted by a porter about Charlie's age in a maroon uniform with a peaked cap who took their cases.

The reception guy, his head almost bowed, a humble, fixed smile on his face watched the couple depart to the lifts, then became aware of Charlie. His expression transformed instantly, and he looked at Charlie with disdain, almost a scowl, 'like I was a piece of dirt,' Charlie thought.

'Yes,' the guy almost barked at him. He was in his mid-to-early twenties, slightly taller than Charlie who was of medium height.

'I'm, eh, I'm here about the...the kitchen porter's job,' Charlie stuttered.

'Liz, know anything about this?' he asked the girl to his right who'd now also finished dealing with her guests.

'Aye,' she replied with a nice smile when she saw Charlie, in such contrast to the guy's coldness. 'One of the KP's phoned in sick.' She addressed Charlie directly. 'Go through the doors to the right there,' she pointed across the lobby, 'go up the corridor to you get to the kitchens, then ask for Adrian. All right?' She smiled even more warmly.

'Yes, thanks,' he felt slightly relaxed and walked across the lobby and through the doors marked "STAFF ONLY" in large red letters.

The opulence and adornment of the reception area was replaced by bare, grubby white walls and a tatty linoleum floor as he walked along the corridor, the smells of various foods assailing him as he approached two red doors, pushed them open and was met with the sight of the largest kitchen he'd ever seen. It appeared to be the size of most of the ground floor. Everywhere, men, all men, of various ages and sizes, all dressed in whites, some quite stained and darkened, were running hither and thither around an assortment of various large, well-used and darkened cookers, or clattering around with pots. The din was deafening; everyone seemed to be shouting at everyone else at the top of their voices.

Adding to the crescendo, every few seconds bells rang, and he heard the creaks of dumb waiters ascending or descending along one wall with kitchen staff running to place or retrieve dishes. He was startled to feel a hand on his shoulder and turned to see the friendly but flushed face of his cousin Gerry in a waiter's outfit of dark top jacket, buttoned at the waist, white shirt, dicky-bow tie and dark trousers, say to him:

'Glad you could make it. It's only past six and we're already nearly threequarters full. It's mental, the gaffers going spare, it's gonny be some night. Here, follow me.'

And that was his hurried welcome to the kitchen as Gerry led him to a set of cupboards against the far wall where he fetched a pair of white overalls. Charlie tried them on. They were a bit large for him.

'Don't worry about the size, you'll fit into them,' Gerry encouraged. 'Right, I'll take you to the boss.' He looked furtively around him, then lowered his voice, saying:

'He's God by the way. Do as he fucking tells you. Ok?' Charlie nodded in agreement.

They walked to the centre of the kitchen, where towering

over a stove with several pots bubbling stood a large, stout man, in his thirties, a mane of dark hair to his neck, large hands with gnarled fingers stirring simultaneously at several pots, shouting a barrage of brisk instructions to all around.

'Chef!' Gerry shouted at him. Charlie gathered that was the only way to get his attention.

'Whit?' The chef turned, revealing a full face, with dark, glinting eyes and an almost furious stare. Charlie cowered while Gerry said in a staccato voice:

'Chef, replacement KP. Charlie Carty.'

There was no greetings or introductions. The chef pointed a stubby, red forefinger at him.

'You ever worked in a kitchen before?' Charlie shook his head abjectly. The chef put his hands in the air, a dripping silver ladle in one.

'What the fuck am I supposed to do?' he shouted at no-one in particular before looking back at Charlie. 'Right, get your arse over there,' he gestured towards three large stainless-steel sinks against the far-right wall, 'and get wired in. The dishes are piling up already. If you're shite, I'll soon let you know. Now move it. And what the fuck are you standing there for like a useless prick?' he suddenly turned on Gerry. 'Get the fuck back upstairs', he ordered. Gerry gave him a "good luck" look before shouting "Chef" and hurrying away.

Charlie picked up the drill quickly, said 'Chef,' and walked rapidly to the sinks. There were two other young guys working at two of the sinks furiously scouring, rubbing and washing an endless array of pots, pans, plates, knives and forks. There was a huge pile beside the middle sink, and he took his place there saying, 'hello, how youse doing?' to the tall, lanky chap to his left and the small wiry guy to his right who both just quickly replied 'fine,' which he thought was a bit rude before he turned the tap on, ensured the water was hot and waited until the basin filled.

When it was filled, he placed a pile of plates in the water and started scrubbing with a cloth, attempting conversation with the two guys, but all he got was monosyllabic replies. He reckoned he was a third of the way washing the plates when he became aware of a figure behind him. Looking around he saw a swarthy, moustached man staring intently at him, before saying:

'Jesus Christ son, if you scrub at that rate, you'll last another hour if you're lucky. Come on,' he made an upward gesture with his hands, 'speed it up, before Ramsay clocks you!'

He really thought he'd been scrubbing at a fast pace. Now he speeded up, a plate every twenty seconds and realised why his companions were reluctant to talk, they didn't have time to.

It was relentless. Piles and piles of plates landed on the board beside him. Just when he'd got through most of one set, another pile was unceremoniously dumped beside him. He seemed to be the plate man tonight as his two companions received constant loads of pots and pans.

Within a couple of hours his feet were aching, his arms stiff and his hands reddening with all the soap, his fingers itching. All around, the noise, the clatter was cacophonous with bells and shouts constantly echoing around him, but the only sound he could clearly distinguish was the boss screaming commands at staff followed by a strident, deferential 'Chef' from whoever was being shouted at.

During the evening the chef came over their way twice. There was a perceptible stiffening in the guys next to him, the scrubbing stepped up even faster, as Ramsay walked slowly past the three sinks. Charlie was convinced he lingered longer over his sink and waited for a verbal fuselage to be directed at him. But he moved past him and away from the three KPs. All three breathed deeply in relief.

Just as Charlie was about to give up and walk out, the tall guy to his left muttered rapidly but audibly, 'it'll start to ease off soon.'

It was reassuring, motivating him to keep at it, and the pace did slow. A short time later the moustached man came to them and said:

'Take twenty minutes.' He asked Charlie directly, 'how are you?'

'Fine,' he meekly replied, hoping his body language wouldn't betray him.

'Ok, take your break.' He followed his companions to a side room with hard backed chairs and well-worn tables where exhausted kitchen staff slumped, stretched and yawned and spoke amongst themselves. Everyone seemed to be smoking, and the room was enveloped in a haze of tobacco smoke.

The two guys sat at a table where Charlie joined them. The tall guy lit a filtered cigarette from a pack of twenty, while the short one rolled his from a tin with a pouch of tobacco.

'I'm shattered.' Charlie loudly declared. The tall guy said:

'If you get through the first couple of hours, you'll last.'

'I doubt it,' Charlie shook his head.

'Fag,' he offered him a cigarette from his pack.'

'I don't smoke, but thanks.'

'Mark,' he offered his hand and gave Charlie a firm handshake.

'Ronnie,' the smaller guy said and gave him an equally firm grip.'

'Is it always like this?' Charlie asked.

'Aye, most nights,' Ronnie agreed, 'especially at the weekends.'

'What's the boss's name? The head chef?'

'Ramsay, Adrian Ramsay,' Mark replied, 'spelt C.U.N.T'

Charlie smiled wearily.

'Avoid him if you can,' Ronnie went on, 'don't attract his attention and you'll be fine. If you do, he'll make your life sheer hell.'

'Aye, I've picked that up,' Charlie said cautiously.

'Just on for the night?' Mark asked.

'Aye. My cousin Gerry works as a waiter here and told me they were looking for a KP.'

'We never see them,' Ronnie said, almost disdainfully, puffing on his cigarette. 'They're front of house.'

'Front of...what?' Charlie asked.

'All the waitering staff,' Mark took up, 'keep themselves in the restaurant upstairs,' he pointed upwards, 'that's called the front of house. We never see them because they don't usually need to come down here.'

'All the orders are sent down by tube to the kitchen,' Ronnie explained, 'and the meals are all sent up by the dumb waiters.

They've got their own staff room as well, so we never mix.'

Others in the room started drifting back to the kitchen. Ronnie looked at a cheap watch on his wrist and finished his cigarette.

'Better get back before we get our arses kicked.'

Charlie couldn't believe the break was over so soon and reluctantly followed them back.

The rest of the night passed quickly and at a less frenetic pace. The whole tempo of the kitchen slowed ever so slightly and even Ramsay screamed and shouted that bit less. At length the flow of plates ceased, and Charlie was reallocated to cleaning chores. He gathered from snippets picked up from some of the younger staff as he cleaned round stoves and hobs that most diners, including guests at the hotel, finished their dinner by half-past ten and the restaurant and kitchen wound down after then.

Finally, about one-thirty he was called over by the moustached guy, whose name he learned was Gregg who was the deputy head chef and taken back along the drab corridor to reception. He hadn't even the opportunity to say goodbye to Mark and Ronnie as he was led into a side office where a man wearing a dark suit sat behind a large desk waring a prominent brown badge on his lapel saying, "Night Manager".

'Replacement KP,' Gregg said laconically but still in a loud voice which seemed strange in this quiet room, before patting Charlie on the back with a brisk: 'ok son,' and left the room.

The night manager, a man about fifty, rose and strode slowly to a small night safe, which he unlocked using a numbered pad. Taking out an envelope he walked equally slowly over to Charlie and counted out a few notes and some coins. He gave him a weak smile, saying:

'Thanks for that son. You'll get home, ok?' handing him the notes and coins.

'Aye, sure,' Charlie replied on autopilot, walked out of the office, past the now empty lobby and reception desk where a lone night porter sat reading a paper, opened the lobby doors and was met with a wave of fresh air which startled him after hours in that stultifying, humid kitchen.

He looked, almost bewildered at the few people walking slowly past the closed entrance to Central Station then realised that from the moment he'd entered the kitchen, he and everyone around him had been at a hundred miles an hour. The night manager and the people in the street were just walking at a normal pace.

He looked at his Timex his mother had got him for Christmas and with a shock saw it was twenty to two. How was he going to get home? Were his night's earnings enough for a taxi? A passing beat cop rescued him. Enquiring what he was doing "loitering" outside the entrance to the Central Hotel, Charlie told him of his evening's arduous work in the hotel kitchen but was unsure now how to get home to Possil at this hour.

The cop took pity on him and informed him if he ran up Hope Street, which was right next to the hotel and station, he would catch a late bus that would take him home. Charlie caught the bus with a minute to spare and was home within fifteen minutes.

His mother had given him a spare key, and he stealthily entered the sleeping house, crept up to his bedroom, quietly undressed, his brother out for the count in the other bed. It took him a while to adjust after the hours of madness in that kitchen. The odours, the shouts, the incessant noise, the itching in his hands and fingers were all vivid reminders of his first ever paid "job", though he regarded that as an extravagant title for a couple of hours' work. Finally, he got to sleep.

He slept through to half-one in the afternoon and was shaken awake by his father.

'It's the phone. That restaurant's wanting to speak to you.'

Fully awake, he ran down the stairs wondering if he'd left something behind or was in trouble, but to his amazement they asked him to come back in that night. He blurted 'yes, sure', but after putting the phone down was uncertain whether he wanted to go back into that cauldron of a kitchen. He swithered all afternoon, his mother saying it was up to him what he wanted to do, and she would support him while his father, in contrast, urged him that 'any job was better than nothing', he couldn't live his life on benefits and needed to 'bring money into the house for your keep.'

He wolfed down an early fish supper, still unsure what to do, but just after four, as if an irresistible force was propelling him, he boarded a bus into town and reported to the kitchen of La Maison Rose. This time he was assigned to peeling potatoes and other tedious cleaning tasks. He survived and was asked back the following night. Two weeks' later he was given a short-term contract,

And so began Charlie Carty's career in the dining trade.

He stayed a year at La Maison Rose. He got bawled at by Adrian Ramsay, but everybody, including Gregg, his deputy, got shouted at too; it was unavoidable. But mostly he avoided his wrath, unlike some of the kitchen staff who were the incessant butt of Ramsay's cruel, twisted, sarcastic humour.

Despite this, he learned a lot in this constantly busy kitchen, picking up tips and trade secrets. Gregg, who could be brusque and shouty when he wanted to - but then that was the default mode in Ramsay's kitchen – seemed to take him under his wing and sheltered him from the worst of Ramsay's ire. Within three months he'd been made a kitchen assistant and put on a three-month contract, though you could be sacked at any moment for the slightest transgression depending on Ramsay's or some of the other senior staff's moods, as Charlie was witness to on several occasions.

Nevertheless, Charlie became inured to the madness around him, blocking out the bullying and focusing on what he was now beginning to enjoy: cooking and preparing food in all its flavours and varieties. Despite Ramsay, there were some talented people in that kitchen, and he gravitated to them and they to him.

He was ecstatic when George, one of the assistant chefs, who also took a shine to him and mentored him, allowed him to cook with minimal supervision a haddock mornay and after getting the nod from Gregg and Ramsay, allowed it to pass upstairs.

Those plates came back clear. George was delighted, Gregg said it "wasn't bad for a first go" and Ramsay chimed in with,

'You're a long way from being a chef yet Carty. Don't let it go to your heid and there's plenty of fuckups for you to make.' That was Adrian Ramsay all right, never say a good word to your staff if you can avoid it.

As the months passed, Charlie was given more opportunities to help prepare and cook dishes. La Masion Rose might be an upmarket restaurant by Glasgow standards but served traditional fare: steaks, hams, fish, usually haddock, occasionally cod, very occasionally, monkfish. There was little innovation, but it allowed Charlie to learn the basics. He was never allowed near the restaurant. He only saw his cousin, Gerry, at family occasions and never again in the kitchen. The KP, Mark, was right. There was a rigid separation between front-of-house and the kitchen, which meant he never got the chance to learn about the hospitality side of the business.

But no matter how well he performed and enjoyed cooking, it was impossible to ignore that the kitchen was being run on brutal lines presided over by a maniac, Ramsay, who was accountable to no one, least of all, the restaurant manager, an aloof figure, who rarely visited the kitchen. As long as the restaurant was busy and complaints minimal, Ramsay was left alone.

There was no courtesy, no compassion and no respect. Bullying, homophobia, misogyny was rampant and contagious; Charlie found himself becoming more aggressive and even started treating the KP's roughly until he checked himself.

THE KITCHEN VIGILANTE - "JUSTICE WILL BE SERVED"

It all came to a head one Wednesday afternoon, as they were gearing up for a big private function in the restaurant for 200 people, when Ramsay unleashed a verbal onslaught on a kitchen assistant called Pat, who was about Charlie's age, for some minor infraction. Charlie had noticed this young lad had been marked out by Ramsay. The lad was slightly built and constantly shook with fear when Ramsay was about, which unfortunately was almost always; he seemed to live in that kitchen.

Ramsay's verbal abuse was even louder and longer than normal, the lad visibly shaking, head bowed over a stove, culminating in the chef throwing a rolling pin at him which just missed by inches. Everybody else looked away, including Gregg, which was normal practice, but something snapped in Charlie. He couldn't believe that he shouted out:

'Aw, for God's sake, leave the poor guy alone!'

Everyone else froze. The silence was palpable. Ramsay slowly turned to him, face flushed, finger pointing; no one had ever spoken to him like that before in his kitchen.

'What...what did you say to me?'

He could have backed down, pleaded for forgiveness, folded abjectly and survived, though Ramsay would have him marked. But Charlie now realised he was heartily sick of a character like Adrain Ramsay and by keeping silent was colluding in his abysmal, utterly unacceptable behaviour. He stood his ground, staring straight at him and more words came out.

'I said leave him alone. I don't know what he's done wrong, but it doesn't deserve that crap you're giving him and throwing stuff at him.'

He said it clearly without quivering, his anger overcoming any fear, though he was astonished at his own audacity. Ramsay smiled, but it was a horrible, oily grin. The chef looked around him, speaking to all the staff who now focused on him in terrified silence.

'Why didn't anyone tell me this wee arsehole had been promoted to head chef?' He let out a mocking laugh, then the smile disappeared to be replaced by an intense, angry glare. Pointing at a boiling pot on the stove in front of him, he yelled at Charlie:

'The next thing I'll throw is this pot at your heid. Don't you ever fucking talk to me like that in my kitchen.' He lowered his voice and growled in a menacing tone, 'now get back to your work and I'll have a word with you later.'

'Naw, piss off.'

Charlie could hear gasps around him as he thew his hat on the ground, unbuttoned his overalls and discarded them too, walked past Ramsay who was stunned into silence, staring him out, and went to the exit. Just as he was about to go through the doors, Ramsay came to and shouted after him:

'You'll never fucking work in a kitchen ever again, I'll make sure of that.'

Charlie turned and gave him the middle finger before leaving, walking back along the corridor, across the reception lobby, out to the bustling surroundings of Central Station and Glasgow city centre.

Then his bravado crashed replaced by a stultifying fear. What the hell had he done? On the cusp of eighteen, he'd just pulled up the head chef of Glasgow's most prestigious restaurant and told him to shove it. Ramsay's last words rang in his ear.

'You'll never work in a kitchen ever again.'

Charlie Carty's fledgling career in the hospitality business was surely over.

TWO

Charlie wandered forlornly around the city centre, not wanting to go back home and face his parents. They were delighted that he was doing well, was enthusiastic about his job and new-found love of cooking (he'd even cooked a few meals at home which went down well, even with Raymond) and was earning a small amount of money.

He'd always put a positive gloss on the job and never spoke of Ramsay or of the chaos and gratuitous aggression in that kitchen. His family were proud of him and to tell them he'd walked off the job in such circumstances would be heartbreaking for them.

'Aw, what a stupid berk,' he shook his head, disconsolately. He also realised suddenly he was skint and only had enough money for his fare home. He wouldn't have been paid until Friday, and he couldn't stomach going back there, asking for what he was owed. It was back to the dole.

He looked around and became aware he'd wandered into the business district of Anderston, which was much quieter than the rest of the city centre. He turned round to head back to Hope Street and his bus home; there was no way he couldn't tell his folks and wanted it over with.

Passing by the site of a newly opened hotel called the New Caledonian, a tall, fifteen storey edifice which was billed as Glasgow's "newest, upmarket hotel," and had been cited as a rival to the Central Station Hotel, Charlie's attention was caught by a notice attached to the signage outside the entrance advertising the hotel restaurant, The Caledon Larder. The notice read:

Vacancies, Hotel Staff, Kitchen Staff wanted: Apply Within.

He remembered now a few weeks back when Gregg had brought up the subject of the new potential rival within Charlie's earshot, Ramsay was scornfully dismissive:

'They'll never last. This town isn't big enough for two quality hotel restaurants. Folk will always come back here.'

Since the calamitous barney with Ramsay, he'd been working on impulse and that memory of the chef's derisive comment impelled him to go through the automatic doors at the hotel entrance and nervously walk up to the reception desk.

The bright, young girl in a smart, dark blue uniform told him to wait at a comfortable seat after he'd enquired about a kitchen staff position. He looked around. The reception area was airy and well-lit where the Central was quite dim. Indeed, behind the opulent façade, the Central was quite rundown, time worn and in need of an uplift. In contrast, the New Caledonian screamed modernity.

After a few minutes a tall man of about thirty with longish, dark hair, twinkling, green eyes and a smile on his face wearing a dark suit and a red tie came up to him and said in a friendly voice:

'Hello, I hear you're interested in working in our kitchen.'

'Yes, uh huh,' Charlie replied eagerly. The man spoke in an English accent.

'Ok, follow me,' the man requested.

They went along a wood panelled corridor until they came to a large room full of long desks where a group of women sat typing or speaking on telephones. The man led Charlie to a glass panelled office at the far end of the room with windows looking over the Anderston Centre of residential flats, shops, businesses and a bus station, while another faced onto the long room. The man sat behind a desk, which, apart from a telephone and a framed picture of a woman and two young children, who he presumed were the man's family, was otherwise clear. Once seated the man asked him, still in a friendly but inquisitive voice:

'Have you any previous experience of working in a kitchen?'

It was an obvious starter. Should he bullshit? He'd gathered a wealth of experience in La Maison Rose, but would the manner of his leaving, not least shouting back and putting the middle finger up to the head chef condemn him for life as far as the hospitality trade was concerned? But lying and not revealing he'd worked in the industry, apart from underselling himself, would be equally fatal when found out. He tried to keep calm and said flatly:

'I worked for a year at La Maison Rose.'

'Under Adrian Ramsay?'

'Yeah. Aye.'

Well, that was it, Charlie thought. They would all know each other. It might be a big city, but it was a small profession and one call to Ramsay, and he was toast and that would follow him around any attempt to get back into any kitchen in the city, Scotland for that matter. He was interrupted by the man asking him another question.

'So, what did you learn there?'

He opened his mouth, but nothing came out. Then stuttered: 'Well I, eh, so, I...em.'

His face went bright red. 'Get out of here, Charlie, don't make such a plonker of yourself.' Then an inner conviction took hold, and he found his voice. He would go down fighting and acquit himself well; after all, he'd worked hard and learnt a lot. And he was off speaking well about his experience and answering the man's questions equably.

After about thirty minutes, the man took out a notepad and a pen from a drawer and asked Charlie to write down his name, address and telephone contact number. While Charlie was doing this, the man checked his watch and said:

'Forgive me, I haven't even introduced myself. I'm Eric Fenwick and I'm the overall manager of the kitchen. I was thinking, it's just after five, would you like a shot in the kitchen, show us what you can do. Say a couple of hours? We'll pay you for it whatever happens.'

Why not, thought Charlie. He was meant to be on shift at La Maison Rose until late.

'Sure, aye,' he agreed.

'Ok, I'll take you to the kitchen.'

They walked to the other side of the building into a large, bright kitchen which gleamed with brand new state of the art kitchen equipment, shiny, clean and sparkling. It was in such contrast to the gloom, grit and stained surfaces of Ramsay's kitchen. He was introduced to a large florid faced man called Henri.

'This is the head chef.' Charlie bristled, after Ramsay who was an extreme negative role model, that title struck fear into him.

Eric continued: 'The lad's worked for a year as an assistant in La Maison Rose.'

Henri broke into a smile and said in a distinct French accent: 'And you survived?' The two men chuckled. Charlie's face reddened again, but he felt reassured and just muttered 'aye.'

'Ok put him to the Garde Manger,' Henri said to Eric, and turned back to his stove.

Charlie followed Eric, wondering what or who the hell a Garde Manger was. They arrived at a large workstation with sinks attached where piles of lettuce and other vegetables were being chopped and shredded by a young guy in whites not much older than Charlie.

'Peter, this is Charlie Carty,' Eric introduced them. 'We're giving him a trial tonight. Get him some whites that'll fit him, and we'll see how it goes, ok'. Eric offered him his hand. Charlie was taken aback, shaking a gaffer's hand; that would never happen in Ramsay's domain.

'Great, I could do with another hand,' Peter said in an equally warm voice.

The night passed quickly. It was busy, frenetic even, but nothing that Charlie couldn't cope with. Peter was a good guide but quickly appreciated that Charlie didn't need much instruction and let him get on with it. Apart from the cleanliness and all the new equipment, what struck Charlie was how relaxed the kitchen was in contrast to the war zone that Ramsay was in charge of. Sure, there was the odd sharp rebuke, but it was nothing compared to what he was used to.

Henri was a commanding presence in the centre of the

kitchen; he was the boss ok, and you obeyed his commands, but he did so without any of the aggression, bluster or sheer, unfiltered spite and anger that Ramsay deployed. Henri's was a quiet authority and more effective for that.

A Garde Manger turned out to be the chef, in charge of preparing and cooking cold dishes such as salads, quiches and flans. As the night progressed, Charlie appreciated how efficient this kitchen was compared to La Maison Rose's. There were designated chefs for various types of dishes: fish, meats, fries, grills, cold dishes where Peter was in charge, even a pastry chef. They were all known as chef de parties, with their assistants all working under the head chef. Eric was the executive head chef, or as he himself had put it, the manager of the kitchen.

At La Maison Rose, Ramsay and his undermanager, Gregg, just allocated everybody: chefs, kitchen assistants, even KPs, to workstations and tasks randomly each night. There was no system, no division of labour; just get to a stove and get the food out and upstairs was the sole credo.

But there was something else. With Eric around, who Charlie saw frequently in the kitchen, Henri too was under quiet but watchful supervision; though it wasn't readily apparent he deferred to Eric. Finally, the waitering staff were constantly in and out of the kitchen, setting down orders and taking up trays to serve, going through a set of swing doors where Charlie caught a glimpse of the customers at tables. He even had a chance to speak with some of them and there was a lot of hurried good-natured banter between waitering and kitchen staff. With a start, he realised he'd never once set foot in the restaurant or met a customer of La Maison Rose who he and his colleagues' cooked food for. This was how a kitchen should be run, he thought.

About ten, Eric appeared beside them. The kitchen was winding down. Peter gave a thumbs up and patted Charlie on the arm.

'A good wee grafter, aren't you?' Charlie blushed.

'Cheers Peter,' Eric said. 'Right, we better pay you for all your work tonight. Don't want your folks thinking we're exploiting you, eh?'

Charlie smiled sheepishly. He now felt apprehensive. Was he going to be kept on? And had Eric made that call to Ramsay? He really wanted to work here in this kitchen. He'd caught the dining bug, and this is what he wanted to do. He followed Eric back to the now darkened open plan to his office with trepidation. From a drawer in his desk, Eric produced an envelope with the usual notes and coins and handed it to Charlie.

'I think you'll find we pay a wee bit more here.' Suddenly, the smile disappeared from Eric's face.

'I phoned Gregg Cooper tonight.'

Charlie's heart sank, he tensed up and awaited the inevitable. Gregg Cooper, of course, was Ramsay's deputy. But Eric resumed his smile.

'He says you've got a lot of character. Like Peter, he says you're a hard worker and you've got the makings of a chef. From what I've seen tonight, I agree with Gregg. And, most importantly, Henri agrees. All right, we'll call it a night. Report at reception tomorrow at eleven to meet personnel and we'll get you signed up on an initial three months' probation. Perform like you did tonight and there should be no problems. Welcome to the team.'

Once more he offered his hand. Charlie couldn't hide his relief as the tension from him released like air from a balloon. He left the hotel virtually skipping, caught his bus home, informed his delighted parents about his new position while glossing over why he'd left his old one and went to bed feeling ecstatic.

He didn't find out if Gregg Cooper had divulged to Eric the spectacular manner of his leaving La Maison Rose. If he had, then Eric didn't seem too concerned about it. The most important thing was that Gregg had given him a good, verbal reference and for that Charlie was very grateful.

Charlie's entry to the New Caledonian Hotel and its restaurant, the Caledon Larder, was another instance of him being in the right place at the right time. In the late 1970s and early 80's, Glasgow was going through a transformation shedding its reputation as a grimy, violent, industrial city and developing a new image as a vibrant destination welcoming to visitors and tourists. What was left of its blackened, soot begrimed tenements were sandblasted revealing the original red sandstone beneath in all its splendour. Indeed, the city was becoming celebrated for having one of the finest collections of Edwardian and Victorian architecture still standing. A new zest, energy and purpose was abroad in the dear green place, the original Gaelic name for Glasgow.

Dining was no exception to this. Led by south Asian, Italian and Chinese pioneers, traditionally conservative Glaswegian palates were being reshaped and turned on to new and exotic dishes; the city was going through a culinary revolution. The Caledon Larder was exactly the type of venue that could capitalise on this and people like Charlie, if they were prepared to work hard and commit, could reap the rewards.

Charlie was aware of this. The restaurant was constantly busy, even more so than La Maison Rose which had its lean periods during the week. To get a table at weekends, you had to book weeks if not months in advance and the hotel was always full.

He took advantage of every opportunity he was given. Henri, with Eric's blessing, gave him stints working under each of the chef de parties, all a good bunch like Peter, and he accumulated a wealth of experience in all areas of the kitchen. This was indispensable because he now had his eyes set on becoming a chef and to do that properly, he had to know all aspects of cooking, serving and preparing food, not least because if a chef de partie or assistant was off, the head chef might have to muck in and maintain the quality of the food.

It was hard work. Days were long, sometimes up to eighteen hours. This was no nine-to-five job. Commitment was everything. If Charlie had any pretensions to be more than just an assistant, he had to be diligent and dedicated and clearly demonstrate that to his bosses.

He seemed to succeed. His three-months' probation flew past, and he was put on the regular staff team. Within nine months, he was appointed a full-time assistant chef de partie with the seafood chef, which was a particular favourite of his. When he'd been allowed to cook some monkfish, seabream or halibut dish with only minimal supervision from his chef, the comments that came back from diners were ecstatic.

Both hotel and restaurant were earning rave reviews, and this buoyed the team up. Charlie felt he and the team, led by Eric and Henri, both with excellent track records in the industry and good people managers, were on a mission to be one of the best, if not the best eatery in Glasgow. Charlie learnt a lot from that job; foremost, that cooking and hospitality were a vocation and only those who treated it like that were likely to advance.

Over the months Charlie discovered there were a few refugees from Ramsay's tyranny working in the kitchen of the Caledon Larder. As for that benighted establishment, eighteen months into his tenure Charlie learned that La Maison Rose was being closed by the Central Hotel management; all the staff were being made redundant, and Ramsay was out of a job. Hell mend him, Charlie thought. The restaurant had been losing custom for quite a while and complaints about the food rising; no doubt customers having experienced the likes of the Caledon Larder had become aware of the mainly stodgy fare being served up to them.

To complete his dining apprenticeship, Eric gave him the chance to work in the restaurant, front of house, learning the art of good, polite and efficient service and the diplomatic skills that went with responding to customer queries or complaints.

He also had a day or two behind the desk at reception and realised there was a lot more to that than just simply booking guests into their rooms. Tact, diplomacy and keeping calm, even though you could be a seething cauldron of emotions inside, were everything, whether in the kitchen, the restaurant or at reception.

After two-and-a-half years though, Charlie started to feel frustrated. For obvious reasons La Maison Rose had a high turnover. Because the Caledon Larder was so well run and a much more benevolent regime than most other kitchens (Charlie learned from colleagues who'd been around a few places that Ramsay's terror was, unfortunately, the norm), few people left. All the chef de parties above him, like Peter, were only a few years older than him. Charlie had become aspirational, keen to get on. That wasn't happening here.

At home things were becoming fraught. The downside of Glasgow's transformation into a bright, modern services led city was a shake out and rapid decline of the city's traditional manufacturing base. Factories, shipyards, mines and steelworks shed their workforce or closed altogether; unemployment increased significantly. Charlie's dad was one of the victims when his wire factory closed. Accustomed to being the main breadwinner in the house, Charlie witnessed his father's pride and confidence sapping as he mooched about the house, aware his wife and son were the only ones bringing an income in and he was dependent on benefits. Inevitably, there were tensions between his parents as arguments broke out and money was tight, relieved only by Raymond getting accepted for university, the first in the family to do so. But he subsisted on a meagre student grant that brought little into the house.

Charlie wanted out. He looked around but couldn't see anything that appealed. Plus, he didn't want to end up in another hellish kitchen run by a psychopath. Eric Fenwick, a good man manager, picked up on this and called him into his office one day.

'I'm picking up the vibes, Charlie, that you're not too satisfied at the moment.'

Charlie was surprised and tried to bluster.

'Naw, everything's fine boss.'

Eric had a way of giving you a penetrating look which went right through you.

'You sure?' he went on. 'You're not here because I've got any issues with your work. You're a good, hard worker, but I just pick things up. So, I'll ask again, how are you?'

Charlie was disarmed. His bluster crumbled and he let loose, telling his gaffer how frustrated he was. He loved working here, but there was little prospect of advancement. He didn't let on about the situation at home but said enough for Eric to respond helpfully.

'I know, I've been there myself, champing at the bit. Kitchens are largely a young man's game and its often-dead men's shoes.' He smiled benignly and leaned closer across his uncluttered desk to Charlie.

'I have to say, cos I don't want to lose you, if you really want to get on in this profession, to become a chef, you need to get as much experience of as many kitchens as you can, even,' he paused and almost sighed, 'if that does mean working in more hostile environments.'

Charlie looked at his boss knowingly.

'I know Mr Fenwick, but there's not much around just now. What I mean is...'

'...There's plenty of places but not much opportunity,' Eric interrupted.

'Aye.'

'So, don't restrict yourself to Glasgow. There's a whole world of hospitality out there.'

That hadn't occurred to Charlie. Eric opened his drawer and retrieved a sheet of paper.

'My brother, Barry, is part owner of a restaurant in London, in the upmarket district of Mayfair, real posh. He's told me they've got a vacancy for a commis chef, but they can't fill it. Sure, they've had plenty of takers, but nobody suitable. Why don't you give it a chance?'

Commis chef was a chef de partie's principal assistant and was the next stage up on the kitchen staff ladder. But it was London! Where the hell would he stay?' He said this to Eric.

'I'd make sure Barry would find you accommodation down there. Look, think about it. You've talent and a really good future in this industry. I wouldn't be having this conversation with you if I didn't believe that.'

'Ok, I'll think about it.'

And he did, ruminated on it for about a week or two, before deciding it was too good a chance to pass up. He let Eric know he was interested and after a telephone interview with Maartin, Eric's equivalent at the Mayfair restaurant and with his sound recommendation, it was wrapped up. Eric's brother, Barry, found him a small flat in Bayswater, not far from Mayfair. Charlie had accumulated some savings (his long hours and working most weekends meant he didn't socialise much) and was able to pay a deposit on the flat. The rent was not too prohibitive and after consulting a map of London, he reckoned he could walk the reasonably short distance to Mayfair.

So, after nearly three years at the Caledon Lodge, in September 1982, Charlie left his family and made his way to London on an overnight coach. He'd been to London only once and found it quite intimidating, particularly negotiating the Underground. But he found Bayswater quite easily and the flat above a Lebanese restaurant was small, but liveable; it came with a fridge, some furnishings and a portable colour TV. It could have been a lot worse: some dreadful bedsit.

Charlie was taken aback by just how cosmopolitan Bayswater was; a later era would describe it as "multicultural". Glasgow was almost completely white, the odd south Asian or Chinese person excepted. By contrast, Bayswater was a sea of different ethnicities and cultures; the street he lived on displayed a variety of emporiums, including restaurants and nightclubs. Indeed, he considered there was probably more restaurants of all sorts, in the surrounding area than there was in the entire Glasgow city centre. There was a good buzz and dynamic about the area; he felt safe and his landlord, an older Arab man, was quite friendly.

In contrast, Mayfair lived up to Eric's terse description. It was posh. Frighteningly so for Charlie, with its neat streets, well-appointed grand terraces with classical facades, ornate features and beautiful squares. It was very formal and such a difference from the relaxed atmosphere of Bayswater. On his first day walking to work, he felt like the proverbial tramp amidst all this splendour and luxury.

The restaurant was French, but not a pretend one like La Maison Rouge. It was the real deal. Half the staff were French which was the normal language among the staff, so Charlie had to quickly pick up a smattering of the language. That was fine as Charlie enjoyed challenges. What was daunting was the aloofness. Even in the warzone of La Maison Rose there was a camaraderie, particularly among the junior staff which was absent here. Maybe it was the language barrier, but Charlie right from the start felt alone.

Unlike his brother, Barry was taciturn and barely spoke a word to him on the few occasions he saw him. The manager, Maartin from Antwerp, was quite formal as was the head chef Alain Ballouse originally from Toulouse. It wasn't La Maison Rose, though there was the odd shouting, but rigid and stiff. In a word, it was cold. And it was relentless. A popular venue, Barry, Maartin and Ballouse were all striving for a Michelin Star, one of the highest accolades of the restaurant world, and lived in constant expectation of a snap visit from their undercover inspectors. On several occasions, Charlie saw the three in a huddle in the kitchen speculating on whether some customers were in fact Michelin inspectors.

The same rigid demarcation prevailed between front and back of house as in La Maison Rose. Except for Ballouse, all kitchen staff were banned from the restaurant during opening hours. Eighteen-hour days were common, and he would come back to his flat dog tired, slumped into a chair in front of the portable TV and instantly fall into a deep sleep.

He was used to hard work in his last two places. But the difference here was the lack of recognition. He wasn't needy and always looking for praise, but just some token of appreciation would have been nice, but there was none, though as usual any mistakes or slipups were pounced on quickly. Charlie felt rapidly alone in this large city, his long hours preventing him from making friends and no one in the staff he felt comfortable with. To compound matters, there was the same issue as the Caledon Larder; almost all the staff were in their twenties and thirties, including his boss. They were going nowhere.

He lasted nine months. Looking around, he saw a vacancy for a commis chef at a large hotel just off Picadilly. On impulse, just as with the Caledon Larder, he had a walk- in interview and got the job. He felt rotten about leaving because Barry was Eric Fenwick's brother and Eric had put out for him. But Barry, Henri and Maartin's response to his departure was typical, nonchalant, typified by Maartin's shrug of the shoulders, though he did give him a good reference.

But there was no real improvement in his situation at the Martindale London, a large five-star hotel in an elegant Georgian terrace run by a multinational group who had hotels across the world. There were uniformed doormen in top hats and scarlet uniforms at the entrance, but Charlie had to use the less salubrious staff entrance at the back. The Martindale London was run on the same rigid, demarcated lines as the Mayfair restaurant, but Charlie found it to be even more corporate and soulless. What really struck him was the indifference to the food from the kitchen staff which he'd never encountered before. All through the worst moments in his previous places, there'd been compensation in the pride and care he and his colleagues took in preparing and cooking dishes. That was completely missing. For all the staff, including the chefs of all ranks, it was a job to get through and finish a shift and the amount of backbiting and bitching was phenomenal. To add to his loneliness, Charlie was depressed and profoundly homesick. After six months and over a year in London, he packed it in and returned home.

He thought he'd get gip from his parents for leaving a job in the Smoke, but they were pleased to see him. Things had improved at home. His father had found work as a courier for a large law firm which got him out of the house, and he enjoyed it. Within days, Charlie was looking for work and answered an ad in his nearest Job Centre for a commis chef at a hotel called the Springwell at the business end of Sauchiehall Street just off the city centre. It was owned and managed by a middle-aged married couple, Larry and Janet Chalmers, and they'd ran it from when they'd bought it from the previous owners in the 1960s.

Charlie had to supress a laugh when he went for his interview with the couple. Larry was six feet four, while Janet was a diminutive four feet nine. They were a pleasant couple who finished each other's sentences and told him their life story. He got the job.

It was a family run hotel, taking up the end of an Edwardian terrace not far from Kelvingrove Park and couldn't have been further from the snobbish hurley-burley of Mayfair or the faceless anonymity of the Martindale. The Springwell was Larry and Janet's baby and the staff their family and Charlie reckoned that compensated for the fact they'd no children. He fitted in rapidly and found his feet.

The clientele were all regulars, either businessmen, trades people or visitors from outside the city who always stayed there when in Glasgow. The kitchen was basic, clean but careworn. There was a head chef, a rumpled man called Craig, with tufts of white hair over a bald pate, whose whites were constantly stained and who'd been there for decades. There was no chef de parties and Charlie was his assistant with a couple of kitchen assistants and a KP. Four waiters completed the restaurant complement. There'd been a vacancy for a senior waiter which Larry and Janet informed Charlie had now been filled and a new girl would be starting 'in a few weeks.'

Charlie loved it. Quite quickly he was treated almost like a son by Larry and Janet, got on well with all the staff, wasn't confined to the kitchen and was able to go into the restaurant frequently and mingle with the customers. His ostensible boss, Craig, was a classic time server whose culinary repertoire was very limited to what had been the usual Glasgow fare of steak, stews and haddock and chips. But the bonus for Charlie was that Craig was neither hostile nor defensive when it came to his suggestions for new dishes and additions to the stolid menu. Craig let him have his way and soon Charlie was adding pastas and other "exotic" dishes to the delight of both customers and Larry and Janet.

He made his presence felt in the kitchen and soon Craig was becoming dependent on him. Charlie could see which way this was going. Craig was probably in his late fifties/early sixties. By Charlie's previous standards, the Springwell wasn't taxing, indeed it was almost laidback. But it was for Craig, and he would struggle without his commis chef. He lived with his wife, who was a doctor's receptionist in Paisley, and they had a large family; Craig was always showing pictures of his brood of grandchildren around the kitchen. Charlie was convinced Craig would retire or be persuaded to in a few years and then he could accede to what he most coveted, becoming head chef of his own kitchen.

Meanwhile the new senior waiter, a girl about 23, same age as Charlie, took up position. Her name was Sarah McBride and Charlie took to her right away. She had glistening long brown hair which she often tied in a ponytail when on duty, sparkling blue eyes, a fetching freckled face and a slim elegant figure. Sarah was a natural with the customers, friendly, supportive but firm when needed with her staff and became the "daughter" to Charlie's "son" for Larry and Janet.

Charlie got on well with her, especially as she had a real interest in cooking. Her father had died when she was young. Her mother worked long hours filling two jobs, so Sarah made all the dinners for her two younger sisters and brother. It was inevitable therefore, given their shared interests that they would gravitate to each other and come up with ideas for new dishes and additions to the menu. One night, just before Christmas, they were both in a small, barely furnished room that staff used during breaks or after shifts.

After the usual post-mortems about the day, Sarah shifted the chat onto movies and declared she would 'love to see ET,' the Stephen Spielberg movie that'd just come out to rave reviews.

'Yeah, I loved Close Encounters,' Charlie said, and launched into 'dee da dee da daa!' in imitation of the film's Alien theme score.

'Aye, all right,' Sarah rolled her eyes. 'Don't lose any sleep expecting Hollywood to phone you if they're doing a remake. Stick to cooking.'

'Aw, you're so cruel!'

'Just realistic.'

'Anyway, when you going to see ET?'

'I'm not. Mom's no interested in that kind of film; she loves weepies. And I'm not going with my sisters cos they'd just fidget and be a nuisance.'

'Well, I'll go with you then.' He said it casually, but he was a bag of nerves.

'Eh...well...eh, aye ok, why not?'

They arranged a day to see the movie. They both enjoyed it and went for a burger in a Wimpy bar afterwards. He asked her out again to see another movie and bought her some perfume for Christmas. On their third night at the movies, they went to a nightclub afterwards and had their first snog. By January 1983, they were an item.

Over the next few years Charlie experienced the happiest days of his life. He continued to court Sarah, and their relationship grew and deepened despite the fact they were in such close proximity to each other over long hours. If Charlie effectively ran the kitchen, Sarah ran the restaurant. This didn't cause tensions or resentment from Larry and Janet. Rather, they seemed to be relieved that day-to-day business could be left in such safe hands.

When not working, Charlie and Sarah were always around each other. He got introduced to her mother, sisters and brother and became a fixture at her home in the east-end of Glasgow. Equally, Charlie's parents and Raymond took to her, and she spent a lot of time there. They were in love with each other. At the start of 1984, Charlie moved into a rented Partick flat, where Sarah joined him a month later, which helped with the rent. They got engaged later that year but decided to put off marriage for a few years until they were both earning more.

Charlie felt safe, like he'd never felt before. Comfortable in his skin, in love with Sarah and completely relaxed and enjoying his job. He was master of his destiny, or so he thought until one day Larry and Janet asked Charlie and Sarah into their untidy office at the back of the hotel. Charlie knew this wasn't going to be good news as the older couple had unusually stern serious expressions. Larry spoke first.

'We asked you in here today to let you know, after a lot of

thought, I mean serious consideration..'

'...We're going to sell the hotel,' Janet interjected.

Charlie and Sarah sat bolt upright, looked at each other and said: "what?' in unison.

'We're both approaching sixty,' Janet went on 'and we've thought long and hard about it but...'

'...It's time we moved on, sold up and...'

'...We're going to ask whoever takes over to keep you all on,' Janet gave them what she hoped was a reassuring look.

Both Charlie and Sarah were dumbstruck. Eventually he asked:

'When are you putting the hotel up for sale?'

'The for-sale notices go up next week,' Larry answered flatly.

'And what if the new owners don't want to keep the staff or us on?' Sarah asked anxiously.

Larry and Janet glanced at each other before Janet shrugged her shoulders, saying, 'Well we can't really control that, hen. That'll be up to them. 'But' her voice raised an octave, 'we'll put in a great word for you all, tell them how mad they would be not to keep you.'

It was meant to be reassuring, but they left the meeting feeling disconsolate and filled with anxiety. Within a week a "For-Sale" sale sign was affixed to the entrance of the building. For Charlie it was like a totem that his idyll and dream of being a chef, in charge of the kitchen and, running the hotel with Sarah, was shattered.

He watched as a few prospective buyers were shown around the hotel over the next few weeks, but none of them to Larry's increasing frustration, pursued the sale any further.

Then, five weeks later, the expansive figure of Dick Forsyth turned up for an appointment to view the hotel and Charlie's career was about to move up to a whole new level.

THREE

Charlie had heard of Dick Forsyth. He was one of a new breed of restaurant owners revolutionizing Glasgow's dining scene and had opened a few new ventures around the city centre which had rapidly become popular with food critics enthusing over them. Why he would be interested in acquiring the quiet, demure Springwell in a location away from the buzzing city centre was intriguing, but then all of Forsyth's initiatives had been a success.

And that made Charlie even more anxious. Because it was unlikely Forsyth would keep on Craig, himself, Sarah and the rest. He would have his own tried and tested people; why change a winning formula?

Forsyth viewed the hotel on a midweek afternoon. He had a large, fleshy red face, a prominent nose and fuzzy, dark hair down to his neck. Charlie reckoned he was in his late thirties, perhaps early forties. He smiled a lot, but Charlie discerned a sharp, alert mind behind his deep, brown eyes as Larry and Janet escorted him around the hotel. He wore an expensive dark suit that couldn't quite disguise his portly frame over a loud, pink shirt and white tie.

Charlie noticed, that unlike the other viewers, Forsyth spent a while talking to the staff, including Craig and Sarah. He was in the kitchen, supervising the staff preparing the evening's dinners when Forsyth came in, Larry and Janet beside him trying not to betray their eagerness. He engaged with everyone, even the KP. Charlie was the last he approached.

Larry gave him a good intro:

'This is our fantastic commis chef, Charlie. A great cook, his ravioli is to die for.'

'Oh, aye,' Forsyth responded, in a commanding, garrulous Glasgow accent that Charlie thought revealed working class roots, 'so, what's your background then, Charlie?'

He gave a succinct summary of his career up to now.

'You survived Adrian Ramsay then? Respect.'

Charlie almost blushed, then recovered, as Forsyth quickly changed the subject and asked:

'Where do you see yourself in five years' time?'

Charlie was perplexed at the question but answered rapidly:

'Running my own kitchen.' He regretted that. The rule of thumb in Glasgow was never bum yourself up; was he coming across as too flash? Forsyth continued to question him.

'Your gaffer here,' pointing to Larry, 'says you've brought a spring to the kitchen and really added to the menu. How did you do that?'

He was conscious Craig was in earshot and didn't want to belittle or humiliate him. Gesturing all around him, he said:

'Me, Craig, all of us in the kitchen and the waitering staff led by a really good senior waiter, Sarah, are a team and we work together with Larry and Janet here to build this hotel into a good solid...' And for the next few minutes extolled all the good changes that had been made, emphasising teamwork but making sure his prominent role in all the changes were highlighted. After that peroration, Forsyth stared at him as if summing him up before patting him on the shoulder, remarking:

'I think you'll get that kitchen quicker than you think,' and moved out of the kitchen, Larry and Janet still at his side.

Charlie breathed deeply. Had he been too forward? Did Forsyth see him as a bullshit and patter merchant? Did Craig and the rest of the kitchen staff regard him as taking all the glory and minimising their contributions? Were noses out of joint?

He needn't have worried. All the staff came up to him led by Craig, thanking him for giving them all such a good write-up, summed up by Craig himself:

'That was great son. I'd have bought the bloody place myself after listening to that.'

He felt relieved. Later, Larry and Janet also praised him, but it was a tense wait to see what Forsyth's next move would be.

A week later, Janet called him into their office, her face drawn.

'That Forsyth chaps' just phoned.' He knew what the outcome was; disappointment etched from her every pore.

'He's not taking it any further.'

'Did he say why?'

'Too many other commitments, he says.' She shrugged. 'Anyway, you all spoke well of the place, you and Sarah in particular. Larry and I were proud of you.'

'Thanks. Is there anybody else interested?'

She shook her head, almost in despair. 'No'.

The uncertainty was awful and impacting on staff morale. Charlie could rarely speak about anything else back in their flat. They both considered jumping ship now and looking elsewhere, though they felt a pang of disloyalty to the couple for doing so, but they had to eat and pay rent.

A fortnight after Forsyth's abortive viewing, Marie, a young teenage waiter, who like the rest of the waiters doubled at reception, came into the kitchen midmorning and said:

'Phone call for you Charlie.'

'Who is it?'

'Widnae say. Just asked for you. It's a guy.'

Intrigued, Charlie went through to the reception and picked up the receiver.

'Hello, Charlie Carty.'

'Hi Charlie,' he recognised the voice instantly. 'Dick Forsyth here. Listen, any chance you can get away sometime today? I've got a wee office in West Nile Street.'

'What's it about?'

'I'd rather no say on the phone.'

Charlie was owed some time and could take a couple of hours off in the afternoon. They arranged to meet at two.

West Nile Street was about a mile away in the heart of the city centre. After a brisk walk Charlie was in Forsyth's surprisingly cramped office, with a secretary and a small partitioned sub-office, where Forsyth held court. His office was on the eighth floor of a bland new building on the corner with Sauchiehall Street in what had been the site of Glasgow's legendary and notorious Empire theatre.

After being served coffee by the secretary, Forsyth, dressed more casually in an open-necked white shirt and dark braces said:

'I'll come straight to the point. I liked your answers to my questions a couple of weeks ago. That place is going nowhere you know. Even if they found a buyer, it'll just be the same ticking over. I thought I could do something with it, but it's too staid and needs too much work and I huv'nae got time for that just now. I reckon you're hungry and want to move fast. This game is quick, and you need to take your chances. I'd like to offer you a position as sous chef in the Queen Mary.'

Charlie thought he'd misheard Forsyth and asked him to repeat it.

'I said sous chef at the Queen Mary.'

That was one of Glasgow's most prestigious restaurants and cocktail bars located just beside Exchange Square slap bang in the middle of the city. It was decked out as a replica of the celebrated Cunard liner the Queen Mary, which had been built in the Clyde shipyards. In a much-publicised deal, Forsyth had recently bought it from the people who'd owned it since it opened in the 1930s.

'You'll no become the head chef there,' Forsyth continued, 'you're no ready for that. But, after a year or two, if I think you're up to it, I could make you head chef in one of my other places.'

'I...eh...don't know what to say,' Charlie stammered, utterly taken aback.

'Aye or Naw, Charlie, I'm to the point. I don't piss about.'

'Aye, of course. Eh...but's there's one request.' He couldn't believe he'd found the gumption to ask this but pressed ahead.

'Well?' Forsyth asked.

'The senior waiter at the Springwell, Sarah McBride,' Charlie paused.

'Aye, a bonny lass, what about her?'

'She's my partner. We live together; we're engaged. Her position's on a shaky peg as well...'

'So, you're wanting me to offer your bidey-in a place as well?' Forsyth asked sharply.

Charlie thought he'd blown it, but was relieved when he smiled and said:

'Aye, all right. But you're not working in the same place, no way. That never works and causes too much grief. I'll find her a position somewhere else front of house.'

'As a senior? That's what she is right now.' Charlie couldn't believe his temerity.

'You don't ask for much, do you?' He shook his head. 'I'll see what I can do. Nae promises.'

They agreed a start date for his new post on a salary, which by non-hospitality standards was quite low, but significantly more than he was getting at present. After, Charlie virtually skipped back to the hotel but kept mum as he wanted Sarah to know first, and she had the day off. He finished about six as it was a quiet night and bought some flowers, a bottle of white wine and chocolates and announced the momentous news to her. She was stunned and delighted.

A month later in the summer of 1985, at the age of 25, Charlie started as a sous chef in the Queen Mary under the head chef Gordon Mearns, who'd been there for about twenty years. In his mid-forties, he was a man of few words, except to issue brusque commands, and like most of that generation of head chefs loathe to dish out praise. He was no Ramsay, though he could indulge in the odd screaming fit, but ran the kitchen with a rod of iron. It was his domain and no mistake. The manager, a slim guy called Don in his late 20s left him well alone as both the kitchen and restaurant ran smoothly.

Charlie spent a year working with and studying Mearns intently, his foibles, likes and dislikes, scrupulously following his cooking styles and managing the three chef de parties, taking a lot of weight off Mearns. As usual, it was fast and constantly busy, but there was, with the exception of the head chef, good banter, staff looked out for each other and there was lively interaction with front of house staff.

Forsyth would pop in occasionally to have a chat with him and appeared to be happy with his progress. True to his word, he'd found Sarah a position as one of three senior waiters at his recently opened, large and frantically busy Parisian Walkways venue at the top end of the city centre. She loved it. They were both incredibly busy, and working tremendously long hours, hardly saw each other, but that only drew them closer.

They kept in touch with Larry and Janet who'd not found a buyer for the hotel as a going concern and instead took a generous offer from a developer to convert the premises into offices and sold up. Fortunately, all the staff found positions elsewhere. The only sad news was the death of Craig, the chef, from cancer; Larry, Janet, Sarah, Charlie and the other staff attended his funeral and got riotously drunk celebrating Craig's memory at the purvey afterwards.

Again, keeping his word, two years after starting at the Queen Mary, Forsyth appointed Charlie to his first head chef's position at yet another of his ventures, the Cullins, a Scottish themed restaurant which allowed him and his new staff to work wonders and serve up beautiful fresh produce that earned consistently good accolades from critics and diners alike.

Before he left The Queen Mary, Mearns had effectively delegated dealing with suppliers to Charlie. This gave him invaluable experience in negotiating a good deal with them, working out who was dodgy and who produced good quality food and developing trustworthy relationships. This was a vital, but often ignored aspect to the hospitality business and Forsyth was delighted at Charlie's acumen in this area and was a major factor in his decision to appoint him as a head chef.

Within a year the manager at the Cullins left and Charlie moved up another level when Forsyth asked him to be the manager, but keeping a watchful eye on the food and his replacement as head chef. Charlie wasn't sure he was ready for it, after all he'd no previous experience of management and said so to Forsyth.

'Nonsense,' Forsyth rebutted. 'You're a manager every day you're head chef. You know your way round a kitchen, you know how front of house works, and you've got the suppliers sussed and you don't take any crap from them. Not forgetting, you love food and not serving shite to punters. What's the problem? You're a manager.'

'I hope you're not making a mistake,' Charlie said earnestly.

'I know I'm not. Go for it.'

It took him about three weeks to start to feel confident about becoming manager of the Cullins. Dealing with restaurant staff and customers was only an extension of dealing with people in the kitchen. It was the same issues stemming from people working in a confined, hectic, fast-moving environment. He was thankful for his many years in kitchens; it was the best preparation in the world for managing a restaurant. Charlie ran the Cullins well, was firm but fair with staff and well-liked, though if you were a slacker, he was onto you, and you were shown the door.

Both Charlie and Sarah were good savers and after five years living together in their small Partick flat, made three momentous decisions in 1989: they were going to buy a house, get married and start a family. They were wed at a registry office ceremony (neither were religious) and had a short honeymoon in Corfu. In September they moved into a new build semi-detached two-bedroom house they'd bought in a small estate near to Anniesland still in the west end of the city. The trio was complete when Sarah revealed she was pregnant in November.

The nineties began auspiciously for Charlie when he was called into Forsyth's city-centre office in early January. That office was even more cramped than when he'd first went there as there were now three secretaries sharing the front space, furiously working at PCs or answering an endless stream of phone calls.

Charlie entered Forsyth's small office, which was more a closet with papers strewn across his desk and on the floor, brought up a chair with a worn seat cover and sat across from his boss who was on the phone. To Charlie he looked older and careworn with tired eyes and bags under his eyes, but then he reflected that he too was looking older when he stared in the mirror while shaving. He still had a good mop of fair hair, but his dress sense had become more dapper, though nothing flash with a taste for dark Hugo Boss suits and expensive Italian loafers; elegant if understated.

He would be thirty this year but worked in a hard, fast and grinding trade where you were only as good as your last review. Could he last the pace as he moved into his fourth decade?

Forsyth finished the phone call and spoke to Charlie, hands in the air looking around him and into the adjoining open plan.

'I'm drowning Charlie,' he said half in jest and half in seriousness.

'Why don't you get a bigger office?' Charlie responded.

'It's more rent for a start. Besides, this place is so handy for the city centre and getting around; I can get to any of my places in minutes. Keeps you all on your toes!' He let out a chuckle before continuing:

'This is why I've asked you here. You see it's not the office space that's the problem. I've just got too much on my plate. I need help.'

Charlie was perplexed. Was his boss going to tell him he was about to resign? His empire was expanding rapidly. Besides the Queen Mary, Parisienne Walkway and the Cullins, he had three other restaurants on the go and a controlling interest in a nightclub, the Hollywood Strip, frequented by celebrities and Glasgow's "beautiful people", and if you didn't fit that category, it was hideously difficult to get in and for that very reason more popular and desirable.

No, resignation wouldn't be the Dick Forsyth way. Single (though there were stories of many liaisons with women), he was immersed in his business which was his life. And Charlie knew, Forsyth wanted more. He had a keen eye on acquiring several other restaurants and even on opening a hotel. He had an insatiable thirst for expansion, so Charlie was intrigued as to where Forsyth was going with this "chat" he'd called him in for.

'It's getting too big for me, I'm the first to admit,' Forsyth went on, holding Charlie in a fixed gaze. He continued: 'So, I need good people to delegate to, and I need to rely on them and trust them. You see I'm looking outwards,' he pointed a finger at the city outside around him. 'Siezing up new opportunities, dealing with the council, the licensing people, marketing, meeting with the media, you know.'

Forsyth had a high profile, rarely out of the local press with numerous TV appearances and slots on radio. A recent fawning article in the Glasgow Herald had glowingly described him as, "one of the new breed of Glasgow entrepreneurs transforming the previously bleak image of the city into a vibrant centre for dining, entertainment and tourism."

'So, what I need when I'm looking outwards, Charlie boy, is people that can handle all that's going on inside.' He leaned forward, looking straight and almost conspiratorially at Charlie, as if divulging a secret. 'I'm,' he made two air quotation marks with his hands, '" restructuring", creating two new positions. An (more air quotes) "executive" manager, who'll oversee all the restaurants and who all the managers will report to. And...' he leaned even closer to Charlie, '...an "executive" head chef, who'll oversee all the chefs.' He relaxed and sat back in his chair.

'These will be my two inside people while I grow the business which is, in all modesty, my forte. I've got Paul McGuiness lined up for the executive manager, and...' he paused and winked at Charlie, '...you as executive head chef. And, as a bonus, I'll make it worth your while. I'm going to cut both of you in for a share of the proceeds.'

Charlie was stunned.

'Well, what do you say?'

'Eh...aye...yes, of course. Brilliant!' In truth, it was an offer he couldn't refuse, particularly with a baby on the way. Forsyth offered his hand and gave him a firm handshake.

'Right, Paul, you and me will meet up in the next couple of days, firm things up and let the world know. Onwards and upwards.'

And that was the start of what Charlie would later describe as "the mad years", a frenetic, crazy period of seven-day weeks and working all hours; a ceaseless rollercoaster of running from restaurant to restaurant, attending to the endless demands, crises and dramas of their staffs and planning for and opening new venues. In three years, Forsyth started or acquired five new restaurants and converted a row of former Victorian townhouses in a salubrious part of the west-end into a deluxe hotel with a fine dining restaurant which quickly became the go-to venue for celebrities staying in Glasgow, boosted considerably when Charlie managed to recruit a top international chef to take charge of the restaurant.

Forsyth continued to have the Midas touch; all parts of the business were booming. Initially, Charlie, Forsyth and Paul McGuiness – an old school friend of Forsyth's - would meet regularly, but after a while this became less frequent, and he would mainly deal with Forsyth on his own. Charlie believed this was because they were so busy, with little time for meetings. And that was fine; Paul focused on the smooth running of the restaurants leaving Charlie to do what he did best: making sure the kitchens were producing and delivering high quality food to happy customers.

Again, Forsyth delivered. In addition to his greatly increased salary, Charlie saw regular sums of cash appearing in his bank account, with no declarations to the taxman. He did worry about this and asked Forsyth about it who shrugged his shoulders, saying:

'It's up to you Charlie. It's your money. You earned it through hard graft. Your call about declaring to Mr Taxman.'

He didn't. And the money went some way to assuaging Sarah who'd given birth to their first son, Calum, in the summer of 1990. She decided not to go back to the Parisienne Walkway in order to look after Calum, though, to get out the house, she occasionally waited on tables at a busy pizzeria close to their home. The extra money went some way to compensate for Charlie's absences from home. Nevertheless, tensions were developing between them.

Charlie was garnering a reputation too; the subject of

many admiring articles in the press, several TV appearances and contributor to a few best-selling cookbooks, which brought more money in. He was becoming something of a celebrity cook himself.

But, in addition to strains at home, the relentless grind was taking its toll. Charlie started suffering from chronic insomnia, and ironically, working constantly around so much good food, ate sparingly and began losing weight. He was running on nervous energy.

One night, seven months after becoming executive head chef, late on a Sunday evening, Charlie was in Forsyth's office at one of their increasingly infrequent meetings with Paul McGuiness. All three mirrored each other, heavy baggy eyes, exhausted and thin: Forsyth's portly frame had significantly diminished over the last year, Charlie had noticed.

They all wore expensive clothes, with Charlie still having an affectation for navy blue suits and Egyptian while soft cotton shirts. On his wrist was a luminous, sliver strapped luxury Swiss watch, his one concession to overt ostentation. It was a long way from stained chef's whites or Moss Brothers.

The meeting was coming to an end. It was after eleven and Charlie had been on his feet since eight that morning. He had a meeting with suppliers at seven the next day and he'd hardly spoken to or seen Sarah or Calum for five days. He rubbed his eyes and yawned.

'Knackered, Charlie boy?' Forsyth asked.

'I am, boss, I must admit,' Charlie agreed.

'Let's unwind a wee bit, eh?'

Forsyth rose and retrieved a bottle of whisky and three glasses from a side cabinet and poured three measures while McGuiness fetched a paper wrap from his inside pocket, opened it to reveal a small plastic bag containing white powder which he poured onto a cardboard coaster he'd brought from his pocket which he put on the desk in front of them. With a card, he divided the powder into neat rows, fetched a ten-pound note from his fine leather wallet, wrapped the tenner into a tube, bent down and snorted the powder into his nose.

'This is a punishing game. We need to relax,' Forsyth said, offering him one of the glasses. Charlie took a sip of the whisky. He rarely drank and didn't particularly like whisky but found it surprisingly smooth.

'Laphroaig,' Forsyth remarked, 'a really neat malt whisky,' before bending down at the desk with his own tenner and began snorting.

Charlie had watched people snorting coke, for he assumed that's what it was, numerous times in movies, but never up close and in person like this. Forsyth passed the coaster, which still had rows of coke on it, to Charlie. Paul, beside him, exclaimed:

'That is fucking brilliant man!'

Forsyth was looking at him intently. After a few seconds Charlie brought his own tenner from his wallet, rolled it into a tube and snorted the glistening white powder.

'Breathe in through your nose,' Forsyth instructed. Charlie inhaled deeply and felt a mild itching sensation as the powder flew up his nose, followed by a powerful sense of elation, almost euphoria. Instantly, he felt alert and had the sensation of his whole body becoming light at the same time as the entire burden of all his concerns, anxiety and tension just evaporated. He felt happy and free, almost weightless and looked at his two companions, both of whom now seemed remarkably revived, even glowing.

'The old Columbian marching powder never fails to do the trick,' Forsyth remarked. 'Here, take a wee sample for yourself,' and offered him a paper wrap. Just an hour ago, the idea of taking cocaine would have struck Charlie as mad. He'd never taken drugs, not even a joint of cannabis. He wasn't particularly against them; it's just the opportunity had never arisen. He took his responsibilities and duties seriously; his work was his dope. But the fatigue, the endless hours, the constant problem solving, were getting to him and he was exhausted, drained; everything becoming a grey blur.

Now he was re-energised, revived. He looked at Paul, who appeared refreshed and ten years' younger than a minute ago as did Forsyth. He accepted the wrap. Forsyth said to him:

'Take tomorrow afternoon off with the wife and the wean. Get some time with them.' Charlie nodded his head vigorously.

'I will,' he declared confidently.

He slept well for the few hours he had before rising the back of five to meet the suppliers but felt tired and worried again as the cocaine wore off, his energy sapping as he drove to work. He did take the afternoon off and had a great time with his wife and Calum. Sarah was delighted at him being home and playing joyfully with their child.

Back at work, though, there was an acrimonious crisis among the staff at the Queen Mary which the head chef demanded he resolve. Charlie felt utterly depressed. Walking into the superb art deco restaurant with its beautiful illustrations of the finest Clyde built transatlantic liners, already busy with diners at six on a Monday night, he went straight into the staff gent's toilet, closed a cubicle door and snorted a line from Forsyth's wrap.

Reinvigorated and feeling supremely confident, he entered the kitchen to a babble of voices from the staff, not least from the histrionic head chef which he cut across, issuing commands and instructions in a commanding, authoritative voice which brooked no dissent. He was in charge all right and the kitchen was back to order, but it was due to his namesake: charlie.

Over the next two years that namesake became his elixir, imbuing him with confidence, boosting his assertiveness to uncharacteristic borderline aggression, and eliminating all doubts and concern. Of course, it was severely time limited; a few hours at most and the comedown was awful, so he had to take more of the white powder and soon had acquired a habit. Forsyth wasn't going to supply him for free; within a short time, he had passed onto Charlie the name of the dealer who supplied both him and McGuiness. In months, Charlie was spending a lot on coke, but the money was rolling in, particularly those "bonuses" from Forsyth.

Contrary to popular conceptions, people who become addicted to drugs, even cocaine and sometimes heroin can function quite well for some time, years even, keeping down a job and sustaining relationships, like a functioning alcoholic. And so, it was with Charlie as he continued to work hard in the twilight and frenzied world of hospitality, managing eventually eleven kitchens, spinning like a whirly-gig as Forsyth's empire expanded.

His relationship with Sarah became more estranged just as, courtesy of coke, his sex drive went through the roof. For the first time he was unfaithful to his wife, having dalliances with several customers and the wife of a fellow restaurateur (although never with kitchen staff).

The work, the relentless pace and the habit meant he never had time to reflect on what was happening. It never affected the quality of his work, and as long as he delivered, his boss (who had also developed a large coke habit) was satisfied.

Three years later, irony of ironies, Forsyth announced he'd acquired the franchise for the Central Hotel, from the new owners, the Martindale Group; the same soulless company that ran the hotel in London that Charlie had hated working in. Fortunately, they were only interested in running the hotel, giving Charlie and Paul a free hand in running the kitchen and restaurant which they were renaming Martindale's in the Dear Green Place.

Forsyth's company spent a fortune refurbishing and modernising the premises and Charlie took great pride in overseeing the renovations and installing the new equipment; this was the first opportunity he'd ever had to design his own kitchen with a seemingly unlimited budget. But, on entering the old La Maison Rose kitchen for the first time in years, he had to exorcise the ghosts of the many horrible memories imbedded in the very walls. But he got past that, and the new kitchen was unrecognizable from those dark days.

He was, of course in charge of the interviews for the Head Chef's position and he could not believe it when Candy, newly in charge of HR for the company, passed him the list of applicants. Adrian Ramsay had applied for his old job. What comes around goes around he thought and took great pleasure in rejecting him for interview. He was tempted to draw a picture of a middle finger at the bottom of the Dear John letter but resisted it.

The opening night of the newly refurbished Martindale in the Dear Green Place was a splendid occasion, the guest list replete with city dignitaries, celebrities and much media attention. Decades later, Charlie still had one of the press photos from that night standing besuited alongside Paul, Forsyth, the Lord Provost of Glasgow in his badge and chain and the CEO of Martindale's hotels. It was the pinnacle of his career with Forsyth's company.

And then it all went pear shaped.

FOUR

It started a few months after the grand opening of Martindale's in the Dear Green Place. Charlie made a routine visit to a valued game supplier for most of the restaurants. His contact was a tall, brawny, hirsute Highlander called Hamish Lochlin, who with characteristic bluntness greeted Charlie with:

'You've not paid us for last month!'

Charlie hadn't taken a line yet, so was feeling quite jangly.

'What?' he reacted as if hit by an electric shock.

'You heard. There's been no payment for last month's supplies.'

Lochlin, with his full ginger beard, was almost in his face, eyes boring into him. He almost stammered:

'Hamish, I'll...I'll see to it right away. It'll not happen again.'

Lochlin relaxed a tad.

'Aye, ok. But if it happens again...' He left the rest hanging.

Charlie's next destination was Parisienne Walkway where Charlie bolted into the staff loo and snorted a line before phoning Forsyth feeling more confident and assertive.

'Aw Charlie, that's shite. I'll see to it right away. Don't want to piss off big Hamish and his squad and end up with a deer's head lying at the bottom of your bed,' was Forsyth's reassuring response.

Lochlin's company got paid within a few days. But then, a month later, two other suppliers complained they hadn't been paid. Forsyth again protested an "oversight", but it took nearly ten days for the payments to be rectified.

Several weeks after that, Charlie walked into a barrage of complaints at all his kitchens. Half the staff in each hadn't been paid and the same with a lot of the restaurant staff. He hurried to Forsyth's office, but he wasn't there. Instead, the HR woman, Candy, looking exasperated and harassed, reassured him, it was down to "payroll glitches" and all the staff's money would come through. It did, but a week later in dribs and dabs.

It went on like that for months. Another supplier not getting paid, staff not getting paid or underpaid. Charlie himself didn't receive his "bonus" in October. Forsyth, on the increasingly rare occasions Charlie got through to him on the phone as he was never in the office, tried to calm him, saying: 'We've changed banks and there's been a whole stream of fuck ups. Don't worry we'll get it sorted. Honestly, bankers, legalised bandits.'

Charlie had no access to the finance side of the business and could only take Forsyth's word for it, but he was growing increasingly worried. Still, for a few months, things calmed down and all payments were met. Then, in late November, as he was gearing up for the incredibly busy Christmas period, on his way to see the head chef at Martindale's in the Dear Green Place, he was asked by the hotel manager if he could have a word in his office.

This was the same office Charlie had been paid for his first night's casual work as a KP nearly eighteen years' earlier. It had been considerably spruced up as part of the refurbishment, but still very recognizable to Charlie. The manager came straight to the point:

'The rent's not been paid for this month.' Charlie's face

drained. He tried desperately to comfort him with the same line he'd had to use repeatedly these past few months.

'Extreme apologies. I'll chase it up right away and I'll make sure it won't happen again.'

The manager's face was impassive. 'I'm hearing this is happening a lot; staff and suppliers not getting paid. They say Glasgow is a village but when it comes to hospitality, it's a hamlet. The rumour mill is going crazy out there. Charlie, this business is run on trust. Lose that and the game's over.'

Charlie could offer no response, just a feeble, 'I'll look into it, I promise,' before darting across the city centre to the office, where, as usual, Forsyth wasn't there. Candy fielded for him again, keeping Charlie at the door, but she looked haunted. He tried to phone Forsyth, but he hadn't been returning his calls for weeks. He tried to get McGuiness on the phone with no luck, and word was he'd only made fleeting appearances at the restaurants and all his managers were up to high doh. Indeed, whenever Charlie appeared at one of the venues, a restaurant manager would buttonhole him with:

'Have you seen Paul?' 'Where is he? I need to see him!'

Something was seriously wrong, but they got through the madness of Christmas and everyone got paid.

He spent Christmas Day at his parents with Sarah and Calum and Raymond, who was now a qualified engineer and a senior manager with a large construction company. His folks were so pleased that both their sons were doing well, but that didn't stop his mother remarking over turkey and the trimmings which Charlie had cooked:

THE KITCHEN VIGILANTE - "JUSTICE WILL BE SERVED"

'You look dreadful Charlie, doesn't he Sarah?' who was seated across from him, Calum beside her.

'Aye, mum. He works all the hours God sends. Calum, nor me, ever see him.'

He knew from the increasingly bitter arguments he and Sarah were having at home that this could be the prelude to a fight over the Christmas dinner table, so he tried to deflect it.

'Come on, it's Christmas. I'm going to take a break in January. Promise.'

'Aye, I've heard that before,' Sarah said wearily. He turned to his father, eating silently beside him.

'How's the hip?' His father had recently retired and was having problems walking and was in a lot of pain; he had an appointment with a specialist early in the New Year.

'Och it's fine during the day, but murder at night. I was saying to your mother...' and he was off talking about his health and deflecting the dinner table talk from Charlie's long hours and terrible appearance. It was true though, he did look dreadful and painfully thin, almost emaciated. By contrast, Raymond wolfing down his turkey at the end of the table was the picture of health.

On the first Monday morning of 1994, Charlie was due to meet the Head Chef at the Cullins about eight. When he arrived, the head was already there, looking surprised.

'What's this about?' he asked Charlie, pointing at a handwritten notice on a piece of white paper attached to the entry door. It read:

Due to emergency work required, these premises are closed

until further notice.

Ignoring the head chef's repeated questions, Charlie tried to unlock the door with the keys he had for all the premises. It wouldn't give and with a deep sinking feeling of despair knew that the lock had been changed. He told the agitated chef to 'get a coffee and I'll be back as soon as I can,' before running up to Parisienne Walkway, to be met with a waiting cleaner which told him everything he needed to know as she also had a key to the premises. There was the same note on the door as there was at the Queen Mary. He didn't dare show his face at Martindale's in the Dear Green Place and incur the hostility of the manager. When he arrived at the West Nile Street office, it was shut and empty. Looking through the glass pane that took up half of the door, he could see the office had been stripped of tables and chairs, only a couple of unplugged telephone receivers lying forlornly on the bare carpeted floor.

Frantically, he tried to contact Forsyth and McGuiness, using a callbox on Sauchiehall Street with no success. Except for Martindale's where he phoned the head chef and told him to alert the rest of the staff, he went round all his restaurants and the west end hotel to inform surprised staff gathering for work and confronted with the paper notices and locked doors that he'd had no "advance warnings" of this and to go home.

Some were stunned, others angry and confrontational and took it out on him. Fortunately, he'd taken a line of coke in a public toilet and was able to handle their hostility, scepticism and despair, but without flannelling them as he genuinely knew nothing.

At home, despite the coke, he felt deflated. To his surprise, Sarah wasn't too upset, in fact she seemed to be quite relieved. She reasoned that they had money in the bank (they were still very thrifty) to last for a while, and with his reputation Charlie should get a reasonably paid job in a good kitchen, and he would have more time with her, and far more importantly, with Calum.

Sarah's soothing words brought him down from his initial dejection. Within a few days he was actually glad to be free of the constant treadmill of crises, dramas and problems. Though he still used the occasional line of coke, it was far less frequently, and he was able to sleep better and relax. He'd been going at it like a jet for years and the ability to take a walk in the park with his wife and child without having to juggle a thousand things in his head was amazing.

He was also lucky in being kept away from the finances in Forsyth's outfit, which meant he wasn't het for anything legally. His phone buzzed for a few days from irate head chefs, but they soon ceased when they realised, he genuinely didn't know anything. Ditto for suppliers.

He was genuinely concerned for his reputation in the hamlet of the dining world and took full advantage of the good copy he'd given journalists over the years to give a couple of interviews in which he expressed great sympathy for the staff who'd been "very badly treated", but emphasised he'd just been in charge of the kitchens, passionate about serving good food and creating outstanding restaurants and had nothing to do with all the "awful shenanigans" that had went on. The published articles reproduced this line faithfully and Charlie was depicted as a "victim" who'd been "shafted" as much as anyone from the "collapse of Dick Forsyth's empire."

Of him, there was no sign. He'd scarpered, leaving a trail of debt and unpaid bills. All the restaurants were closed and staff left on the scrapheap unpaid. It was little comfort at the time that most of the venues were up and running under new owners and staff back in work within months.

Because Forsyth couldn't be found, Paul McGuiness copped it for everything; he'd signed most of the contracts, leases, deals and so on – a cynical but smart move on Forsyth's part. He'd also vanished but was apprehended at Heathrow Airport trying to flee the country on a false passport. As McGuiness was awaiting trial on countless charges of false accounting, fraud and obtaining monies by deception, Charlie gave a few statements and depositions for the court basically repeating that he'd dealt solely with the kitchens, suppliers and managing staff, which was basically the truth. He was never called to court to give evidence. McGuiness was found guilty and went down for five years.

Meanwhile, after a few months of relaxing, Charlie was starting to feel restless and at a loose end. He'd managed to wean himself off coke with his own willpower and the assistance of a private counsellor who didn't come cheap, but he found to be very effective. She convinced him that addiction to anything was a matter of ingrained habit and patterns of behaviours in your head in trying to cope with crises and anxiety. The key was to deal with these entrenched negative habits and behavioural patterns by developing the skills and resilience to confront and overcome the triggers that could lead to him relapsing. As these triggers were entirely work related, and he was now out of that environment, this was relatively straightforward. With her assistance he was off cocaine entirely after a few months.

There were no immediate financial concerns for Charlie and Sarah, but they couldn't live on her paltry wages from the pizzeria for ever. They took a holiday back at the same resort in Corfu where they'd had their honeymoon; their passion and love rekindled. So much so, that when they got back, Sarah announced she was pregnant again. Charlie was ecstatic, but it also galvanised him to find work.

The thought of working under a head chef once more appalled him. He was looking to run his own place, mindful of all the pressures, including relapse triggers, that might induce, but he was confident he could now deal with those. Despite Glasgow's flourishing dining scene with new ventures opening constantly, he couldn't see any good opportunities.

Then he got a call from Gregg Cooper, the former assistant head chef at the old La Maison Rose who invited him to lunch with a "proposition". After they'd reminisced and had a good laugh about the Adrian Ramsay days, Charlie listened attentively as Gregg told him there was a bank branch recently closed not far from where he and his wife lived in Giffnock, an affluent suburb, just outside the Glasgow city boundary. Gregg thought it would be a great spot to turn into a restaurant. Would Charlie like to look at it?

Initially dismissive that a former bank could be transformed into a restaurant, he reckoned there would be no harm in paying a visit. The former bank was a solid, detached single-storey building made of dark brown sandstone with a paved entrance at the front and a car park in the rear surrounded by a lawyer's practice and a dental surgery. A lot of work would be required to refit it as a restaurant, but there was an extensive basement where the vaults had been which could serve as the kitchen. It was located off a busy main road, and apart from a few takeaways and a pub, no other restaurant for miles. The more he investigated it, the more appealing it became for Charlie.

He'd always got on well with Gregg, who'd been a good support and mentor. Ok, he could be shouty, but that was the norm back in the day. Gregg was a good chef, and Charlie could have him focus on the kitchen while he covered front of house and suppliers. Sarah, also initially apprehensive about the idea, came round, especially with the thought of another baby on the way and their diminishing savings.

With Sarah's help, Charlie drew up a business plan and took it to various banks to raise the finance. Two dismissed it, but the third accepted on condition that they raise one third of the money needed themselves. This was daunting and meant he, Sarah, as well as Gregg had to draw on their savings and both parties had to put their houses up as collateral. That was a lot of pressure, but by now Charlie had sold himself completely on the idea and the prospect of owning his own restaurant – albeit in partnership with Gregg – drove him on.

It took nearly a year to refurbish and kit out the building. Inevitably, costs rose, and they had to eat into more of their savings. Then there were further delays caused by holdups in obtaining a drinks license and issues raised by their neighbours. Charlie and Sarah hadn't helped matters by wanting the interior decked out in terra cotta and other exotic furnishings that would give the place the feel of a cosy trattoria. During that hectic year, Sarah gave birth to their second child; a boy they named Caleb.

Finally, in the autumn of 1995, their savings virtually extinguished, with no income coming in, they opened the restaurant. Sarah had come up with the name: Deep South, as it was right at the very edge of the southside of Glasgow.

Charlie's friendly contacts with reporters came in handy once more, and the opening earned good advance press, epitomised by the headline of one article in the Evening Times which declared:

Renowned Glasgow Chef, Charlie Carty, goes Deep South.

Their opening night was a great success, and their first ten days were fully booked. Reviews were excellent. But then there was a lean period of three weeks. Charlie and Sarah were living on their nerves; they'd worked out their savings would dry up completely by February. Fortunately, bookings and walk-ins picked up. Further good reviews followed. By early November they were fully booked for the Christmas period. Income started to pour in, though there wasn't much left after overheads and the bank was paid. But it staved off disaster and by the beginning of 1996, Deep South was busy most nights and you could only secure a table at the weekend months in advance.

It was back to the grind for Charlie; persistent eighteen-hour days and all the issues that came with running a popular restaurant. But he was in charge of his own place, Sarah had his back (and kept an experienced, keen eye over the waitering staff), Gregg was an old hand in the kitchen and Charlie picked up with the suppliers, regaining their trust, even with Hamish Lochlin.

They were all tried and tested and knew what they were doing. Deep South was a success; there'd been nothing like it in the vicinity and the well-heeled locals flocked to it while other customers came from all over Glasgow and beyond. To cap it all, six months after they opened, a flamboyant TV chef called Claud Todd, who presented a popular BBC TV cookery programme with a huge audience, popped in unannounced, raved about the place and asked to make an episode at Deep South. It was broadcast six months later and Charlie and Gregg played prominent roles throughout the programme along with Claud Todd. The response was huge and after it they were taking bookings from across the world and the money rolled in which meant Sarah was comfortably able to spend as much time as she needed at home with Caleb. Charlie was eternally grateful he'd went for that lunch with Gregg.

About a year after they'd opened, Charlie was covering in the kitchen for Gregg who'd taken a night off. Around half-nine as the tempo was beginning to ease, one of the waitresses came up to Charlie to say that a customer had requested if he could speak to him to relay how much he and his wife had enjoyed their food. Front of house was normally his focus anyway, so Charlie washed his hands and went to meet the customer.

He was a young but distinguished looking black man in his early 30s wearing a beautifully cut, dark suit which seemed to Charlie's untrained eye to be bespoke. His wife next to him was a beautiful looking woman also in her 30s and just as elegantly attired in a lovely aquamarine full length dress. Charlie introduced himself. The man rose and gave him a firm handshake as did his wife who remained seated.

'The seafood spaghetti aragosta was absolutely delicious,' he spoke in a rich, velvet voice. The man exuded gentle authority. 'That is my favourite dish. I've dined across the world, but I've never had it as succulent as that. The taste, the texture, the sauce, everything,' he pressed his fingers together, his face lit up, 'was perfect.' His wife vigorously nodded her head in agreement.

'Thank you very much. I'm so pleased you both enjoyed your meal,' Charlie responded fulsomely. Praise like this from customers, made the job for him. There were very few jobs where you could get instant positive feedback like this.

'Oh, enjoy is such an understatement,' the man protested, 'it was incredible! Please, take my card.'

The man proffered a distinguished looking white business card fringed in black. Charlie gave it a cursory glance but didn't really read it. In exchange he gave him one of his own cards.

'If you're ever in Glasgow again, it would be a pleasure to

have you dine with us once more.'

The man sipped the remains of his coffee while his wife rose to leave. Charlie commanded a waiter to fetch the couple's coats and escorted them out. Back in the kitchen he studied the business card. It read:

His Excellency Monsieur Aristide Nzamba

Finance Minister

Republic of MapAlindi

'Bloody hell!' He showed the card around the staff in the kitchen. 'An African minister. 'Jesus, we're certainly on the global map now!'

Back home later, he and Sarah looked up an atlas. MapAlindi was in central Africa just north of the equator. Neither he nor Sarah had ever heard of the country.

'If he and his wife ever come back, we might get a holiday there,' Sarah said.

'Aye, you never know. But he probably says that to all the head chefs he meets,' and Charlie placed it in his collection of business cards.

At the turn of the year, after a long bout of chronic illness stemming from his arthritis, Charlie's father died. Part of Charlie was relieved that his father was out of his misery but that didn't mitigate the loss. His mother was all alone now in their Hamiltonhill house which she'd no intention of leaving. Raymond, now going steady with a girl called Louise he'd met at a nightclub, and Charlie alongside Sarah, were determined, despite their busy lives, to visit and keep her company as much as possible.

Things rolled along nicely for a few months when a blast from the past walked into Deep South one fine spring evening. Charlie was flitting between the kitchen and restaurant and recognised him right away: Eric Fenwick, his old manager at the New Caledonian Hotel. He was now in his fifties but looking well on it. He was with his wife. They hugged, exchanged greetings and Eric introduced his wife, a petite brunette named Maxine.

'You're looking great, and this place is doing very well,' Eric said fulsomely after Charlie pulled up a chair and sat beside them.

'Aye, can't complain,' Charlie agreed with the restaurateur's characteristic understatement.

'You walked away from the Forsyth mess unscathed.' Charlie blew out his cheeks and gave a deep sigh.

'That was close. Learned a lot from that.'

'Still no word of him?'

'Vanished off the face of the earth.'

They moved on to talk of pleasanter memories from the past and after a while Charlie left them to enjoy their food. He rejoined them over coffee where, after praising the food, Eric disclosed that his visit wasn't entirely casual. He'd left the New Caledonian years earlier and had relocated to London to work for a company called Landis Cuisine where he was the executive head for acquisition and development.

Charlie had heard of Landis Cuisine. A French company originally from Bordeaux, they'd become a rapidly growing player in the dining trade and were opening restaurants in the

UK, mainly in London and the south-east.

'I'll come to the point, Charlie,' Eric said, sipping his coffee. 'Glasgow is now on the culinary map and Landis are interested in opening a venue here. Better still, we want to skip all that time and research malarky, take on a good, going popular concern.' He looked around the restaurant. 'This place looks fantastic. You've done brilliantly here.'

'You want to buy me over?'

Eric was blunt. 'Yes. You and Gregg. We'll make you a really good offer, keep you two in charge, but you'll have the benefits of all that Landis can bring you: bigger supply chains, even better marketing, lower overheads, reduced costs. I don't expect you to reply right away but think about it.'

He did and discussed it with Sarah and Gregg. They'd ran the place for eighteen months and had ridden a wave of success. But would it last and could they continue to do it all on their own? They still had the enthusiasm, the hunger and the thirst that a new challenge brings, but both he and Gregg were tired and had to admit they could do with help. Furthermore, success attracts competition. Giffnock, a culinary desert prior to Deep South, now had several restaurants about to open. The challenges would only intensify.

Charlie also had to consider that his mother was taking his father's passing very badly. Formerly outgoing, she'd become housebound, wasn't eating much and the house was beginning to become untidy. Raymond's job took him across Scotland, while Sarah was busy with the two kids, and he was tied to the restaurant. He was concerned about his mother and that he couldn't look after her as much as he wished. All in all, with Gregg's agreement, he agreed to start negotiations with Landis.

It didn't take long. Eric and Landis's people cast a sharp eye over the premises and within a few weeks made a generous offer, including keeping both Gregg and Charlie on as both joint head chefs and co-managers.

Charlie trusted Eric, but the thought of answering to someone else didn't suit him. He discussed it with Gregg who was happy to stay on as sole head chef. With Sarah's agreement he decided to sell his interest in Deep South. It was quick and amicable and completed by early summer. Landis took over, Charlie pocketed a generous sum and was able to spend more time with his visibly ailing mother.

For four months Charlie split his time between his mother, helping Sarah with Caleb and Calum (who was now at primary school), spending good quality time with both, and giving paid advice to other restaurateur's. One of his clients said to him that rather than doing this unofficially, why not set himself up as a consultant? Following this advice, Charlie created Carty Cuisine Consultancy and received a stream of paid appointments.

In late October he received a cryptic call from an agency in London asking him if he'd be interested in coming down to view "an interesting option relating to his work in the restaurant and dining business." The caller refused to give any further details and after agreeing with Sarah there could be no harm in 'a wee trip to London and seeing what was on offer,' he agreed to a meeting with the agency.

The appointment was in a large building made from Portland stone not far from Marylebone Station in central London. He went to a discreet office on the third floor which appeared to be a rented office and not their permanent base and was met politely by two men in sharp dark suits. The meeting which Charlie rapidly became aware was really an interview, lasted two hours. He was questioned intensively about his experience and background. Finally, the two men seemed to relax slightly and one of them said:

'We work with and represent a very exclusive list of clients. One of those clients is the current president of the central African country of MapAlindi.'

Charlie's ears pricked up; that name rang a bell with him, but he couldn't quite remember why.

'The president's long serving executive head chef, effectively the president's personal chef, recently passed away suddenly and he wishes to appoint a new personal chef. We have been asked to recruit for that position and a person close to the president has strongly recommended yourself.'

Of course, Charlie remembered now, the guy in the immaculate dark suit who'd been in with his wife at Deep South extolling the food, the finance minister of MapAlindi. Christ, he must have made quite an impression, he thought.

The other man went on:

'The position will be well remunerated, the accommodation is well appointed and in the grounds of the presidential compound and you will have total control of the kitchen staff who will answer to you, and of course, all relocation costs for you and your family will be paid for.'

'I've got two young children, the youngest only eighteen months,' Charlie pointed out.

'We understand and there will be excellent nursery and education provision for the children.'

Charlie was stunned. 'I wasn't expecting this.' They both smiled.

'Could we ask you to think it over, but get back to us quite soon,' the first guy said. 'The President and First Lady are keen to have a new personal chef in place.'

Charlie went back to Glasgow in a daze and spent days mulling it over with Sarah. Offers to become the personal chef to a president weren't common and Charlie was attracted by it. But they would have to leave everything behind and there was his ailing mother. Raymond, his brother, came up with the solution that allowed them to accept the offer.

He'd just recently bought a secluded villa in the sedate suburb of Bearsden just outside the city and moved in with Louise, who worked part time in an elderly care home. Raymond suggested that their mother move in with them. The old lady doted on Louise (as she did on Sarah), who was experienced in working with older people and she would be delighted to help look after the mother.

His mother was reluctant at first, but they talked her round, and she moved in with Raymond and Louise. With that off his mind, Charlie accepted the offer, and they arrived with the kids in MapAlindi in the late autumn of 1997.

It was, of course, a culture shock in every sense; the tropical weather, the sights, the sounds, the colours. Aristide Nzamba, the finance minister, who turned out to be President Olivier Nzamba's nephew, greeted them on arrival with his gracious wife and helped them settle.

The president's "compound" was a beautiful white, stuccoed, extensively pillared palace, heavily guarded and the couple were allocated a villa in the large grounds of the compound. They were introduced to the President, a small man who wore a bright, scarlet uniform with a braided gold cap, epaulettes and a host of medals pinned to his chest (he'd been the army chief of staff and had come to power in a coup a decade earlier). He was quite formal as was the First Lady, but polite and wished Charlie and his family well and looked forward to the delicious food that he would cook for them which his nephew had praised so highly. No pressure then, Charlie thought.

He got to work in the kitchen with a staff of about twenty who were good and competent and rapidly took to him. What helped was that the previous chef had been quite a tyrant along the lines of Adrian Ramsay, so the staff welcomed Charlie's brisk, efficient, but above all fair approach and he secured their willing co-operation. He also uncovered a whole series of corruption and kickbacks with the presidential kitchen suppliers which Charlie, with the enthusiastic support and influential help of Aristide Nzamba, sorted out. Aristide, who became friendly with him and often invited Charlie and Sarah to dine with him and his wife, was invaluable, alerting Charlie to the president's favourite dishes which he served to him with additional flavours and enhancements earning him positive feedback from the main man himself.

They settled in, Sarah loved it, Calum had his own personal tutors and Caleb's nursery was first class. They had the freedom to roam the grounds of the presidential compound with the kids which were like a mini tropical forest with "ponds" that were more like small lakes and a variety of exotic wildlife.

Compared to the norm, the hours weren't too long either. He was in complete charge of the kitchen. Aristide had his back, and the President and First Lady were pleased with what he was serving up to them. On several occasions he travelled abroad with the president's extensive entourage, including on one occasion a state visit to meet the US President, where Charlie worked, to his disbelief, with the chefs in the White House: quite a journey for a lad from Possilpark! As a bonus he was inducted into the Chef des Chefs des Chefs, an exclusive club for personal chefs of heads of state.

Aside from the odd tropical downpour and the sticky humidity, the weather was in such contrast to the prevailing, grey drabness of the west of Scotland which could be so depressing and cast a gloomy pall over everything. Even cloudy days in MapAlindi were bright.

Raymond phoned frequently updating them on his mother. She had settled into her new home, was eating well and looked and sounded much better than she had on her own. Louise was a tonic for her, and this was the final factor that convinced Charlie he'd made the right decision for himself and his family.

There was a beautiful beach resort about forty miles from the presidential compound and the capital where he, Sarah and the kids would go to on his days off with a security escort. They had the unspoilt beach to themselves, the kids paddling in the blue seas, while Charlie and Sarah swam into the breakers against the background of the dense tropical forest. It was picture perfect. MapAlindi and the lifestyle suited Sarah. She looked fantastic, her browned, tanned skin glowing and looked stunning in her bikini. Charlie loved her more than ever and they were happy, very happy.

One Saturday they came back after a delightful day at the resort, Charlie's deputy under his strict instructions attending to the President and First Lady's evening meal. On arrival at their villa as the short tropical dusk was descending, their telephone rang and the operator at the compound switchboard informed Charlie that there was a call from 'a member of his family.'

And everything fell apart, and Charlie was set to embark on a radically different path.

FIVE

He assumed it was Raymond and concerned his mother. When the connection was made, he said urgently:

'Raymond, is it mom?'

But a different voice answered hesitatingly.

'Eh...no...it's not Raymond, it's Gerry.'

Gerry? The cousin who'd tipped him off about the vacant KP's position at La Maison Rouge all those years ago. He hadn't seen him for years. Why would he be calling Charlie?

'Hello, Gerry, everything all right?'

Gerry's voice continued to waver.

'I'm...eh... really sorry to tell you...'

'Is it my mother?' Charlie interrupted. There was a short pause, then:

'No, it's not your mom Charlie.' Another pause. 'It's Raymond.'

'Raymond?' Charlie was surprised and startled. There was something dreadfully wrong here. 'What's up with Raymond?'

'Aw, this is terrible. I...I don't know how to tell you Charlie.'

'Just get on with it!' Charlie demanded.

'There was an incident involving Raymond.'

'Incident. What do you mean incident?'

'He was attacked.'

Charlie noted that ominous 'was'.

'Attacked? Where?'

'In the city centre.'

'How?' And Gerry told him the sparse details of what he knew.

'I don't know all the details, Charlie. Raymond was at

a night out in town, and he was walking home, and he got attacked and beaten up. I don't know who it was; it was some guy and he's been arrested, and they've got him in custody.'

'Was it a fight? Raymond never got involved in a fight in his life! Does he know the guy? Is it somebody he knew that he worked with?'

'Charlie, I really don't know all the details.'

'Ok, how is he? Is he in hospital?' There was a long dreadful pause before Gerry resumed.

'He was badly injured.'

'How badly? What hospital is he in?'

'Charlie, I'm really sorry to tell you, he's dead.'

'What'?

'He never made it. He was dead when he arrived at hospital.'

Charlie was stunned. He asked: 'Does my mother know?'

'We've not told her yet. She's not been great recently.'

'Louise?'

'She's in bits, absolutely shattered. Listen, Charlie, sincerely that's all I know. Any chance you could get back here as soon as you can?'

'Aye, Gerry, I'll make arrangements and get back. Don't tell my mother until I get home.'

'Sure. Really sorry, Charlie.'

He ended the conversation and let Sarah know who broke down in tears; she was very fond of his brother. They comforted each other before, in a daze, Charlie contacted Aristide and told him what had happened. He, in turn, let the President and First lady know and arranged for a plane to fly him, Sarah and the kids to Glasgow. Within forty-eight hours he was back in his hometown for the worst possible reasons.

He met Gerry off the plane, and they went straight to Raymond's house in Bearsden where it finally fell to Charlie to let his mother know. It took a while for it to register with her, but when it did, the look of utter anguish and pain on her face was appalling for Charlie to see. He hugged his mother closely and broke down with her, sharing the grief. He also tried to comfort Louise, but she was bereft, virtually numbed with distress.

Leaving Sarah with his mother and Louise, he went to the city mortuary where he'd arranged to meet the two CID officers heading the investigation into his brother's murder. The senior of the two cops, a tall morose looking man in his thirties identified himself as Detective Inspector Tumelty and led him into a windowless, tiled air-conditioned room where his brother lay under a shroud on a stainless-steel trestle in the middle of the room.

He'd watched this scene countless times in movies and TV shows, but it was so unreal for him to be at the centre of it. DI Tumelty asked if he was ready to see his brother's body. Charlie nodded he was, he just wanted it over with. A sallow faced mortician pulled back the shroud. He supressed a gasp as he saw Raymond's head swathed in bandages, his skin blotched and discoloured, nose broken and his opened eyes lifeless. It was a shocking sight and Charlie could barely murmur:

'Aye...aye, that's him.'

The mortician pulled the shroud back over his head and Charlie was led to another room where the DI and his colleagues filled him in with the details of his brothers' vicious slaying.

Raymond had been at a colleagues' retirement leaving party at a bar in the Merchant City. He'd left just after closing time with his workmates, but couldn't get a taxi, a typical situation on a busy weekend night. As no one else was going in Raymond's direction, he walked on his own across the city centre until he reached a quiet street with a bridge behind Queen Street railway station. A couple were walking about fifty yards behind him as Raymond crossed the bridge. They saw a man on the opposite side, staggering, suddenly turn to him and shout "whit you looking at?"

Raymond ignored him and walked on. Charlie knew that's what he would do to avoid trouble, but the guy walked stridently across to Raymond and aggressively confronted him. Raymond tried to run away but the man, powerfully built, grabbed his shoulder and punched him on the face, which probably explained his broken nose. Raymond collapsed and hit the deck, and the guy proceeded to kick him in the head. The couple walking behind shouted at him to stop but the man produced a knife. They were petrified and watched in horror as the guy continued his assault on Raymond.

At this point the DI stopped his narrative and asked Charlie: 'Do you want me to go on?'

'Aye, please.'

Not content with kicking him on the ground, his attacker then stamped and jumped on Raymond's head, before delivering a final kick to his slumped body before moving on. The couple, paralysed with fear, nevertheless could distinctly hear the assailant saying, as he walked away, 'nae cunt gets wide wi me'. They watched him, still staggering, walk under the newly constructed Buchanan Galleries shopping centre and turn into Buchanan Street. Raymond lay comatose while the couple screamed before a passerby ran down to the nearby George Square and alerted a passing police patrol.

Raymond's injuries were catastrophic; Charlie was later to learn that his brain was effectively squashed like a sponge and despite the heroic efforts of paramedics who were on the scene in minutes, died on the way to hospital.

Following the couple's description, the attacker was detained walking down Sauchiehall Street and subsequently charged with his brother's homicide. DI Tumelty was not able at this stage to disclose any further details about the attacker as 'inquiries were continuing.' Charlie thanked the officers and left the mortuary, his stomach churning.

As there was no doubt about how Raymond had died, his body was released into the care of an undertaker and Charlie was able to proceed with the funeral arrangements. On a windswept, bleak autumn day, Raymond was cremated; the service overflowed with friends and colleagues. Charlie read a brief eulogy and there was a mournful, sedate purvey which he couldn't wait to get away from.

His mother didn't attend the funeral as she was too unwell, virtually incapacitated by her youngest son's passing. They'd kept the horrific details of his murder from her but that didn't detract from the impact the loss had on her. She was only in her late sixties, but she was already very frail and had never really recovered from her husband's death. Her grief was palpable and severely compounded her ailing health. She needed constant care and attention which Louise, Raymond's girlfriend, was in no fit state to give her. After the funeral, Charlie had to get back to work in MapAlindi. Sarah elected to stay with the kids to look after his mother for a few months until more permanent arrangements could be made for her. The plan was she'd rejoin him in Africa with the children.

He flew back to MapAlindi and attempted to get back into a work routine. All his staff, the President and First lady, Aristide and his wife were all very sympathetic, the President telling him if he needed more time off to go back home, to take it, but he declined and threw himself into his work. This distracted him, but at night alone in the villa compound, his mind dwelled on the memory of his lovely, young brother, a pleasant, hard-working guy and the unspeakable way in which he'd died, a total waste at the hands of a drunken thug.

Through Gerry and Sarah, Charlie learnt more about the murderer which they'd gleaned from press reports and what the police were able to divulge to them. He was 22 and his name was Jo Jamieson. He lived with his mother in the Barmulloch housing estate or "scheme" as they were called in Glasgow, on the north side of the city. Though details were scant, it seems that on the night he murdered his brother, Jamieson had been drinking in various bars in the city centre.

Quite well on, he'd been ejected from one bar for pestering women and then refused entry by stewards on the door at several other pubs. Witnesses reported that he'd been growling at people as he staggered through the city centre streets. His pent-up homicidal rage exploded at Raymond. There were few other details Charlie was able to pick up about him.

Meanwhile, Charlie's calls with Sarah were becoming increasingly concerning. His mother was becoming more confused and constantly yearning for Raymond. Louise had moved out of the Bearsden home; it's memories too much for her. Charlie understood this. She was only in her early thirties and had a whole life in front of her.

His mother's sister, Gerry's mother, had moved away to Fife some years ago and had her own health problems with rheumatoid arthritis so was in no state to look after her. She'd lost contact with her brother who'd moved to Australia decades ago. In short, apart from Sarah and himself, there was no one else able to provide the care his mother needed.

Over a few weeks, they had long conversations about the situation and finally agreed: it was best that Charlie returned home to look after his mother with Sarah. Besides, the kids needed stability, and Caleb was at the age where he was about to start primary school.

Charlie informed the President and the First Lady along with Aristide, who were completely understanding and resigned his position. Along with his time at the Springwell Hotel with Larry, Janet and Craig, and of course where he'd met Sarah, MapAlindi was the second happiest period in Charlie's life, and he regretted leaving as the plane flew him home for an uncertain future in his hometown.

His mother's health did improve when he came back although she still pined for Raymond and was constantly asking when he was 'coming home,' which caused Charlie great distress. Sarah missed MapAlindi and the lifestyle she'd grown accustomed to but knuckled under and focused on settling Caleb into his first school which Calum also attended and looking after his mother with Charlie.

He revived his consultancy and quickly obtained some good commissions. Their savings had been replenished (they'd hardly spent anything in MapAlindi as everything was provided for them), they'd no major debts and they were financially secure. Though still missing MapAlindi, Charlie had rapidly re-established himself in Glasgow. Apart from his mother, his main concern was the upcoming trial of Raymond's killer which opened seven months after the murder in the spring of 1998.

He wasn't called as a witness but attended every day of the ten-day trial at the imposing High Court building in Glasgow where he got his first glimpse of Joe Jamieson, aside from some grainy press pictures taken of him in custody. Right away Charlie, viewing Jamieson in court from the public gallery, could see that Raymond would have been no match for him. He was tall, well-built and muscular with short, fairish hair and eyes that betrayed no emotion. Throughout the proceedings, he remained utterly impassive.

Charlie, of course detested him on sight; this was the monster who had killed his brother in the prime of life and his expressionless demeanour only added to Charlie's anger.

Jamieson pleaded not guilty, and the trial began with the police and various witnesses, including the young couple who had witnessed the savage attack on Raymond, giving evidence on the assault and his arrest. The stewards on the door at the pub where Jamieson had been ejected from testified, he'd persistently annoyed and harassed several young women and it had taken three of them to get him out the venue. Other stewards reported he'd been verbally abusive and threatening to them when refused entry.

Hearing this, Charlie had his head in his hands wanting to shout at them, "why didn't any of you bastards not call the police?" but he stayed silent hoping the prosecution counsel would, but he never did.

The evidence against Jamieson was overwhelming and his defence was reduced to nit picking about identification which the witnesses easily dealt with. On the fourth day as the prosecution was concluding their case, the defence threw in the towel and announced Jamieson had changed his plea to guilty. Charlie let out a huge sigh of relief as this charade, as he saw it, could come to an end.

What remained of the trial consisted of the prosecution summarising their case and the defence attempting to make pleas in mitigation on the basis that Jamieson had a "troubled upbringing at home", his culpability was diminished that fateful night as he was suffering from grief brought on by his father's recent death exacerbated by alcohol. He'd acted on impulse and wished to convey his sincere sorrow and regret to the family of Raymond Carty.

Listening to this, Charlie wanted to scream out:

'Absolute fucking bollocks! Look at that bastard sitting there with not an iota of pity, remorse or feeling. The only regret that animal has is being caught."

But still he kept his peace. Before sentencing, the judge read out a list of Jamieson's previous arrests. It only heightened Charlie's anguish as a litany of assaults, threats and charges was revealed since his early teens and which had only ever resulted in him being imprisoned for a year. Charlie was astonished: how was a thug like this allowed to walk the streets with a charge sheet like that?

Finally, the judge sentenced Jamieson to life in prison and ordered the court officers to 'take him down.' On reflex, without thinking, Charlie shot up, unable to contain himself any longer and shouted:

'Rot in hell you fucking beast! I hope someone gets to you in the showers and knocks fuck out of you and...' but he was interrupted by the judge furiously banging his gavel ordering Charlie to be quiet and instructing court officials to escort him from the courtroom.

He calmed down slightly in the court foyer and apologised to the officials, explaining he was the victim's brother.

'Don't worry about it, big man,' one of them replied, 'I'd do the same if it was someone belonging to me. At least he's off the streets for a good long time.'

He felt relieved and reassured by the official's remark and thanked him, before leaving the court. Back home he let Sarah know the verdict. They hugged and held each other tightly for a long while.

Later that evening Charlie Carty resolved to move on with his life. Joe Jamieson was, as the court security guard had pointed out, away for a long time where he could do no harm though he wouldn't lose a second's sleep if some serious harm did befall him in jail. But mostly Charlie wanted to forget about Jamieson, extinguish him from his thoughts as far as he could and concentrate on cherishing Raymond's memory and look after his mother.

Above all there was his beautiful wife, his rock, his unwavering support and their two incredible boys. That was light. That was the future. That was hope. And that bastard Jamieson couldn't take any of that from him.

After a few glasses of wine, putting the boys to bed and ensuring his mother was settled, Charlie and Sarah made sweet, intense love as a virtual purgative for the past few months of darkness and horror. Later, in the post-coital glow, with Sarah lying in his arms, Charlie was determined to rebuild his career on his home turf.

Chef Carty would be back, bigger and better than ever.

SIX

It's often the most trivial, chance turn of events that can result in momentous outcomes. For Charlie Carty the path that led him to infamy and notoriety began in the Horseshoe Bar in Glasgow city centre one Sunday evening. He'd been out with four fellow restaurant owners enjoying the karaoke in the upstairs bar. It wasn't often, given their hectic schedules that five leading restaurateurs could get together for a couple of hours, so they were enjoying the moment.

They'd been out since the early afternoon and consumed a fair deal of alcohol; unusual for Charlie who drank sparingly. But the company was good, the atmosphere convivial and the quality of the singing fairly decent, and in one or two cases, excellent, aided by an entertaining and hilarious MC who dished out praise when earned to the singers, and caustic comments to any audience member who dared to heckle.

By about six though they'd had their fill of karaoke, and the standard of the singing had appreciably deteriorated. When one very stout, red-faced man in his sixties took the mike and proceeded to demolish the standard classic My Way, one of Charlie's company, Bob Carlton, now the owner of the Queen Mary, remarked:

'Christ, he's howling!'

They all agreed, and Charlie urged: 'Time to leave boys and head downstairs, eh?'

There was nodding heads all around as they collected their pint glasses from the table and went to the large ground floor bar below. It was busy but mercifully bereft of music and they found an empty corner table where they continued their afternoon, now early evening session.

Charlie was beginning to feel squiffy and decided it was time for home. He needed a pee first, excused himself and made his way to the gents. The bar was a long, elongated horseshoe shape – thus the name – with an assortment of tables, nooks and crannies around it. Charlie's table was towards the rear of the bar on the left; the gents was at the bottom of the right side. He could have chosen to walk down the left side across to the gents, but there were loads of people cluttering the passage, so on a whim he made his way round the top of the bar towards the right side. And that whim changed everything for Charlie's future.

For as he made his way down that right side, a tall man sitting beside a woman on a stool at the bar, suddenly got up temporarily blocking Charlie's path but allowing him to see over to the tables on the right-hand side. He froze. The man in front moved away freeing Charlie's path to the loo. Recovering, he turned back a few paces, noticed a space at the bar next to a wooden support column, ducked in there and looked over again to confirm what he'd just seen.

Halfway up the bar just in line of sight, was a table with five people around it. Three of the people, two girls and a guy in their twenties were engaged in an animated conversation. Separated from them by a few spaces were a couple, an attractive looking blond woman and a fair haired, powerfully built man with his arm around her. Both were in their early thirties, wearing expensive looking clothes and were to Charlie's eyes, an item.

'You getting served mate?'

Charlie was shaken out of his trance by a passing barman.

'No, your fine pal.' The barman moved away.

He realised his breathing was shallow and his heart racing, almost palpitating. He focused on the gantry in front, concentrating on his breathing, reducing his pulse and becoming calmer. Once he'd recovered, he forced himself to have one last look across the bar to confirm who the guy was sitting at that table. The close-cropped hair, the build; it definitely was him; the unmistakable figure of Joe Jamieson, his brother's psychotic killer. He watched in fascinating disgust as the couple kissed closely, virtually a snog. Charlie couldn't stomach any more.

It was him. Older, mind, but unquestionably him. He'd studied that face intently for ten tormenting days at the High Court in Glasgow and in numerous press photos; a face which he never, ever wanted to see again. The face of the murderous thug who'd viciously, almost randomly snuffed out his brother's life. A face he'd tried to suppress from his mind these past ten years as he picked up his life.

And now the bastard was here, in front of him in a crowded bar with a woman on his arm while Raymond was just a memory; all that potential wiped out by that drunken violent brute sitting there enjoying himself. Charlie wasn't sure if he could take on the guy; he'd be fifty next year but was lean and athletic, working out most days, jogging, taking part in marathons, but he couldn't care. Sheer unadulterated rage was coursing through every fibre of him. 'Go for him, go for the shite, kick sheer utter fuck out of him' was Charlie's immediate impulse. But he knew he had to control it, get a grip. With an immense effort, he turned round and walked back to his table; his hands he realised were shaking so he kept them in his pockets. As he approached, Bob Carlton let out:

'All right Charlie? You're as white as a sheet.'

He attempted a smile. 'Got a dodgy stomach, fellas, it's just came on me, last couple of minutes. Think I'll head for the road.'

There was lots of hugging and promises that 'we need to do this again' and 'look out for yourself' before Charlie departed the increasingly raucous bar, walked the short distance to the taxi rank outside Glasgow Central Station and took a cab to his home in the exclusive gated community in the affluent village of Bothwell outside the city, he, Sarah and the boys had moved to eight years earlier.

By the time he arrived home, he'd sobered up, but the anger hadn't subsided. On the cab ride home, he decided not to tell Sarah; it would only upset her. She was on her own in the house; Caleb, now fourteen and at a private secondary school in Glasgow was at a friend's house nearby, while Calum was in his second year studying economics and history at Edinburgh University staying in student digs. He was immensely proud of both and didn't want that evil prick, Joe Jamison, to intrude back into their lives.

'How was the afternoon with the guys?' Sarah asked as she helped him off with his jacket in the large hallway. The house, a detached mock-Tudor villa with six bedrooms, was far too large for them, Charlie thought. He was not an ostentatious man; a product of his working-class Glasgow upbringing, but Sarah loved it and her taste in furnishings were far superior and tasteful compared to Charlie's.

'Aye a great day, thanks,' he replied as he walked with her into the living room. 'A good laugh. We were at the karaoke upstairs in the Horseshoe. Some of the singers were brilliant, but a few were quite dodgy to say the least.'

'I've heard there's some great acts that perform there. Do you want a cup of tea?'

'No, listen, I had to leave the guys a wee bit early there because I wasn't feeling great. Just a sore stomach so I think I'll have a lie-down.'

'Aye, you're not used to drinking on an empty stomach, are you?'

He shook his head, agreeing with her. 'Too right.'

'Get up the stairs, have a rest for a few hours and I'll make up some sandwiches for you. Best keep it light with a sore tummy,' she said solicitously as she gave him a deep kiss before going upstairs.

Nearly twenty years married, and he still loved her so deeply. He cringed every time he thought of his mad coke habit during the frenetic Forsyth years and his many dalliances. Thank God that was long over. He couldn't do without Sarah.

So, how was he going to deal with the fact that Joe Jamieson was out walking the streets Charlie reflected as he lay on the bed, curtains drawn. But how could he be out? He'd been sentenced to life and the judge had pronounced that to be fifteen years, and that meant he had at least another five years to serve behind bars. So, what the fuck was he doing with a woman in his arms, drinking in the Horseshoe Bar on a Sunday afternoon?

Was he mistaken? No. It was definitely, undeniably him. He sat on the side of the bed, his head in his hands. His thoughts a frenzy of emotions.

He'd spent the past ten years after the trial rebuilding here in Glasgow, opening four restaurants which were all doing well. His consultancy had flourished, and he'd even expanded stateside, opening two restaurants in New York and one in San Francisco. The New York venues had performed well, and he'd sold them for a good profit, even though the San Francisco place had not done so well, and he was lucky to get out from it with only a small loss.

Still, he'd made enough to buy this villa, and he'd learned the hard act of delegation by hiring and selecting a good, reliable group of managers and head chefs, though he still worked long hours, but nowhere near as much as previously, so his work/life balance was far better. He'd also learned from the Forsyth disaster to maintain a careful eye on cash flow, keep the overheads down and resist the temptation to go for constant expansion. All told, he was reasonably wealthy and secure and was now an established player on the Glasgow dining scene.

The sight of Joe Jamieson upset everything. It also brought back the painful memory of his mother's last few years. Her dementia rapidly worsened and both Sarah and Charlie nursed her. What made it worse was that in her occasional semi-lucid memories, she cried out for Raymond which only compounded Charlie's grief and anguish. He was convinced that his mother's slide into advanced dementia was hastened by her youngest son's sudden disappearance from her life. For Charlie, Jamieson had not just murdered Raymond but effectively killed his mom. And that only made the sight of him swanning around Glasgow even more sickening.

He barely touched the sandwiches Sarah made him and couldn't sleep, Sarah beside him blissfully unaware of the torment consuming her husband. Several times during those long hours he was tempted to wake her and inform her but resisted. Finally, in the hours before dawn, he determined to find out as much about Jamieson as he could. Had he been released from prison or was he on some extended weekend release programme? If he was free, for what reason? And why hadn't the authorities the decency to let him know?

If Jamieson was now free to stride about Charlie's hometown, he wanted to know what he was up to and where he was staying. After he'd found that out, he'd decide whether to tell Sarah. That gave him a resolution and a purpose.

A regular customer at one of his restaurants was a senior partner in a law firm. Charlie had got to know him quite well and had laid on private dining nights for his staff and associates at short notice and good rates. He'd already divulged to him about his brother's murder, so had no qualms about asking him: if his brother's assailant was sentenced to fifteen years in prison then:

"How the fuck am I convinced I saw him drinking with a bird beside him in a city centre pub last night a good five years before he's due to be released?' He couldn't help anger creeping into his voice. The lawyer sighed deeply and answered:

'Ah, Charlie, you're not the first to have that happen to you. The fact is fifteen years rarely means that. If you're man behaves well and causes no trouble while serving his time in prison then, unless the judge specifies he must serve the full term, he automatically qualifies for release after three-quarters of his sentence. When was the trial?'

'1998, eleven years ago,' the implications of what the lawyer had just said sunk in.

'Yeah, well that explains it. If he's not caused any trouble inside, he'd have been released last year. Plus any time he spent on remand would also have to be taken into consideration.'

Charlie almost exploded: 'How the fuck was I not told? I mean...sorry, I'm just so angry about this.'

'I understand, Charlie, but there's no right for the victim's family to be informed when a prisoner's released.'

'That's shocking!'

'I know Charlie, but that's the way it is.'

He thanked the lawyer, astonished that murderers and thieves could be automatically considered for release before their sentences were spent. Jamieson would now be 32, well enough time to resume his life, whereas Charlie had to endure the loss of his brother for life, not to speak of his mother's death. Now, that was a life sentence. Where was the justice in all this?

Charlie had to hone his anger; find an outlet for it. Now he'd confirmed that Jamieson was out of prison, he had to build up a picture of him. How could he do that? He was no detective. As soon as he thought that word, inspiration came to him. He phoned Bob Carlton at the Queen Mary. After reassuring him his 'dodgy tummy' had cleared up, he asked:

'I remember you had some problems with pilfering from your kitchens last year, but you couldn't get to the bottom of it?'

'That's right,' Carlton agreed. 'Lost thousands.'

'So, am I right in thinking you hired a private detective?'

'Sure did, Charlie. Worked wonders and got to the bottom of it. Nailed every single one of the bastards.'

'I might need to use them myself.'

'It'll cost you, but it's worth it. Is it theft from the kitchen?'

'Aye, something like that. What's the company's name?'

'It's a guy called Alistair or Ali McMahon. He runs an outfit called AMAC Private Investigations. It's really him and two other people, a man and a woman. To be honest he comes across as a bit seedy, but he's very effective. He'll do the business for you.'

'All right Bob, give me his details.'

He made an appointment to see McMahon at his office in a late Victorian red sandstone block just off Argyle Street in the centre of town. There was an array of companies listed on the brass plate at the entrance to the building and "AMAC Private Investigators" was listed on the sixth floor. Access was by an old-fashioned caged lift encased in iron which creaked slowly up to the sixth floor.

He walked halfway along a deserted uncarpeted corridor until he found a brown stained wooden door with a bronze stencilled plaque bearing the name of the company. Charlie knocked and a gruff voice shouted: 'Aye?'

He entered and was hit by an overwhelming smell of cigarettes relieved only by an open window which blew a draught into the cluttered room. There were piles of papers and ring binder files everywhere: on the floor and on the three wooden desks, behind one of which sat a thin sallow faced, heavily wrinkled man with rheumy, watery eyes with prominent bags under them. Charlie guessed his age could be anywhere between 30 and 50. He wore a tattered check shirt and beckoned for him to sit on a wooden chair in front of him.

'Mr Carty?'

'Yes.'

Among the pile on McMahon's desk, Charlie noticed a crammed ashtray; he reckoned that the private dick was on a minimum of 30 a day. Bob Carlton's description of him as 'seedy' was an understatement. Ali McMahon lived up to every image of a private eye Charlie had seen in movies or read in books, down to the messy office; he even suspected there was a bottle of whisky in a drawer.

'What can I do for you?' he drawled.

Charlie inhaled deeply. There was no point in prevaricating, and he went straight to the point.

'My brother was viciously murdered eleven years ago. The piece of dirt that did it was caught and jailed. I thought he was in for fifteen years, but I've just found out he was released after ten.'

'How did you find out?' McMahon appraised him carefully.

'I saw him at the weekend in a pub.'

'And your blood's boiling,' McMahon said curtly.

'Is it that obvious?'

'Aye. I hate fancy language, Mr Carty, but to be frank you scream smouldering rage.'

Charlie looked at him carefully. He and his office might look a state, but he was sharp. McMahon went on:

'Did he see you?'

'No. He was in a crowded pub. I saw him from a distance.'

'Ok, what do you want me to do? I'm not going to kill him for you.'

Charlie sighed. 'I know. I want you to find out as much about him as you can. Where he lives. Is he working? How is he earning a living. What his movements...I don't know...habits are. I...' McMahon interrupted:

'...You want a full profile of him?'

'Aye.'

'Why?'

They looked at each other carefully before Charlie replied:

'The fucker's sharing the same city with me, my wife and kids. I don't want them to come across him like I did. I want to know where he is and what he's up to.'

McMahon opened a notepad on his desk. 'All right Mr Carty, tell me his name, when your brother was killed, when this guy was sentenced and anything else you know about him.'

Charlie recited as much as he knew about Jamieson, which wasn't in fact a lot, but it seemed to be enough for McMahon.

Closing the notepad he said:

'That's fine to start with. If I need any more information from yourself, I'll be in touch. But, of course, before we go any further, let me tell you what my rates are.' He paused. Charlie braced himself for it.

'This should be a quite straightforward investigation. There might be some trailing of the target which might cost a bit more, but the standard fee will be £250 per day. That's not every day; we've got other investigations going on but covers the days we're on this.'

Charlie swallowed. 'How many days will it last for?'

He opened a drawer in his desk and brought out a ball of string. 'If I unravel this, how long do you think it would be.'

Charlie got the message. That was a prop McMahon probably employed with every new client as it would be a standard question.

'Ok. 250 a day.'

'If we're getting nowhere after two weeks, which I doubt, we'll review.'

McMahon drew up the paperwork which Charlie and he signed, shook hands -the private dick had a surprisingly strong grip for such a thin man – and left the office wondering just what he'd done and the expense. He could afford it; he had substantial savings. Both he and Sarah were still careful with money and the businesses were doing well, despite the recession and credit crunch which were gripping the country. Sure, footfall at all his venues was down slightly, and like other restaurateurs in the city he'd had to raise prices, but it wasn't catastrophic, and he was certain he could ride it out.

But £250 per day was a drain if the investigation went on for a while, and despite Bob Carlton's recommendation of him, he knew nothing about private investigators or whether McMahon would string him along. However, he'd made his choice and signed up. Now, he would have to see what the results were.

McMahon phoned him twice over the next few weeks to say he and his team were making 'steady progress.' On the second call, he informed Charlie that his inquiries necessitated going into a third week at least. Very reluctantly, Charlie agreed worrying if he was being taken for a ride. He resolved if McMahon requested a fourth week with no detailed progress report, he'd call a halt.

But, immediately after the third week, McMahon asked him into his office. When he got there, the private dick handed him a typed report sheathed in a brown folder which ran to fifteen pages.

'I'm a paper man,' he said. 'I've got a PC but I'm loath to use email. Anyway, our findings are in there. Take it and read it and let me know what you think.'

'So, is he...'

'...Mr Carty, just read it, before you ask any more questions,' McMahon butted in. As Charlie rose to leave, the private dick leaned across his desk and handed him a piece of paper.

'My bill.'

'Bank transfer, ok?' he asked after looking at the bill.

'That's fine. Payment within fifteen days please.'

Charlie left with the folder and went home. Sarah was out; Caleb was at school and Calum at uni. Nobody but Bob Carlton knew he'd hired McMahon, and he didn't know precisely why, assuming it was about theft, and Charlie wanted to keep it that way.

Settling down with a coffee in a comfortable armchair in his living room, Charlie, with some trepidation, read the report. It was brief, but Charlie quickly appreciated, was comprehensive and entailed a lot of in-depth background work. The report was divided into three sections. The first was a brief description of Jamieson, his criminal record, sentencing and prison record plus date of liberation – which Charlie mostly knew about already. Plus, there was some new information which he didn't, including where he was living (in his mother's house, a former council house which was now owned by a housing association; she'd died a few years ago and Jamieson's brother had inherited the tenancy and allowed him to stay there since his release). The report confirmed the house was in the Barmulloch area of north Glasgow and listed the address. Jamieson was unemployed and living on benefits.

The next section recounted Jamieson's background. He came from a working-class family of two brothers and a sister. His mother worked as a cleaner while the father was involved in petty crime and on the fringes of a local crime family. Nevertheless, his two older brothers made decent lives for themselves, one as a car mechanic and the other working in a local bakery while his sister went on to university and became a teacher.

From an early age, the report went on, the killer ran

around with local gangs and hardmen and made a succession of unforced, bad decisions. Violence became second nature to him; the police were never away from his mother's door. Despite fines and receiving a year in prison, the law proved no deterrent. By his early twenties he had a long history of violent attacks fuelled by a fondness for pills and cheap wine. He became an enforcer for one of the local gangs and came close to killing his victims on several occasions. But he was too much of a loose cannon even for them and they ditched him.

He'd never held down a job and started drinking heavily, becoming more aggressive and volatile, culminating in the frenzied, random attack on Raymond who was in the wrong place at the wrong time when Jamieson came across him enraged at being forcibly ejected from a bar for pestering women and refused entry to other bars. The section ended with an account of his trial, subsequent imprisonment and release the previous year with good behaviour after serving two-thirds of his time.

The last section detailed Jamieson's current activities. He was released on license and had to see a community justice social worker every few weeks. He was also back on benefits.

Through "discreet surveillance and other methods", the investigators discovered, despite his supervision, he was back working as an enforcer with a money lender for a local outfit intimidating and terrorising people to pay the extortionate and crippling rates being demanded. He was making a comfortable living from this, but his volcanic temper meant he'd got involved in fights and violent assaults and the rumour was he'd been pulled up by the outfit and the money lender for stepping out of line. He'd hadn't been arrested and breached his parole, yet, as his victims were too terrified of him. But it was only a matter of time before he severely injured or even killed another victim.

Charlie read this with despair. Jamieson was back to his old lifestyle. There was no atonement, no remorse and certainly the killer had not reformed. It was a mockery of his brother's fatal ordeal and the hell he'd put him and his mother through. The rage that had engulfed Charlie since he'd came across Jamieson in the pub weeks earlier only intensified.

Finally, the report highlighted that he spent a lot of time, especially at weekends with a girlfriend named Denise in her late twenties who worked in a city centre department store and lived in a private housing estate not far from Barmulloch. Charlie surmised this was the blonde woman he'd seen him with. The significance of this information was that, apart from working the streets on his enforcement activities, every Friday he drank in a notorious pub in the area described in the report as "a haunt for gangland enforcers, petty criminals and similar elements". Jamieson would stay in the pub until closing time and walk the ten minutes to his girlfriend's house.

Charlie finished reading the report, opened a short pocket notebook and wrote down the most important details from the report before taking it to a windowless room at the back of the house which he used as an office. He'd just recently bought a shredder and fed the report to it, bagging the strings of paper that spewed from it before binning the bag. He went back to the living room and poured a generous dram of Laphroaig; a tipple he'd acquired a taste for from his Forsyth days and sat back in the armchair digesting the report's findings.

Charlie Carty was a fair man, a family man, hardworking and had played by the rules all his life. But this was too much. Joe Jamieson was only in his early 30s, free to continue his criminal activities while he had to wrestle daily with his brother's loss. The law seemed to be of no use and there was every likelihood that Jamieson would maim or kill another poor victim.

As he savoured the whisky in the quiet of his living room, Charlie considered that he wasn't a vengeful man, but this was exceptional, far out with anything "normal". He thought carefully about his next move until he heard a car pulling up in the driveway. It was Sarah returning. He put the kettle on to make her a cup of coffee and greeted her with a big hug.

He knew clearly now what he was going to do.

SEVEN

It was a hot sweltering mid-August night with thunder in the air as Charlie sat behind the wheel of the non-descript grey twelve-year-old Ford Fiesta looking over at the pub. He had the car windows open as it was stifling, not helped by the pungent aroma of battered fish wafting from the fish and chippy he was parked behind.

It was near closing time, and he'd arrived about fifteen minutes earlier. His gamble was that Jamieson had broken his Friday routine and wasn't in the pub. As on two previous occasions, he could have tailed him from his girlfriend's house and guaranteed he was in the pub. But for his alibi to work he had to take the risk of being here just before closing time.

He'd had dinner earlier at a restaurant in the town of Greenock, twenty-five miles away from Glasgow on the Firth of Clyde. Charlie had a genuine interest in acquiring the restaurant and diversifying out of Glasgow. He'd spent the evening with the current owners over an excellent meal, which Charlie couldn't really enjoy as he was so tense about what he planned that night but focused enough to progress a possible purchase. They'd left the restaurant about ten thirty and the owners gave him a lift the short distance to a new hotel complex on the riverfront that Charlie had booked into earlier. He bid them farewell at the hotel entrance and he made a point of asking reception for an alarm call at seven before going to his room.

There, he changed into a dark sweater, blue anorak, black

jeans and donned a brown-haired wig that covered his balding grey pate, before leaving the room. The reception area, foyer and adjacent bar of the hotel were all quite busy that Friday night and no one appeared to notice him as he slipped out and went to the far end of the hotel car park where he'd parked his car, a black 2006 Mercedes Black ALG. There was a fast link to Glasgow on the M8 motorway and Charlie bombed up it, careful though to stick to the speed limit, and was in a lock up behind a railway line at Hyndland in the west end of Glasgow by quarter past eleven.

In the lock-up he transferred to the dirty grey Fiesta he'd bought second hand at a car auction several weeks previously and quickly negotiated the quiet streets across north Glasgow and was outside the pub in Springburn by half eleven. All good so far, he thought, and fervently hoped Joe Jamieson was in that bar. He heard a bell ringing in the pub which he presumed was for last orders.

An increasing number of people were leaving the pub quite refreshed, laughing and joking loudly. On his previous two recces outside the pub, he'd noticed the alarming number of men entering and leaving (the clientele was almost all male) who had prominent scars or chib marks on their faces. Ali McMahon's report had not exaggerated; the pub was rough. In Charlie's less reserved estimation it was a haunt for low-life, and he sank as low as he could in the front seat of the car, behind a row of shops, including the fish and chippy, in line of sight of the pub, but as unobtrusive as he could be. The sticky heat was becoming unbearable, so he put the anorak on the back seat, but it was still uncomfortable with the wig on. He was keen to get this over with.

Time seemed to go by agonisingly slowly as closing time came and went and more people staggered out to the increasingly desperate tones of the bar staff shouting, 'that's your time now, come on, do your talking outside!'. By about quarter past midnight, Charlie was becoming increasingly concerned he'd either missed Jamieson in the melee of people exiting the bar or he'd broken routine and not gone there that night.

Then, about five minutes later, he saw the gangly, fair haired figure of Jamison in a white T-shirt and green cotton shorts and sandals, emerge, light a cigarette and spend another couple of minutes engaging in the proverbial long goodbye with several other shady figures, all beery and red faced and after some hugging, he made his way, staggering but not too drunk, to his girlfriend's on his own.

The sight of the bastard pissed, enjoying himself like that with not a care in the world only confirmed Charlie in the righteousness and justice of what he was about to embark on.

He gave it a few minutes before he slowly drove along until he saw Jamieson in the distance walking along a quiet road paralleling a railway line. He parked here and waited for him to turn left onto the road ahead. Charlie knew that he'd walk along this road for about fifty yards until he would make a further turn left into the only road that allowed access to the estate where his girlfriend lived.

He waited a further minute and drove slowly to the upcoming road. To his left, utterly oblivious, Jamieson was approaching the access road. In front of Charlie was an industrial goods yard and railway maintenance depot. A wall on the other side of the road surrounded the estate, divided by the access road which Charlie could see Jamieson lurch into.

He drove left, then halted at the start of the access road. Jamieson was twenty yards ahead. A further forty yards beyond, Charlie knew from previous recces, was the avenue where his girlfriend lived. His heart was racing. It was now or never. He thought of Raymond and of his mother. The red mist descended. He turned into the access road and accelerated. The road was completely deserted. 'Go for it, Charlie, go for it,' he almost shouted to himself as he rapidly approached him.

At the last-minute Jamieson became aware of the speeding vehicle behind. He half turned as Charlie mounted the pavement and struck him, his face startled and alarmed, before his body seemed to spring in the air, describe a circle before hitting the windscreen with an enormous, sickening thwack. Charlie was concerned he'd smash the windscreen, but it held, before Jamieson bounced off the bonnet and landed hard on the pavement.

Charlie braked the car. There was a crack in the windscreen, but it didn't look as if it was going to shatter. He looked over at Jamieson slumped on the pavement, legs askew. Was he dead? Had he carried out the act he'd set out to do? Would he need to reverse and drive over him?

Then, he noticed with incredible satisfaction, almost joy, a pool of blood developing around his head. That's exactly what he'd done to Raymond, broken his head. Charlie couldn't help himself. He pulled down his window and shouted exultantly: 'That's for my brother ya cunt!'

Before turning the Fiesta around and screeching down the access road, his heart racing, adrenaline pumping. At the top of the road, he turned left and slowed down on the drive back to the lock up. As he drove back, he was concerned that he might bump into a passing police patrol alerted to the growing crack in his windshield, but he arrived at the lock up unmolested. He discarded the wig which he put into a plastic bag and with a cloth performed a thorough wipe down of the front car seats, dashboard and steering wheel.

This was just a precaution as his plan was to leave the Fiesta in the lockup for a few days, hire a trailer and take it to a breaker's yard and have it crushed and melted. Once he'd wiped the Fiesta, he got behind the wheel of the BMW and drove back to the hotel in Greenock, heart still pounding, but beginning to slow. He entered the hotel unobserved about half-past one, just as streaking lightning flashes in the distance heralded the storm that had been threatening all evening.

He didn't sleep, his mind racing. In the morning, after showering and before breakfast, he tuned the room TV/radio set to Radio Scotland and the eight o' clock news bulletin. There was a brief report about a man found seriously injured on a residential street in the Springburn area of Glasgow. He'd been taken to hospital and police were appealing for witnesses.

Charlie tried to keep up appearances by appearing at breakfast but could only manage a few spoonsful of cereal. So, Jamieson wasn't dead, yet. And if he wasn't dead, would he regain consciousness? And what were the grim implications of that?

After breakfast, Charlie checked out and drove back to Bothwell. Sarah gave him her usual big hug, inquired how the night had gone in Greenock; was he going to go ahead with the deal to buy the restaurant? Charlie answered as normally as he could but his demeanour piqued Sarah's acute radar.

'Are you all right?' she asked. 'You seem flushed.'

'Aye, I'm fine,' he tried to brush it aside. 'I'm just knackered, running about mad everywhere.'

'And that's why you pay managers to deal with that,' she came back sharply

'Sure, it's just difficult to break the habits of a lifetime sometime.'

'I know,' she said more soothingly,' 'but I don't want you burnt out and dropping dead like I've seen too many others in this trade.'

'I won't,' he promised as she hugged him again and gave him a long kiss.

'Right, I'm away to get my hair done, back about three.'

He watched her leaving, thanking the Lord or whoever that he'd met her. It was their twentieth wedding anniversary in a few months, and he was still very much in love with her.

Half-an-hour later he emptied the wig and clothes he'd been wearing for the "Act" into a large brazier, keeping a careful watch that the smoke wasn't too thick or billowing over into neighbour's gardens, though the wooden fences were a good height. After a few hours, there was nothing but ash and by the time Sarah got back there was not even a lingering smell of smoke.

There was no further mention of the incident on local radio or TV bulletins, but a report in the Daily Record tabloid newspaper on Monday morning revealed that Jamieson was in a coma after a "hit and run". Police were appealing for witnesses. There were no further details nor any mention of Jamieson's past.

He hadn't banked on Jamieson surviving the hit and it gnawed at him as he tried to carry on as usual at the start of the week. On Tuesday evening he arrived back from a meeting with his managers about eight. He wasn't hungry and ate a light meal before joining Caleb in his room playing a computer game after ensuring he'd completed his homework. He was paying good money for him to attend the private school, and he was determined, as was Sarah, that he'd do well at school as his older brother had before him.

Just after nine, he heard the doorbell followed shortly by Sarah shouting up:

'Charlie, could you come down?'

At the bottom of the stairs, his wife looked worried. 'It's the police,' she said, almost in a whisper. 'They want to speak to you.'

A grip of tension and fear engulfed Charlie which he tried to hide by walking up to the two dark-suited guys in their thirties with brown folders at their sides. They screamed cops.

'Hi, how can I help gents?' Charlie said breezily as they flashed warrant cards.

'Detective Sergeant Maxwell and DS Carmicheal. Mr Carty?' the one identifying himself as DS Maxwell did the talking.

'Sure.'

'We'd just like to ask you a few questions about an incident that took place last weekend. Last Saturday morning to be precise. Could we come in?'

'Of course,' Charlie beckoned for them to enter the living room. Sarah followed. Charlie invited them to sit on the leather armchairs while his wife offered tea or coffee which they declined. Once settled, Maxwell retrieved a large orange journal from his folder and flitting between eyeing Charlie carefully and the notes and paperwork in the journal. He described how there'd been a hit and run in the NorthPark estate near Springburn just before one on Saturday morning. The victim had been seriously injured and was lying in a coma in hospital. The detective stopped talking and an awkward silence hung in the room broken by Sarah.

'What's this got to do with us?'

Without taking his eyes off Charlie, Maxwell explained:

'This is just routine Mr Carty, but the identity of the victim is a Mr Joseph Jamieson.' After a pause, Maxwell asked:

'I have to ask, but do you recognise that name?'

Charlie knew there was no point in bluffing, but Sarah got in front of him.

'That's the same name as...'

'...the guy that killed my brother,' Charlie finished for her.

'Yes,' DI Maxwell confirmed. 'It's the same man.'

'But he's in prison. He got life!' Sarah declared.

Charlie stayed silent as the detective corrected her. 'No, he was actually released last year with good behaviour.'

Sarah looked astonished. 'What?' Then looked at her husband: 'Did you know he was out?'

Charlie also feigned surprise. 'No. He's been out walking the streets and no one in authority lets us know? That's terrible.'

'I'm sorry, but that's the way it is. I just need to eliminate potential suspects. Can you tell me where you were on Friday night and Saturday morning?'

'Sure, I was in Greenock, spent the night there. I'm looking to buy a new restaurant.' He went on to detail his movements that night, including who he was with and his stay in the hotel. Both detectives took notes.

'So, you went to your room in the hotel about ten-thirty?' Maxwell asked.

'Yep.'

'You didn't go down to the bar at all or leave at any time?'

'No, I was really shattered. I ordered an alarm call for seven am, watched some telly and conked out.'

'And when did you check out?'

'Oh, I had a shower, breakfast...I would say about nine, nine thirty.'

'And you got home here at...'

'...he arrived about half ten,' Sarah answered.

The detective stopped writing as did his colleague.

'Well, that seems fine. We will of course check this out, but that's just routine; as we say a process of elimination.'

'Do you have any other brothers, Mr Carty?' It was Carmicheal, who spoke for the first time.

Charlie shook his head, 'no'.

There was a long silence before Carmicheal went on:

'There was a woman out walking her dog at the time of the incident. She was about fifteen yards in front, and she witnessed the car deliberately mount the pavement and knock over Jamieson. She couldn't see the driver clearly, except that he was male. But she did distinctly hear him say,' he referred to his notes, '" that's for my brother you cunt,"'.

A sharp pang of tension coursed through Charlie. He felt his face reddening, the faces of the detectives and Sarah staring at him. He tried to control the trembling that wanted to take control of his body. Eventually, he blurted out:

'I told you I was in Greenock.' A thought came to him. 'There might be other guys that he's attacked who've got brothers, you know.'

DI Maxwell came back. 'We've gone down that line and so far, we've found nothing. Jamieson threatened and assaulted a lot of people, mostly punching, kicking and slapping them, a good few of whom were women, but your brother was the only person he's ever murdered.'

He put his hands in front of him. 'As I said, gentlemen, I was nowhere near Glasgow on Friday night or early Saturday morning.'

'I'm sure that'll check out Mr Carty,' Maxwell said assuringly. 'Do you drive a car?'

'Yes, a Mercedes ALG.'

'Is it here?'

'In the driveway.'

'Can we have a look at it? Again, just routine.'

He led them to the car. Carmicheal asked him, 'did you drive this to Greenock and back?'

'Yes.'

They inspected the car, particularly the front and bonnet, for a few moments.

'Aye, that seems ok,' Maxwell said before proffering Charlie his card. 'If I need to, I'll get back in touch with you. What's the best number to contact you?'

Charlie gave him his mobile number. Looking closely at him, Maxwell said:

'If there's something you've forgotten to tell us, phone me. Thanks Mr Carty.' He nodded to Sarah, 'Mrs Carty.' They walked to their car parked in the gravel driveway and drove away.

Back in the living room Sarah asked him straight: 'You were in Greenock that night?'

'Of course I was!'

'That'll all check out with those detectives?'

'Yes, of course it will.'

'You just went pale there when the detective told you what the witness heard.'

'I was fucking shocked, like you, that the bastard was out.'

That seemed to reassure her. 'Yeah, I suppose.'

'Besides, as they said, he's attacked loads of people as well as Raymond. Just because he's not murdered them as well doesn't mean that one of their brothers couldn't have gone for him.'

She took hold of him, wanting to believe him. 'That's true. Well, he's got his comeuppance now.'

Hugging her closely, he said soothingly to her. 'It's fine,

but I do need a whisky.'

'Pour me one as well.'

He barely slept that night, despite a couple of whiskies. He tried to focus at work, but the prospect that Jamieson might come out of his coma and had recognised him before the car struck filled him with dread. He reckoned his alibi was solid though and that kept him going. By Thursday afternoon he was beginning to relax a little when his mobile rang as he was in one of his restaurants. Despair hit him when he realised it was Maxwell's number who came straight to the point.

'We'd like to ask you a few more questions, Mr Carty'.

Trying to keep the panic in his voice down, Charlie replied: 'I thought I'd told you everything on Monday.'

'Aye, but there's one or two follow-ups we need to go through with you.'

'What are they?'

'Not on the phone, Charlie. We'd like you to come in. We can get a car to pick you up.'

'No, no. I'll come in,' he said eagerly; the last thing he wanted was for the CID to appear at one of his restaurants or in front of his staff. Charlie also noted that the detective's use of "Charlie" rather than the more respectful "Mr Carty", hinted at something more ominous.

'It's ok Charlie, we're on the move just now. Where are you? We'll pick you up.'

His mind was racing. 'Am I in trouble?'

'We just need to clarify a few things, Charlie. Where can

we get you?'

Maxwell was pressing him. He named the restaurant he was at. Charlie agreed to wait outside for them. They were there in five minutes. On the silent car journey to Stewart Street police station on the northern boundary of the city centre, he chided himself for not having called his lawyer. But he specialised in commercial law as that was all Charlie required legally, never having been in trouble with the law before.

He was taken to a windowless interview room where Maxwell went back through his Alibi up to the point where he'd gone up to his hotel bedroom apparently for the night.

'And you stayed there all night, didn't move once?' Maxwell asked.

'No, I told you, I was very tired, slept right through to when reception called me with my alarm call at seven.'

'Do you own any other car besides the Mercedes?' Carmicheal asked.

'No,' Charlie answered, rather too quickly he thought.

'Sure, about that?' Carmicheal pressed.

'Aye.'

The detectives looked at each other before Carmicheal opened a folder and took out two large square black and white photographs. He slid one across to Charlie. It was quite blurry and was a front shot of a car turning into a street; in the background were some houses. Although, the quality of the picture was poor, he knew it was taken at night. What he also knew was that the car was a grey Fiesta. His recently acquired Fiesta which he'd used to slam into Joe Jamieson.

He could feel panic stirring in him but held onto a morsel of hope as the registration number wasn't clear. Maxwell took up the narrative:

'That picture was taken from a recently installed CCTV camera at a railway repair works just across from the street that leads into the estate where Jamieson was knocked over. The picture was taken about a minute after the hit and run based on the testimony of the dog walker. We think it's the car that hit him getting away from the scene.'

'By the way,' Carmicheal added, 'the victim's regained consciousness.'

By a massive effort, Charlie kept it together. 'Oh aye,' was his terse response, aware both tecs were again eyeing him closely. After a short pause, Carmicheal continued.

'He'll live. But the medics reckon he's suffered irretrievable brain damage and will need care for the rest of his life. So, he'll not be able to say who drove that car at him.'

Two thoughts pulsed through Charlie. First, he hadn't killed Jamieson as he'd planned, but he'd placed him in the next worst place; a living death for the rest of the swine's life and that partly atoned for Raymond. The second was another morsel of comfort as Jamieson couldn't identify him now. But that was instantly annihilated by the second photo Maxwell shoved across the desk to him.

All Charlie's attempts to remain cool and calm evaporated as the colour drained from him. The photo revealed a late middle-aged man, of medium height, entering the front entrance to a hotel foyer. It was much clearer and better than the first photo. He was barely aware of Maxwell saying to him:

'That was taken behind the reception desk of the Clyde Marina hotel in Greenock at 1.20 am last Saturday morning. The man in the picture looks a hell of a lot like you, Charlie.'

'The wig, the fucking wig!' Utter despair took hold of Charlie. The man in the picture was balding as was Charlie because he'd discarded the bloody wig after the hit and run. He couldn't wait to take off that wig as he was driving back because it was so heavy and hot on him, not thinking it through that the hotel's CCTV would pick him up, minus wig, when he came back.

Still, the barrack room lawyer in him thought all this was circumstantial and almost before he'd even thought it, blurted out:

'Sorry boys I forgot to mention, the thunder woke me up and I couldn't get back to sleep, it was hot in my room, and I just wandered outside for a couple of minutes to get some fresh air.'

'In the pissing rain?' Maxwell asked with a sour, cynical expression on his face.

Charlie shrugged. 'I just stood under the canopy.' It was desperate but plausible he considered. There was a knock on the door and a man in plain clothes poked his head in, saying:

'Sorry for interrupting, but can I see both of you for a minute?' The two tecs went to the door, shutting it behind them.

Charlie exhaled sharply. He tried to keep his wits together. It looked bad, but without the registration number, they couldn't pin the Fiesta to him, and he had been in Greenock that night and people do leave their rooms briefly during the night even during a storm. No, a good defence brief could hack away at this. The tecs coming back into the room broke his reverie. Carmichael said:

'I'm going to ask you again, Charlie, besides the BMW, do you own another car?'

He shook his head. It was Maxwell's turn.

'We've got a much better picture from another camera on Hawthorne Street, and it clearly shows the registration number on the Fiesta. We're putting it through DVLA just now. Should get a result quite soon. So, you're absolutely sure you've got nothing to do with that car?'

Charlie knew his last defence was crumbling. He'd arranged for the Fiesta in the lock up to be sent to the breaker's yard the following day, but that was rendered redundant if they could trace it to him because he hadn't even tried to disguise his name when he bought the car at the auction. He was an amateur at this. As if to highlight this, there was another knock on the door, a uniformed cop came in, handed Maxwell an A5 sheet of paper and a much smaller slip of paper before leaving. A smile came over Maxwell's face. He turned the A5 paper around.

'The internet's an amazing tool, Charlie. You can sometimes verify folk's stories in minutes. Just downloaded this from the online PC in the open plan.'

Charlie looked at the picture. The A5 sheet displayed the front entrance to the Clyde Marina Hotel presumably taken from its website. There was no canopy at the entrance and nobody in their right mind would have ventured out in the driving rain in the middle of a storm, unless they were coming back from somewhere such as parking a car after being somewhere else. Then Maxwell showed him the slip of paper.

It was the registration number of the Fiesta. Maxwell said: 'That camera gave us the registration number and DVLA have just confirmed the Fiesta was purchased second hand at a car auction in Easterhouse five weeks ago by you Charlie.'

He knew it was over. Carmicheal spoke up:

'Charles Derek Carty, you're being arrested and charged with the attempted murder of Joesph Patrick Jamieson on the...' Carmicheal recited a litany of serious charges including attempting to conceal the crime. When he'd finished, Maxwell added:

'You're being detained here for a while as we go back over your story. Time to get yourself a lawyer, Charlie.'

His commercial lawyer recommended a good criminal defence lawyer, who huddled with him in another windowless room in the police station before he was questioned again. He confessed all to the lawyer who advised Charlie that his alibi had disintegrated and the evidence mounting against him was overwhelming. It would be best if he pleaded guilty with a mitigating plea that he was driven by the loss of his brother in such harrowing circumstances and the subsequent death of his mother, combined with the shock of the revelation that Jamieson had been released unbeknown to Charlie, and the devastating upset of coming across him abruptly in the pub. That might get him a reduced sentence. Charlie agreed. He knew he'd made a complete hash of it.

Back in the interview room with his lawyer present he admitted to the assault on Jamieson. He was detained overnight in the police station and was allowed a call to Sarah who was stunned and broke down when he told her he'd been charged and why. That was even harder for him to bear than being detained. He was glad when the call was over.

Next day, in handcuffs, he was taken to Glasgow Sherriff Court for an initial appearance. His lawyer had warned him there was almost no chance of him being bailed given the gravity of the charges, particularly attempted murder. But he would ask for bail, given it was Charlie's first offence, he'd been of previously good character, a family man and a hard-working member of the community.

Apart, ironically, from attending Jamieson's own trial for the murder of his brother, he'd never been in court. It was both frightening and surreal to be led from the manky, graffiti strewn cells underneath the court to the dock. He saw Sarah, her face a picture of anguish, her eyes reddened with weeping, in the public gallery next to a bewildered, distraught looking Calum. The only relief was that fourteen-year-old Caleb wasn't with them – he knew his wife wouldn't have let him come – but he would soon learn about his father.

The proceedings were mercifully brief as he pleaded guilty. His defence lawyer did put in a strong case for bail, but as expected, this was rejected by the sheriff, and he was remanded in custody. He heard Sarah sobbing as he was taken down, back to the cells.

An hour later he was escorted onto a long white prison van,

known as a sweat box, where he was placed in a barred, cubicle sized cage, one of twelve with six on each side divided by a corridor at the end of which a security guard stood silently at the rear entrance. Once all the cages were occupied with other prisoners the van made its way on the short trip across town to Barlinnie Prison. The other prisoners in the cages were a good deal younger than him and he felt ancient. A young guy in a cage opposite who looked to be in his late teens shouted across to him above the noise of the engine:

'Auld yin, whit ye going to the big hoose for?'

"Big hoose" was the local Glasgow term for Barlinnie. Charlie thought for a second before answering and was upfront as he no longer had anything to lose.

'I tried to kill the cunt that murdered my brother.'

The young guy smiled back at him. 'Fucking respect big man. Take it he's no deid?'

'Naw, but he's a vegetable. That'll do me.'

The young fella gave him the thumbs up followed by the others. At least some people understood him.

After the juddering journey to the grim Victorian prison, he was processed and admitted into C Hall, the remand wing of Barlinnie where he was allocated a cell to share with the young addict Mick. They barely acknowledged each other that first night which was difficult; he could hardly sleep knowing he was in prison, there was the sound of Mick grinding his teeth and the various noises coming from the other cells, but he somehow got through that first night.

As he had admitted to all the charges, there was no case

to defend or prosecute and his sentencing date at court was set for only three months away; most remand prisoners had a much longer wait. He adapted well to prison. As with the sweat box, he earned the respect of his fellow inmates as he continued to be upfront when asked why he was there. After a shaky start he got to know and like Mick, despite normally despising drug addicts. He'd always considered his own cocaine habit in the 1990s as somehow different from injecting heroin users from the schemes but began to realise that was just sheer hypocrisy and double standards.

He mentored Mick as best he could, and an almost father-son relationship developed between them (Mick revealed to Charlie that he'd only seen his father fleetingly in childhood and he'd died from an alcohol induced burst liver when he was twelve). Charlie felt a real loss when Mick left C Hall after two months following his trial where he was sentenced to two years for armed robbery and assault and resolved to help him as best he could when the lad was released.

Otherwise, he kept his head down and the three months on remand passed quickly, helped by being given a passman or trusty role inevitably helping with the food deliveries to the Hall and assisting with serving meals.

The worst aspect for Charlie was visits from his family. Sarah couldn't help looking appalled and upset during her visits, made worse by her constantly asking him how he could have got himself and his family into this mess. Calum paid frequent visits on his own or with his mother who also brought Caleb along on two occasions. He was delighted to see his boys but always felt ashamed and depressed afterwards that they had to see him there.

The sentencing at the High Court, the same court where Jamieson had been tried, lasted only a day. Charlie's lawyer made a strong plea for a reduced sentence given the special circumstances of the case. In his summoning up the Judge made a great deal about people not taking the law into their own hands and enacting vengeful justice, but the lawyer's plea seemed to make an impact as he was sentenced to seven-and-a-half years; attempted murder could earn up to a life sentence. His lawyer informed him that with good behaviour he should be out in five years.

He was sent back to Barlinnie in the sweat box and admitted to D Hall for sentenced prisoners. His time on remand meant the prison didn't spook him; indeed, he was surprised at how well he coped with it, which he put down to his inner strength and ability to withstand adversity. They made them tough in kitchens and Charlie was a product of that environment.

As the door shut on the first night of his minimum five-year stretch, chef Carty, celebrity chef, former personal cook to a President and prominent restaurant owner, had no regrets he was in the Big House for quite a while. Of course, he'd rather not have been caught and spend any time in jail, but at least Raymond's murderer was now enduring a proper life sentence and not swaggering around boozing, shagging, threatening and hurting people. He stretched up to the pane of glass and the bars behind it, sneaked a look at the prison courtyard and the walls surrounding it and stared up at the pitch-black sky.

'All right bro,' he declared. 'Job done.'

EIGHT

He chose the bus on a whim. Originally, he'd intended to go directly to the southside, but a number 9 heading southwest came along first, and he jumped on it. He'd just recently bought a Zone Card which allowed him to travel across the city at a discounted rate for a month. Charlie had rarely used public transport, but now he had a lot of time on his hands, it was a good way of seeing parts of the city he'd rarely visited or ever been and passed away the time.

Just over two years out of prison after serving five years, he went upstairs, having to negotiate past one young guy on his right just past the stairs, whose legs were jutting out to the passageway, immersed in his phone and oblivious to other passengers going by. He sat midway up also on the right and checked his own phone.

There was one message from Sarah. She agreed to meet him for coffee the following week. That made him feel good. It'd been a while since he'd last seen her and he missed her desperately. He put the phone back in the side pocket of his jacket and became lost in his own thoughts as the bus wended its way across the Clyde.

The last year of his sentence, first at Letham Hall in Barlinnie and then a final few months at a Training For Freedom open prison near Dundee had gone well. Bob Carlton, the owner of the Queen Mary who'd been with him that fateful night he'd come across Joe Jamieson in the Horseshoe Bar, had supported him throughout his sentence, visited him frequently and gave him a position in the kitchen of his restaurant for Charlie's final year. That'd been a great help as he'd performed well and was the final step in letting the prison authorities and parole board confirm his early release.

Before his imprisonment he'd rebuilt his business after returning from Africa and recruited a group of skilled managers to oversee his four outlets. Though he was worried how they'd perform when he was inside, they'd done well, and the business continued to thrive.

Then, in a surprise move, after he graduated from university with a good upper first, Calum announced he was going to take a postgraduate course in Hospitality Management. It was surprising as Calum had never shown any interest in his father's profession. The course involved a practical work assignment and Calum chose to work in one of his father's places, a bar/diner in the east end of the city called the Camlachie Arms. It was a busy venue, next to two shopping malls, a clutch of new build housing estates all built on reclaimed previously derelict land and close to Celtic Park and astride a major road junction.

When he'd announced his interest in buying it nine years back, some people in the trade were taken aback as all Charlie's other ventures had been high end restaurants. The east end of the city wasn't regarded as a lucrative area for dining. But Charlie had reckoned it was going through a transformation and that particular location, a good distance from any other pub or restaurant, was ideal.

A former pizzeria franchised to a large chain, Charlie

got a good price for it and put a lot of money into it, building extensions, creating a beer garden and developed a venue appealing to families, a spot for event hires and also catering for regular drinkers. It worked. There was nothing like it for miles. People flocked to it. Bookings for Sunday roasts were full for weeks in advance and it was in demand for birthdays and special occasions. It rapidly became one of Charlie's most profitable outlets and the manager, a solid, hard-working guy in his thirties named Des, kept it flourishing after Charlie was sentenced. Indeed, his notoriety earned the bar a certain cachet with the clientele as there was a lot of sympathy for what Charlie had done among local people.

Calum flourished on his placement and had met a girl named Alice working in the bar for the summer. She was a social work student, and they were now going steady. Charlie liked her and was delighted for his son. Things were going well, he reflected, and the dark memories were receding.

He was also nearing the end of his monthly supervision with a community justice social worker which was a condition of early release. It wasn't a major burden as he had no intention of getting into trouble again. He met with the social worker (there'd been four since he was released, all female and a lot younger than himself) in a dingy area office in the west end, but it was just a formality and soon those meetings would be over and his connection to the criminal justice system finally sundered.

Some shouting up front alerted him from his reverie. They were passing the colourful frontage of the Grand Ole Opry country music venue just before the gushet at Paisley Road Toll, where the road divided at the distinctive Angel building with a landmark gilded statue of a winged angel protruding from its roof.

Two guys, both in their late twenties, were hurling racist abuse at a young black man sitting on the seat behind the stairhead. Behind him, the guy with his feet sticking out onto the passageway with his mobile still in his hand was grinning which seemed to egg the two guys on. The men were clearly quite drunk and animated, screaming vicious invective while the man sat ashen faced, cowering. There were two other passengers on that top deck, all of whom stared impassively out of the windows, feigning indifference.

The tone and aggression were getting worse. Charlie felt helpless, humiliated and ashamed at the plight of the black man. Then he saw the two guys get up and walk down the stairs, still showering abuse and making threats. Suddenly, on an impulse Charlie got up and walked to the stairs, noticing the black fellow was shaking; he wanted to apologize to him, but kept silent and descended the stairs.

The two guys were now loudly talking to the driver as he pulled up at a stop, the driver just smiled at them as he opened the doors. Charlie was wearing a white cap and pulled it down over his head as he left the bus.

He stood at the stop pretending to read the bus timetable information as the two men drunkenly weaved their way across the road and headed towards a pub about sixty metres up the road at the bottom of a row of brown sandstone tenements. He watched them stagger into the bar.

He had no idea of what he was going to do or why he'd got off the bus. He just knew he was bloody angry at the conduct of the two "twats" and their licence to do what they wanted unchecked. For Charlie couldn't help thinking it was all on a spectrum from Joe Jamieson being allowed to walk the streets and pick up his life after killing his brother, to these two screaming, shouting and threatening someone because they were a different colour with no one stopping them. Was there no sanction? He knew if he'd intervened on the bus, they would have turned their wrath on him; he was roughly the same height as them and quite wiry and fit, but probably not a match for both. Or was he just making excuses for himself?

But these guys needed to be stopped, otherwise they would go on until they did someone real harm. Anger again surged through Charlie, and he left the bus stop and walked across the road to the pub which had two entrances. He avoided the one where the two guys had entered and choose the far one at the end of an adjoining street, pulling his cap down even tighter across his head.

Shafts of sunlight were refracted through the dusty air as Charlie walked into the otherwise gloomy interior. A bar took up most of one side and a few customers were scattered around some tables. Focusing directly in front of him, Charlie approached the bar where a young bar tender came up to him. Without being asked, Charlie said out of the side of his mouth:

'Lager mate.'

Wordlessly, the barman slid away and poured his pint.

Charlie concentrated on controlling his breathing and relaxing as much as he could until the bar man came back with the beer. He grunted "thanks,' paid the guy, then took his change and sat at an empty table. Trying to remain calm, he took in his surroundings as furtively as he could.

It was pretty desolate as most pubs are in broad daylight when two-thirds empty. The few other customers were all male and over 50, drinking singly or chatting in low voices, with two flatscreen TVs providing a background commentary on tennis and racing. The only animated chatter was from the corner leading up to a small kitchen and staff area, with toilets off to one side, where the two guys were: one feeding a puggy and occasionally dropping a coin with a clang, while the other one sat at a nearby table urging him on to beat the machine.

Charlie noted one CCTV camera above the puggy looking out over the front of the pub; it was fixed, and he estimated his table was just outside its range. He'd made no impression, just a nondescript middle-aged man wearing a scruffy white cap with a grey anorak and a pair of jeans. That suited him as he sipped his beer.

Then he noticed the guy at the puggy walking to the loo, the other viewing his phone at the table. He was still working on impulse, but with controlled anger and determination as he stood up and made his way to the gents. He didn't look at the CCTV, ignored the other guy at the table and opened the toilet door. There was another door in front of him giving access to the gents. Entering, he saw a row of four urinals to the left, two wash hand basins to the right and two cubicles in front. The guy was at the second urinal and seemed to barely notice Charlie as he appeared to walk across to the cubicles.

Charlie stopped, summoned up an impression of Raymond, then with every effort of his body, lunged at the guy, propelling him against the urinal and wall with tremendous force, his urine splashing against his trousers and jumper. Before he had a chance to say anything, Charlie with his right hand, battered the guy's head against the hard, white tiled wall, then kicked his legs from under him, causing him to slump to the damp floor on his back.

Blood poured from the bridge of his nose as Charlie, now completely fired up, delivered a vicious kick to his genitals, his flaccid penis flopping about, before stamping on his mouth. He could hear a sickening crunch, as more blood gushed from his mouth, gurgling sounds emanating from his throat. The guy lay on the floor, terror stricken and prone.

Charlie moved back a pace. He felt an exultant energy take hold, ran at the guy and kicked his head with all the strength and momentum he would a football when he occasionally played five-a-side. The guy's head lurched from side to side as Charlie continued kicking it ferociously another five times. He stopped. He wanted to stamp on the guy's head, just as Jamieson had done with Raymond, but couldn't do it.

Instead, he recovered, the anger and the energy subsiding. The guy was bloodied, groaning and gurgling. Charlie stood over him with loathing, feeling utter contempt for the guy.

'That'll teach you to fucking noise up some innocent fucker on their own on a bus. And tell that prize arsehole you fart about wi, I'll fucking take his heid aff as well!'

He turned away and caught his reflection in the mirror above the basins. His face was flushed, but there was no blood on him. Taking a deep breath, Charlie opened the door and left the gents, straddling past the other guy still sitting, twiddling at his phone, stared determinedly ahead, cap firmly down on his head and exited the pub.

From talking to the experienced lags in Barlinnie, Charlie knew the key was to get away as fast as he could but not to create any impression, least of all to be rushed or appear panicked or look frantic. He walked resolutely away from the pub, past shoppers and passersby, a grey blur.

Until, in the distance ahead, he espied the welcome sight of a black cab with its yellow for hire sign on. Unhurriedly, he stretched out his left arm, saw the cab's indicators come on and stopped as it drew up.

'Lauriston, pal just opposite Bridge Street Subway,' he ordered the cabbie.

Traffic was still quite light in the early afternoon, and it was only a few minutes before they arrived at the destination, Charlie staying silent, making no eye contact with the driver and slumped in his seat.

Opposite the subway station, Charlie paid the driver with a small tip, crossed the road and caught a bus to Shawlands in the south of the city, before backtracking and boarding a bus to the city centre. He wanted to avoid train and subway stations or anywhere that would have CCTV.

Once in the city centre, he contemplated going into a

pub; he could have done with a drink, but knew he had to lay low, not create any conspicuous trail for at least a few hours. So, he got another bus to the west end. Sure, buses now did have CCTV, but unless an incident happened on board, their footage was not inspected as a matter of routine. Finally, after hopping on and off a few more buses, Charlie arrived home at his expensive art deco penthouse flat just off Great Western Road in the affluent Kirklees area of the west end, which he'd bought after being released and breaking up with Sarah.

He poured himself a generous measure of Laphroaig, sat in an armchair and tried to relax, a multitude of thoughts swirling around his head. Had anyone identified him? Would he be caught? If he was, as he was still under license he'd be whipped straight back into prison and would receive a substantial additional sentence. Could he last another stretch inside? There would be no chance of a reconciliation with Sarah. And what would Caleb and Calum think of him?

But he had no remorse whatsoever about kicking the shit out of that guy. The only pang of regret was not knocking the daylights out of the other one. But fifty percent was better than none. No, those two were racist scum, preying on innocents going about their business trying to make a living and an honest buck.

They were too many anti-social types like that getting away with it or only receiving some pitiful slap on the wrist. Charlie had surely broken that guy's jaw, dispensed a painful kick to the balls, caused him to pee all over himself, above all he'd been attacked and humiliated in what was probably one of his regular haunts, by somebody he didn't know. That would make him and his sidekick anxious and insecure. Exactly how they made their victims feel.

Ok, it wouldn't completely atone for Raymond, but, as he sat there sipping the delicious whisky, feeling more relaxed, more confident there'd be no comeback on him, Charlie felt good. This was revenge, sweet revenge.

Later that night, Charlie discarded all the clothes he was wearing, including his shoes, and sealed them in a plastic bag. Next day he burned them in a large brazier he had at the rear of the Camlachie Arms. Over the next few weeks, he studied the local papers, listened to newscasts and watched regional news programmes for any items on an assault in a pub off Paisley Road West. There were none.

Within a few months, Charlie felt confident there would be no repercussions. He had gotten away with it. He felt good and knew he would do the same again if the circumstances arose.

NINE

'What do you make of that, Charlie?' Malky, a regular customer at the Camlachie Arms asked him as he rinsed out a pile of glasses in the basin behind the bar.

It had been an exceptionally busy lunchtime on what was a freezing cold Thursday in February. Just after twelve, Des the Manager had phoned to say the place was jumping, one of the staff had called in sick and was it ok for him to contact the manager at another of Charlie's venues, to borrow a body.

Charlie was mildly put out as Des, always the most risk averse of his managers, could have done that on his own; he didn't need Charlie's say-so. But then he perked up as he was looking at a gloomy winter afternoon doing nothing.

'Des, in future, just phone who you want to if you need to fill a place. Listen, I'm bored shitless, so I'll be there in twenty minutes and give a hand.'

He'd made it in fifteen and it'd been a very busy shift, helping to take orders, serving customers, pouring drinks, wiping and cleaning. He loved it, got a buzz from it. As he often reflected, he'd never really left the basics of the trade. At heart, he was a KP.

'What's that then Malky?' Charlie responded as he started drying glasses.

'In the paper here,' he waved a copy of the Evening Times in his face pointing to an article. 'Some bastard attacked a woman going to her work and he's got a fucking community sentence! Honestly, here, read it.'

Charlie put down the glass and the cloth and took the paper off Malky. He was a stout man who always wore a crumpled, faded brown jacket and whose large girth virtually sprawled over two bar stools. He was in his early sixties, had taken early retirement and along with his two mates, Sam and Bert who were the same age, came into the bar every day about two and spent the rest of the day decamped at the bar and putting the world to rights while knocking back pint after pint. They were harmless, but above all good customers; those vital regulars that were the lynchpin of the bar trade. Charlie always indulged them.

'All right, let's see what's got your knickers in a twist, Malky.'

He read the article. The bar/diner was now quiet. A few remaining diners were relaxing at their tables over drinks, waitering staff were furiously clearing and wiping tables after the lunchtime deluge and apart from two other customers, there were only Malky, Bert and Sam at the bar. It was the lull before the evening rush, so Charlie had the time to read the article.

A twenty-six-year-old man named Kieron McPhail had been found guilty of attacking a thirty-nine-year-old woman under the Central Station Bridge in Glasgow city centre at six in the morning as she was making her way to her work as a cleaner in a nearby office. McPhail, who was a stranger to her, had been kicked out of a homeless hostel for aggressive behaviour and had been drinking cheap wine. Minutes earlier he'd been ejected from Central Station, Glasgow's main railway terminal, at the exit for low level trains beneath the wide bridge which was known locally as the "Heilanman's Umbrella" as allegedly in past times Highlanders sheltered there during rainstorms.

For no apparent reason whatsoever, he'd verbally and physically assaulted the woman, who'd suffered what were described as "superficial injuries." Charlies guessed that this was largely down to luck as McPhail would have been too drunk to do her any real damage. Nevertheless, even if she hadn't been seriously injured the woman would have been badly shaken by the assault, and her confidence in going out on her own or her faith in the criminal justice system to look after her and dispense justice, severely dented.

But there was the rub. McPhail had been arrested and charged with umpteen counts of assault but was given a non-custodial, community sentence as he had pleaded guilty. This despite the fact, as disclosed in the article, he had a plethora of previous convictions for assault and aggressive behaviour.

That woman, just trying to make her way in the world eking out a living cleaning offices, paying her taxes, playing the game, is assaulted by a random stranger. But her attacker, despite a string of previous charges, is free to wander the streets, subject only to whatever strictures imposed by the community sentence.

'What the fuck is wrong with these people?' Charlie thought to himself as he put down the paper. What was going through the mind of the judge or "sheriff" as they are called in the equivalent of a magistrate's court in Scotland, not locking that bastard up?

Charlie shook his head, 'fucking outrageous.'

'Honestly,' Bert said from the side, pointing at the newspaper, 'these sheriffs need a kick in the arse letting a thug like that back in the streets and not put in a cell.' They were nods of agreement from all four of them. Sam put in:

'If it was me, I'd...' But Charlie was distracted by a customer looking for service at the bar.

He finished about six and went home but took the copy of the paper with him leaving Malky, Bert and Sam to continue putting the world to rights and sipping lots of beer.

Over a ready meal, he reread the article. It just made him angrier, especially the details of the sentence. McPhail received 200 hours in the community spread over two years. Precisely what he would be doing "in the community" wasn't disclosed. 100 hours a year or roughly two hours a week for attacking a woman on her way to work.

For Charlie, that said so much about the Scottish criminal justice system. That a wretch like McPhail could get off so lightly was nothing short of shocking and diabolical. Again, there was no justice.

Raymond had played by the rules, only for his killer to be free after a mere ten years. Now this woman must live with the appalling thought that her attacker's punishment was an unpaid job somewhere for a couple of hours a week! Was that really what justice was about in modern Scotland?

The more Charlie brooded on it, the angrier and frustrated he became. It had been five months since he'd doled out the kicking to the guy in the pub and there'd been no comeback;

nothing whatsoever. He reflected that this was either because the guy himself, his mate and possibly whoever oversaw the pub, had decided not to report it: A not uncommon occurrence in the circles where crime happened frequently.

Or it had been reported but just not hit the media's radar. He'd scoured everywhere, including online and Glasgow's scurrilous underground crime scandal sheet, The Digger, which reported on the slightest detail of every assault and robbery in the city, but there was total silence everywhere. It was more likely Charlie reasoned that this was because the guy had decided not to report and had declared his injuries to medical staff were the result of an accident.

In sum, the guy would have had no idea of who'd attacked him or why. Charlie was completely off the radar for that one. Which gave him an idea and that made him feel better as there was somewhere for his anger and frustration to go.

It'd been six years since Charlie had last been in the building that housed AMAC Private Investigators. It hadn't changed much. The same brass plate with the same array of company names and the ancient, caged iron lift which wheezed its way to the sixth floor. If anything, the building was dingier and tackier than before. He made his way along the corridor to Ali McMahon's office with the same wooden door and grimey plaque. He'd arranged the appointment for three and it had just gone past. He knocked on the door and heard a familiar voice say, 'aye?'

Charlie had thought carefully about approaching the private investigator. He'd provided invaluable information which had allowed Charlie to plan and set up his revenge attack on Jamieson. The botch ups and carelessness that had ensnared him and put him in jail were entirely Charlie's. But that was the issue. Without the information supplied by Ali McMahon's team, he could never have carried out the ambush. But that made McMahon an accessory. Of course, Charlie had never blubbed about the PI's role.

Questioned by DS Maxwell about how he'd managed to trace and find Jamieson, he'd been vague and just said he'd asked a few questions. CID never really pressed him; after all Charlie had confessed and they'd got their man. But Ali McMahon would know well how it was that Charlie Carty knew where to ambush Joe Jamieson at his most vulnerable.

He entered the office. It was as untidy and dishevelled as ever, clutter everywhere and piles of files on his desk, a veritable fire hazard. McMahon looked even more emaciated than he had before, his sallow face more washed out.

'Mr Carty, we meet again,' his voice slightly raspier than before. 'Take a seat.'

Charlie sat across from him. He decided not to bring up the subject of Jamieson unless the private eye did so.

'Thanks for seeing me, Mr McMahon,' he looked him straight in the eye. 'I've got, ah, someone that I'd like some background information on.'

'Oh aye.'

'Yeah.'

He waited for McMahon to say something about the

previous time Charlie had engaged his services. This was his opportunity. Would he just ask him to leave given what Charlie had done with the last information he'd provided him with? But there was an awkward silence as they appraised each other. Charlie broke first.

'Aye, you see I'd just like to know more about someone.' Charlie felt quite strained.

'In what respect?' McMahon asked. Charlie shuffled in his chair.

'Usual stuff, where he lives, his movements, habits, you know.'

'Why?' McMahon's gaze was clinical which unnerved Charlie further.

'I'd just like to find out more about this guy, if you could help me.'

'I'm not here to judge people Mr Carty. I just supply information, discreetly. I only ask that the people I supply that information to are also discreet.'

Charlie nodded his head. 'Of course.' He started to feel less tense, more relaxed.

'So, who is this person?'

Charlie handed over a folded A4 sheet from his pocket. McMahon looked over it. Rather than use his own handwriting, he'd used a computer at one of his other restaurants, The Hungry Puffin, to print out the barest information he had on McPhail from the newspaper report, which was basically his name, age, the charges he'd been convicted of and the date of the assault.

'Ok,' McMahon said after scanning the note, 'we can get to

work on this. Our rates have increased since we last engaged on some work for you.'

'That's fine.'

'I'll update you weekly and we should be able to get you a full report in several weeks.'

Charlie felt relieved. McMahon hadn't subjected him to intensive questioning about his motives, nor more importantly shown him the door.

'Thanks, Mr McMahon,' he rose and shook his hand which was damp but firm. It struck him the only difference in the messy office this time, apart from the laptop on his desk rather than the PC he'd had the last time, was the absence of the smell of cigarette smoke and full ashtray. Possibly, he'd given up, though the wrinkles on his skin appeared to belie that. As he opened the door to leave, McMahon remarked:

'All I ask Mr McMahon, is that you use maximum discretion about your contact with us for the purposes of this enquiry. I cannot be held responsible for how a client uses our information on one occasion. I'm not psychic. But that defence becomes a lot thinner on a second occasion.'

They looked at each other. McMahon was letting him know there was a deal here. The private eye knew full well what Charlie could use his information for. That wasn't deterring him from supplying it. But the stakes were higher now. AMAC would definitely be viewed as an accessory by the law if Charlie was to do something similar to McPhail as had happened to Jamieson and their role was revealed. McMahon was taking a chance and was depending on Charlie to keep stum. He felt a responsibility to the private dick but also, he realised, an affinity. McMahon was on the same page as him.

'Mr McMahon,' he stood in the doorway and in a calm but deadly serious voice, continued: 'I would never mention you in any circumstance, I can assure you. Good day.' He closed the door behind him.

That evening, Charlie met with Sarah for a pre-arranged dinner at the Queen Mary. Bob Carlton had laid on a booth for them at the side of the main restaurant, assuring them a good deal of privacy. Charlie was grateful to him for this as he wanted to use dinner as the pretext to see where he was in getting back with her. Charlie had chosen a vintage Saint Emilion Grand Cru as the wine and the starter and main courses were excellent and relaxed both of them. They spoke of the boys and how well they were doing; Caleb their youngest had moved down to London to study engineering at Imperial College and after a rocky start settling in the big city, much to his parent's anxiety, he was now, thankfully, thriving. Sarah had just visited him the previous week as he'd moved out of student accommodation for his third year and was now in a flat near King's Cross.

'That was a dump years ago,' Charlie remarked midway through their main course.

'I know,' Sarah replied 'and I would have had kittens thinking he was staying in a terrible part of town. But it's all been done up and the flat he's in is lovely, really nice.'

Her face lit up, happy and content that her youngest son

was settled. She looked great and like Charlie kept herself fit and trim.

'You look lovely,' he said with genuine affection.

'Thanks. You keeping yourself well?'

'Aye.'

They hadn't divorced and hadn't even discussed that. Sarah kept her hand in at waitering at an Italian in town and Charlie's managers could call on her if they needed an experienced hand to help out. She still stayed in the comfortable villa and gated community in Bothwell and apart from her earnings, Charlie provided her with a generous income.

They discussed Calum's growing relationship with Alice who they both liked.

'He's thinking of moving in with her. She's got a nice flat in Battlefield,' Sarah announced.

'That's great,' Charlie was delighted. 'She's a lovely girl and she'll sort him out.'

'Aye, she will,' Sarah agreed.

'Just hope that Caleb meets someone nice when he's down there.'

'I think he has.'

'What? Didn't know anything about this.'

They were interrupted by the waiter clearing their main dishes and handing them the dessert menu. After they'd chosen and ordered, Charlie resumed.

'So, what's happening? Who's the lucky girl?'

'Well, it's not a girl.' Sarah's eyes were boring into his as the implication dawned on Charlie.

'It's a bloke?' She nodded.

'Yeah. A chap called Lawrence.'

Charlie was stunned. The idea that one of his sons would be gay had never occurred to him. He didn't regard himself as homophobic, but he had no experience of or didn't overtly know of anyone who was gay. Certainly, in the past hospitality had been a hotbed of homophobia along with misogyny, rampant sexism and visceral racism. It would have been hell if someone had outed themselves in Ramsay's kitchen. Like the rest of society, the industry was changing fast, and Charlie's HR people would be on top of any display of anti-gay discrimination in his kitchens.

But Caleb being gay struck him sideways. The entire culture and background Charlie had been raised in until the last couple of decades was firmly anti-gay. Indeed, up until 1980, being gay was illegal in Scotland and could be punished by a severe fine or imprisonment. And God help anyone revealed to be gay in the grim confines of a Scottish prison such as Barlinnie.

But things had changed remarkably. Acceptance of people's sexuality and for what they were was the norm. So why was Charlie so dumbstruck? Caleb was his son, his flesh and blood; he loved him and that love was unconditional. Why should his sexuality change that? Was there some atavistic impulse in him that thought being gay was unmanly? Sarah read him perfectly.

'Stop that!' She commanded. 'Caleb's our son. Nothing ever will change that and how he chooses to live his life is for him and him alone. Our job is to support and love him. I've met

Lawrence and he's lovely. Sometime soon, Caleb will bring him up to Glasgow and as his parents you and I will welcome Lawrence just as we would if Caleb brought a girl home.'

The desserts arrived. Charlie had affogato and as he poured expresso over the ice cream, he realised the key words in what Sarah had said were acceptance and love. Caleb was his youngest son and nothing in the world would change that.

He stopped pouring and took hold of Sarah's hand, looking straight into her moist eyes. 'Of course, I'm looking forward to meeting Lawrence.' Sarah clutched his hand and put her head towards his.

They parted after the dinner and Charlie didn't press about getting together again; it just didn't seem appropriate after the revelation about Caleb. The important thing for the moment was that Caleb knew his mother and father would accept him for what he was. Reconciliation with Sarah would, hopefully, come later.

Ali McMahon's report on Kieron McPhail was pinged to Charlie's inbox ten days later. It made depressing and predictable reading. There were lots of echoes of Joe Jamieson. McPhail was living with his single mother in Royston, a part of north Glasgow that was always given the tag as an "area of multi-deprivation". He was unemployed and had never really worked, having dropped out of one college course and being expelled from another. He'd been suspended numerous times at both primary and secondary school for aggressive behaviour, including attacks on other pupils and teachers.

But in line with the policy of avoiding excluding pupils in the belief that this would make their situation worse, he was never expelled though Charlie could only consider that McPhail would have made his teacher's and fellow pupil's time in class a misery.

He'd graduated onto petty theft, mainly shoplifting. In another disturbing echo of Jamieson's case, McPhail had been arrested, charged, convicted, detained in Young Offender's Institutions or put on rehabilitation programmes, but always reoffended. Nothing seemed to work. A succession of youth workers, social workers, criminal justice workers and even a psychologist had been assigned to him over the years with apparently no impact. He'd also passed through a plethora of third sector agencies working on "alternative to custody" programmes, all of which he eventually dropped out of with seemingly no sanction.

For Charlie, McPhail, as with Jamieson before him, just appeared to be recycled through the criminal justice system. Whether locked up for a short period or sent to this and that programme, he either dropped out or came back into the community and within weeks or months, reoffended, was back in custody or put on yet another programme working with yet more workers, dropped out, reoffended and so on.

This recycling culminated in McPhail being kicked out of the house by the usual exasperated mother, turfed onto the streets, where he entered a homelessness shelter, in which after a few nights of increasingly violent behaviour fuelled by cheap wine, he was thrown out, staggered into the city centre, where blitzed out of his mind, he came across the innocent cleaner on her way to work and assaulted her; his paralytic state being the only reason he hadn't done more damage to the woman, though that was of little comfort to her.

McMahon's people had managed to get access to a Social Enquiry report on McPhail which argued strongly for mitigation, blaming an "unfortunate relapse into persistent alcohol misuse" and that he had been making "some progress" toward "controlling his violent impulsive behaviour" and "a non-custodial sentence" was recommended along with "engaging with a community programme" and enrolling in "a behaviour modification initiative".

Charlie was appalled. Giving McPhail another chance, not giving up on him and keeping him in the community trumped locking him up and protecting the community from this violent, aggressive thug. Like Jamieson, Charlie considered McPhail to be wound up tight like a rocket ready to explode and if unchecked, escalating rapidly to killing someone and all those agencies so concerned to rehabilitate him would be complicit in this catastrophic madness. Well, Charlie was the man to halt that escalation.

McPhail's community sentence was working with a gang of offenders on various projects. Currently, during the school holidays, he was painting fences and walls at a secondary school in the east end of Glasgow.

But the location of the school, the times when McPhail was working there or his mother's address (where McPhail was back staying) were not specified. This struck Charlie as strange given all the other details in the report about him. Then he reckoned McMahon was holding this back from him, lest Charlie did "something" with that information.

Charlie was determined to stop Kieron McPhail from murdering someone and to give him the "justice" he'd thus far escaped from a fatally flawed and weak criminal justice system. But he had to pinpoint and locate McPhail. And only Ali McMahon could help him with that.

The whisky bar was stowed on a sultry afternoon. It looked like thunder was in the air as Charlie ordered a dram at the crowded bar, and saw McMahon sitting at a table on the raised floor at the rear of the pub. He pushed his way through the mixture of locals and tourists and sat beside the private eye who was nursing a Guinness on the table.

'It's mobbed in here.' Charlie stated the obvious by waying of an opening.

'Aye, the tourists lap up the specialty whiskies,' McMahon concurred.

The pub was noted for its vast range of whiskies which attracted people from across the globe and Charlie picked up a curious mixture of American, French, German and Scandinavian combined with local accents around him.

'So, why do you want to see me?' McMahon came to the point.

Charlie reckoned he knew the reason, but McMahon was being cagey. He'd phoned to arrange an appointment, but the PI immediately said they should meet in a pub and not his office and suggested this time in the whisky bar. Charlie barely had time to say "yes" before McMahon said brusquely, 'Ok, I need to go, I'm with a client,' and put the phone down.

'The report on...' Charlie began, but McMahon interjected sharply:

'...no names!'

Charlie drew breath. 'All right. What you sent about our mutual friend. You haven't told me where he stays or where he's carrying out his community sentence.'

'That's right, I haven't,' McMahon stared straight back at him.

'Is there a reason for that?'

'I thought that would have been obvious, Mr Carty.'

'You mean what happened after my last encounter with your firm?'

He sipped a good measure of the Guinness before replying, 'yes, you could say that.'

'They never charged you and you were only doing what your client asked you to do.'

'Yes, they never charged as they didn't need to. You were caught red handed and you folded with little resistance.'

Charlie looked down at the table. 'True, but I learned a lot from that, but I assure you, this time, whatever happens, I'll never divulge your name if the cops come sniffing. I won't grass you.'

Charlie looked straight at McMahon. He was convinced he wouldn't mention the private eye's name to the CID.

'How do I know that?' McMahon asked squarely.

'You don't.'

A silence ensued before McMahon asked directly in a low

voice, after taking another sip of his ale:

'If I told you the details you're looking for, is it your intention to knock fuck out of him like you did the other guy?'

Charlie didn't answer but just looked directly at him. After a minute, McMahon said:

'I think I know the answer. Do you see yourself as an equaliser?'

'A what?'

'You know what I mean. A Glasgow version of Denzil Washington or that British actor, Woodward, seeking justice or vengeance or whatever.'

'Look, Mr McMahon, that cunt battered a woman on her way to her work and gets a pitiful community sentence,' he said the words with contempt. 'He's got previous for assault and violence up to his fucking neck and he's working up to doing to some poor bastard what that piece of shite Jamieson did to my brother. He should have been put away ages ago, but nothing and nobody's doing that. Somebody has to.'

'And that's you, is it?'

'Aye, if no one else will. I don't want anyone else having to identify someone they love lying with their head caved in on a slab.'

A flash through the frosted windows of the pub followed by a clap of thunder broke the pensive silence between them amid the hubbub and clatter around them. Charlie realised he hadn't touched his whisky and took a generous swallow. As the bitter taste of the liquor hit him, a thought occurred to him.

'Listen, I was always going to be in the frame for the attack on Jamieson. But this guy we're talking about has absolutely no connection to me. Zilch. How could anybody connect me to whatever happens to him? I've no skin in the game.'

'That's true,' McMahon responded, 'but it's how clever you are at covering your tracks. You weren't too great the last time, were you?'

'Granted, I ballsed up big time. But I've learnt a lot, and I don't want to spend any more time inside. Besides, even if I do fuck up, which I don't intend to, I'll never finger you or your team. Christ, I'm taking a chance even telling you this.'

McMahon swallowed the remains of his pint, placed the empty glass on the table and said:

'Ten years ago, my sister got mugged in Govan in broad daylight. The guy that did it also got a community sentence, a curfew and a tag. She wasn't badly hurt, just shaken, but when she saw her attacker walking down the street months later, it panicked her. She's never been the same since. Being in the profession I am, I kept an eye on him. Two years later my sister's attacker put a guy in a wheelchair.'

Abruptly, he stood up, fetched a piece of folded paper from his jacket and laid it beside Charlie's glass.

'Discretion, Mr Carty, discretion,' and left the table, edging his way through the throng. Charlie watched him depart the pub before picking up the notepaper and unfolding it. It listed three items: An address, including postcode, in north Glasgow. The name and address of a secondary school, also in Glasgow and two sets of timings. One for Tuesday mornings and the other for Thursday afternoons.

Ali McMahon had just let Charlie Carty know where Kieron McPhail was living and where and when he was currently serving his community sentence.

The CCTV cameras were on the approaches to the underpass from east and west. It was a fair assumption that between then they covered the length of the walkway underneath the busy dual carriageway. The street leading to the east approach was the best for Charlie's plan; it had a small park to the right and a wall behind a disused warehouse on the left, giving way to a red sandstone church that led onto a residential street of four-in-a-block houses and a row of small shops. This part of the street was almost a pathway before the descent to the underpass.

Charlie had performed a couple of recces and worked out when was best for his "resolution of delayed justice" as he decided to call it. It was the school holidays and most of the traffic through the underpass was from the school, so few people ventured through it on Tuesday mornings just after eleven thirty.

McMahon's earlier report had provided Charlie with a description of McPhail, and he'd used a car park across from the school next to a business park as an observation point. He'd seen a group of about a dozen young people, mostly young guys but a few girls among them, all in splattered blue overalls, making their way into the school, presumably to commence their community sentence time painting fences or walls.

Thankfully, McPhail was easy to spot. Tall and lank with a black bonnet over his head, on Tuesday mornings and Thursday afternoons he walked to and from the school on his own never mixing with the other offenders who seemed to give him a wide swerve. About two hours later he would walk away from the school through the underpass and the virtual pathway, still on his own to the residential street that led to a bus stop. Most of the others left the school and walked past the car park and the business unit to shops and bus stops on the other side of the underpass.

For the recces and the actual day of the "resolution" Charlie wore a grey anorak, dark blue jeans, dark green sweater, brown training shoes and a white baseball cap with no logo. All of which he intended to destroy.

On the Tuesday morning he'd selected, Charlie parked a maroon second hand Toyota, bought at a car auction recently, on a quiet side street, next to some brown tenements a couple of hundred yards from the underpass. Wearing the same clothes, he'd worn for the recces, but carrying a long object wrapped in plastic from his left arm, Charlie walked onto the street with the four-in-a-block grey houses and made his way along it past the church, until it narrowed before the underpass. He only saw a tradesman and a postman as he stopped just short of the descent to the underpass out of range of the cameras.

He brought out his phone and pretended to text with his right hand, long package still in his left, while leaning against the wall behind the warehouse. Out of the corner of his eye he was aware of someone emerging from the underpass. Stained blue overalls, white trainers, fair hair, tall, fast walker, but with a grey cap this time; it was McPhail, as usual on his own. Charlie rapidly scanned behind him; there was no one else walking through the underpass and the rest of the street before him was deserted.

Charlie stopped texting and brought the phone to his right ear, grunting 'hello', the brim of his own cap wound tightly over his forehead, almost obscuring his eyes. McPhail walked past him. Charlie had rehearsed his next move numerous times in the privacy of his flat in front of the full-length wardrobe mirrors in his bedroom.

With a fleeting move he dropped his phone into his anorak pocket, quickly slipped off the plastic wrapper revealing a large white baseball bat with a black handle, walked noiselessly a few paces until he was right behind McPhail and with all the force and fury he could muster swung the bat at McPhail's head. There was a sickening, crunching sound as wooden bat met skull, McPhail's cap flew into the air and he crumpled to the ground, legs collapsing beneath him.

Blood gushed from the back of McPhail's head as Charlie cracked the bat across the front of his face, causing it to flatten and become a bloody mass, before swinging the bat with full intensity on both his left and right kneecaps. McPhail screamed in agony, his legs and body writhing in spasmatic, jerky movements. After a final swing at his knees Charlie ceased, stood erect and walked calmly away, leaving the pulpy, bloody mess of McPhail lying behind.

His choice of location was perfect. The street was still

empty; trees and bushes at the edge of the small park hiding the sight and by the time Charlie walked into the residential part of the street, McPhail's painful screeches had receded. He went into the small side street, placed the bat covered in blood stains back in the plastic wrapper, went into the Toyota, placed the bat on the floor below him, started the engine and drove away. In the boot of the car was a glove and ball in case he was pulled over by the cops and had to justify the bat.

He avoided main roads, dual carriageways and above all any motorway, as all would be covered by CCTV and wended his way to Govan on the southwest of the city, to a breaker's yard where for cash up front, the Toyota would be crushed and dismembered there and then, no questions asked.

Having paid the cash and with no paperwork involved, Charlie walked half a mile to the car park at Govan Shopping Centre next to the subway station, where he picked up his own car and drove back to his Kirklees flat.

Stripping off the sweater, the jeans and discarding his anorak and trainers, Charlie sealed them in paper bags as well as the plastic wrapper for the cricket bat. In his spare room, he placed the bloodied bat on a trestle table and with a large hammer systematically broke the bat into smaller wooden pieces, including the handle, which he also sealed in paper bags.

After cleaning up around the flat he drove to an industrial incinerator near East Kilbride on the southeastern outskirts of the city where, for another fee, he inserted the bags into a large waste burner.

By four he was back in his flat savouring a Laphroaig.

One of the lags in Barlinnie had called it "being forensically nude". That is, having absolutely no trace on or about you that could link you to a crime. Well, Charlie Carty reflected over his second fine whisky, he was as forensically nude as it was possible to be of any connection to the attack on Kieron McPhail.

He seriously considered that he hadn't wanted to physically hurt McPhail, or the guy in the pub before, or even for that matter, Joe Jamieson, his brother's killer. He wasn't a violent man. In fact, he'd never been involved in a fight in his life. It was terrible that it had to come to this. All he would have wanted was for the likes of McPhail and the others to have been locked up and prevented from carrying out their attacks on innocent people going about their lives. But they hadn't. And for that reason, Charlie pinned the blame on a feeble system run by well-meaning but ultimately deluded and dangerous do-gooders.

What was it McMahon had called him in the pub? An "equaliser". He played that around in his head. Maybe that's what he was with these two guys and the attempt on Jamieson that had backfired on him: Chef Carty, Equaliser. He smiled to himself. He liked that. Whatever, he had absolutely no regrets about the actions, the "resolutions of delayed justice" he had embarked on.

The first news of the attack came in a report on local radio news the next morning followed by a brief item in the regional TV bulletins that evening. They all described a twenty six year-old man, "identified as Kieron McPhail" as having been "seriously assaulted" with "severe injuries" and taken to hospital where his condition was "said to be serious but stable."

The first newspaper report was on the Thursday morning in the Daily Record followed by the Glasgow Times. Both were sparse. Kieron McPhail had been the victim of a "savage attack" and police were looking for the culprit or culprits as there were no witnesses. There were a few more reports in a similar vein, but then it petered out.

Although part of him was always tensed up for a knock at the door from the cops, by the turn of the year Charlie considered himself to have gotten away with it and had successfully accomplished two resolutions of delayed justice.

Crucially also, there had been no response from Ali McMahon. By that silence, Charlie considered McMahon to be a supporter. There was at least one other person out there who understood what he had done and why.

TEN

He plated up the monkfish, spruced with his own parsley and lemon sauce and took them over to Sarah sitting at the oakwood dining table in what Charlie like to call the 'dining area', but was really no more than a glorified alcove off the main sitting room in his flat.

'This looks delicious,' she beamed in expectant pleasure at the dish on the table.

'Wire in doll!' Charlie said in his broadest Glaswegian, 'there's mair wi that came fae.'

He walked back to the kitchen and fetched the side dishes of roasted vegetables and new Ayrshire potatoes, came back to the dining space and put them on the table before lifting the vintage Rioja from the table and poured two glasses for them.

'To health and happiness,' Charlie declared.

'Health and happiness,' Sarah echoed.

He'd purchased six bottles of the reserved Rioja which had cost a fortune but as he savoured the wine after tasting the richly flavoured monkfish and saw the contentment and beaming smile on his wife's face, he considered it worth the price.

'It's gorgeous, Charlie,' she said, patting her mouth with a napkin, 'you've surpassed yourself.'

'Aye, it's rerre hen,' he kept up the broad Glaswegian.

It was often said that cooking great food was the key to a man's heart for a woman. For Charlie with Sarah, it had been the reverse. From their courting days back at the Springwell, through all the craziness of the following years when he could,

Charlie would serve up a good quality dish and put all his chef's skills into ensuring it had the right balance of the three key components essential to make outstanding food: presentation, flavour and texture. Tonight's serving had all three and by her 'oohs' and 'ahs', Sarah certainly seemed to be in seventh heaven.

Outside, a light dusting of snow covered the gothic Victorian tenements of the city's west end and sprinkled across the wide boulevard of the Great Western Road causing traffic to slow.

It was a cold and wintery January night but inside Charlie's sumptuous apartment it was all toasty and snug. He experienced a dayglow warmth envelop him as the beautiful wine coursed through him and the food hit all the pleasure spots, mirrored by Sarah. He felt an intimacy, almost post-coital in its intensity, developing between them. And this convinced him that her response to what he had to say later would be positive.

It had been a good couple of months. All his venues were doing well, despite the ongoing cost of living crisis, and the Christmas season had been exceptional. His bank balance was healthy.

The boys were doing well. Calum had moved in with Alice and their relationship was thriving. In November, Des, the manager of the Camlachie Arms, announced he was resigning with immediate effect. He'd been suffering from chronic arthritis and his doctor had ordered immediate rest and relaxation, something the hospitality trade was never going to deliver.

Charlie was devastated at the loss. Apart from being genuinely affected by Des having to leave as he was a bloody good and hard-working manager who knew and could read his earthy east end customers well, he was a decent guy who Charlie respected and trusted. He would miss him terribly. Besides, recruiting someone of Des's calibre was going to be difficult.

Then Calum offered to step in 'for a temporary period.' It was a risk, especially with the frantic festive season approaching, but he'd performed well on his placement and so was familiar with the diner and the customers. But a placement was a long way from running the place. Would his oldest son have the skillset to run a hectic bar/diner, deal with customers and manage staff in the frenetic hothouse atmosphere that was hospitality when it was full on? It was deep-end stuff.

It had worked out well. Sure, Charlie was there to help and proffer advice, but rapidly Calum had picked up what was needed within days. He was a natural for the trade. Great with the punters and flexible but firm with staff. Charlie was confident there'd be no issues there and felt assured that his business was going to be in safe hands whenever he decided to retire. He was also, of course, incredibly proud of Calum, though tried hard not to show it with typical west of Scotland blunt humour and caustic wit. But after a mad shift with a healthy turnover and tired but content staff relaxing over a complimentary drink at the bar, Charlie could be spotted beaming with pride at his son's natural affinity for his father's chosen profession.

As for Caleb, his youngest, he'd hadn't the opportunity yet to visit him or his new partner, Lawrence in London. Instead, they'd come up to Glasgow for Christmas and stayed with his mother in Bothwell. Charlie was trying to come to terms with

Caleb being gay and Sarah had warned him to do nothing by way of looks or remarks that would make him or Lawrence feel awkward.

Christmas Day was one of the busiest in the hospitality calendar and Charlie had troubleshooted between his various outlets, but he'd really nothing to do except lend a hand serving pints and waitering tables.

It meant Christmas chez Carty was on Boxing Day in Bothwell. It was fantastic. Charlie, as ever, cooked and served the turkey and all the trimmings with Calum assisting. The food was devoured and the wine flowed. Charlie watched his p's and q's particularly around Lawrence and earned a withering glare from his wife on only a few occasions which swiftly brought him into line. But he took to Lawrence who for Charlie was quintessentially English with his posh "BBC accent", confident and assertive but not overbearing or arrogant. He and Caleb matched and were obviously happy and content with each other. Any residue of discomfort or distaste he had, evaporated; Charlie was not quite a New Age man, but he'd shed a load of the cultural prejudices he'd grown up with.

Boxing Day was a huge success as was the Hogmanay party held here in Charlie's flat a few weeks earlier. He'd introduced Lawrence to the delights of Laphroaig which the Londoner seemed to enjoy, everybody had taken a turn at belting out a song to the accompaniment of Charlie's karaoke audio system he'd recently acquired and had a great time.

It was all going well. Certainly, lurking in the background and popping uninvited into his head at various times were the ghastly spectres of Jamison and McPhail, not to speak of that racist twat he'd ambushed in the pub toilet. But as soon as they emerged into his consciousness, he managed to vanquish them. Indeed, by now after the delightful holidays, they increasingly seemed to be part of someone else's life. What he desired most now was a quiet life; in a few years, especially if Calum continued to do well in the trade, Charlie envisaged himself retiring early and leaving the business in his oldest son's capable hands, there to be called upon for sage advice when needed.

But a major part of settling down for Charlie was to be with the love of your life. And this was what tonight was all about. As he cleared the plates and put them in the dishwasher, and then got the desserts ready, nerves overcame him. For he was shortly going to suggest to Sarah that they get back together again.

It was nearly five years now since they'd separated and he desperately yearned to be reconciled and living under the same roof as her. He loved her deeply as much, if not more so, than when they'd first met.

He'd made fresh chocolate mousse which he knew would be a light counterweight to the rich seafood. It was also one of Sarah's favourites and she gasped with joy when he brought the mousse through and exclaimed:

'Fantastic!' Then she gave him an inquisitive stare. 'So, what you up to Charley Carty?'

She was on to him. Always could see through him and his manoeuvres.

'When we finish these, all will be revealed.'

They destroyed the desserts, but it wasn't until coffee and some superb Belgian chocolate truffles that he felt able to come out with it.

'Ok, I'm fed up living on my own and I think it's time we thought of getting back together.'

The instant he said it the atmosphere changed. Sarah's visage transformed from smiling anticipation to concern and tension. She put her wine glass on the table and her hand to her mouth. Charlie sensed this wasn't going to go well.

'Oh Charlie, I...' She stopped, unsure what to say next. She took her hand from her mouth and looked away from him, eyes closed. 'I don't know what to say to you.'

'You don't want to get back?'

She shook her head and finally looked straight at him, eyes wide open.

'I was going to tell you.' She looked away, stirred her coffee cup needlessly, and then back at him. 'I've met someone else.'

Charlie froze. An icy shudder went through him. He was prepared for her to respond she needed more time, needed to think more about it, but that there was someone else in her life, would never have occurred to him.

'What?' he asked, almost with incredulity. His voice was strained, but calm and composed.

'You heard me, Charlie.'

'Who? Where? When?' His arms were outstretched in bewilderment.

She drank more wine. 'Before Christmas. I got involved

with someone.'

'Who?'

'In San Vittorio.' That was the Italian restaurant she waitered part-time at.

His eyes were as wide as saucers. She continued.

'It'd been building up for a while.'

'Who is it?'

'Luigi Martello.'

'Aw for fuck's sake! He's married with three kids.' Martello was the manager of the restaurant.

'The marriage is a sham, been so for years and the kids are all in their twenties and thirties.'

The anger building up in Charlie burst. 'That sleazy, dago bastard! The...'

'...now stop that,' she vigorously interrupted him. 'He's a good, kind man.'

'Oh, I bet he is,' Charlie almost spat out contemptuously.

He was dumbfounded. He shook his head. 'I just can't believe this.'

She put her hand on his. 'I'm really sorry, Charlie, but I've thought long and hard on this. What we had was great, but it's over now. I'll never stop loving you, but not in that way.'

He took his hand away from hers. 'No, but you love him that way!'

'Charlie, I didn't want you to find out this way.'

'Oh, were you gonny send me an email or put an announcement in the paper?'

She rose from her seat. 'Aw Charlie, there's no point in

me staying.'

'That's right, just walk away, don't discuss it.' She'd brought out her mobile and began texting.

'We can't talk just now because you'll just end up screaming and shouting.'

'Do you fucking blame me?' his voice was raised.

'I've just called for an Uber,' she came back. 'The cab will be here in three minutes.'

It was a Monday on a snowy evening, and they were just off the Great Western Road. Of course, the cab would only take minutes. He watched in a stunned and angry silence as she retrieved her coat, silk scarf and handbag.

Her phone pinged. 'That's the cab. I'm really sorry you had to find out this way.'

'You let me cook that fucking meal,' he said slowly with anger.

She'd reached the sitting room door and stopped. 'I'll phone you in a few days. I know you hate me right now but thank you for that lovely meal.' She closed the door; an instant later he heard the front door.

He sat alone at the dining table, completely deflated, his anger ebbing replaced with an awful emptiness. He'd spent most of his life with her, built and shared a career with her. The mother of his two kids. The thought of her out of his life was devastating. He put his head in his arms and did something he hadn't done since he was a little boy, cried. Not even when he'd heard of Raymond's death or seen his brother lying on that mortuary slab had he broken down. But he did now, sobbing, his whole body shaking.

He stayed in his flat for five full days, not washing, hardly eating, barely sleeping, lost in a miasma of grief, sorrow, anger and loss. There were loads of calls and texts from business associates and Calum, all of which he fielded by texting he was feeling "exhausted" and was "taking a few days off". Sarah phoned on the fourth day. He didn't answer. She texted, but he didn't respond.

On the fifth day, he showered, shaved and tidied the flat up. Feeling tired but determined he drove to the Camlachie Arms where Calum was both surprised and relieved to see him.

'I was about to come to your flat. I've been phoning and texting you for days'

They were in the restaurant area. It was Friday lunchtime, and the place was heaving.

'Needing a hand?' Charlie asked his son.

'Could do with some help in the kitchen.'

'Ok.' As he was about to go to the kitchen, Calum asked:

'You all right, dad?'

'Your mother's got a new man,' he answered him directly.

'I know,' Calum responded, just as directly.

'Caleb?'

'Aye, he knows too.'

A waitress came clattering out the kitchen fully laden with plates. As she passed them, she said out of the corner of her mouth but out of earshot of customers:

'Dishes backing up.' At the entrance, six customers walked in waiting to be seated.

'We'll talk later,' Charlie said to his son and made his way to the kitchen.

THE KITCHEN VIGILANTE - "JUSTICE WILL BE SERVED"

Bob Carlton and Charlie were enjoying late night cocktails in Logos, a private members club part owned by Bob in Royal Exchange Square slap in the middle of the city. The Square was a collection of distinguished Georgian terraces now housing offices, shops, restaurants, bars and nightclubs surrounding the magnificent Graeco-Roman edifice, the former Royal Exchange, now Glasgow's modern art museum. In front of the museum was a bronze statue of the Duke of Wellington which had attained global iconic status when an unheralded genius decades earlier, presumably half-cut, had placed an orange and white traffic cone on the duke's head.

Ever since, despite the authorities many attempts to prevent it, legions of traffic cones had adorned the statue and become a part of the city's image.

They were sitting in the penthouse rooftop bar looking down on the crowded square. It was after eleven on a Saturday, but in early June with the long Scottish summer nights in full swing, the sky was still in twilight. Queues were starting to build outside the various late-night bars, including Logos where members were allowed to sign in two guests. Of course, Bob and Charlie didn't have to queue and were waved in by the stewards at the door.

They'd arrived by taxi twenty minutes earlier from a new restaurant that was earning a good name in the Dennistoun area just east of the city centre. Run by a husband-and-wife team, Jenni and Leon in their late twenties, Marchetti's was a new addition to the city's flourishing Italian dining scene. The food was standard Italian fare but cooked, prepared and presented with flare and tasted delicious. Both Bob and Charlie had been really impressed which was saying something for the jaded palates of two experienced restaurateurs who'd eaten and seen it all.

'I don't know what he'd done to that prawn ravioli but it sure was stunning,' Bob extolled sipping at his Black Russian.

The 'he' was Leon Marchetti, who presided over the kitchen while Jenni oversaw front-of-house.

'Aye,' Charlie agreed over his Margarita, 'they're doing something right. I had to book it for a Saturday five weeks in advance.'

'Great service though, even if it was full house tonight,' Bob praised.

'True, she was full of chat and bubbly, but the boy Marchetti, when he came out the kitchen, had a torn face the whole night. He needs to let her be the only one to deal with the punters.'

Bob sipped his cocktail through the straw before saying:

'I think she's putting an act on as well.'

'How do you mean?' Charlie asked.

'Apparently they're coming under heavy pressure from a wee start-up team in the east end.'

'Oh aye, who would they be?'

'Two brothers, the McGarvey's, based in Shettleston. Tam McGarvey, the older one, started out as a lieutenant for the Chisholm's, but he's now branching out on his own with his younger brother Mark. They still courier and run dealers for the Chisholm's, but they've started doing protection rackets and running girls on their own in their neck of the woods. Word has it they might even make a move on the Chisholm's when old man Sammy finally snuffs it.'

The Chisholm's were a notorious Glasgow crime family who'd dominated the city's drug trade for the past thirty years. They'd ascended to the top after a vicious struggle resulting in a large body count in the nineties. Now they controlled most of the city's heroin and cocaine supplies along with newer, even more potent substances such as fentanyl and nitazenes. At the helm for three decades was Sammy Chisholm, a chiselled underworld, ruthless autocrat, now afflicted with a severe respiratory illness – reputed to be emphysema, not helped by a 30 a day habit – that was beginning to restrict his hitherto unbridled rule.

Ruling by fear, including over his two weak sons, the mob boss's grip was beginning to falter and into the looming power vacuum, the lieutenants and other parties were starting to jockey for position. Despite being awash with drugs, Glasgow had been relatively peaceful when it came to gang wars and that was because one family and one patriarch was in control. Now with that in doubt a bloodbath was predicted as numerous players made bids for dominance. And one of those players was the McGarvey's.

Protection rackets were endemic in hospitality, even affecting the big chains. You were open to the public, vulnerable, largely operating in isolation, so you had to make some accommodation with local gangsters. Bob and Charley had. But it was relatively small scale. There was a limit to what a business could afford by way of protection before it went under, and you killed the goose. Seasoned operators like Sammy Chisholm knew this.

But eager, aggressive wannabes like the McGarvey's, didn't appreciate this, as Bob made clear to Charlie.

'Word has it they're hitting the couple for nearly fifty per cent.'

'Fuck's sake!' Charlie blanched. 'Nae wonder your man Leon has got a sourpuss on him.'

'Can you blame him? I know the type. Tam McGarvey's ruthless, he's got a reputation to make, and he'll push for more than half,' Bob explained.

'That couple will soon be working for nothing.' Charley shook his head in despair at the thought of it. 'Soon their whole business, everything they've worked for, their savings, will go down the Swanee. It's abominable.'

'Tam McGarvey couldn't give a fuck; he'll just move onto somebody else. It is shocking,' Bob said with an air of resignation.

'Is there nothing that can be done?' Charlie asked.

'Well, the polis are useless; they canny be there twenty-four/seven sitting in the kitchen all the time. That's no gonny happen. Time was you could have asked auld man Chisholm to tap Tam Maguire on the shoulder and tell him, "haud it, you'll kill the business that's giving you money," but those days are gone it seems.' Bob put his hands in the air. 'There's nothing it seems can be done. I really feel for that young couple.'

Charlie was silent, ruminating on what Bob had told him. The anger, which had dissipated since his attack on McPhail nearly ten months ago, resurfaced at the blatant injustice of what was happening to the Marchetti's. His brooding contemplation was interrupted by Bob declaring,

'Hi, let's change the subject. Look who's just sat over there?'

Charlie glanced over at a table by the far window. Two women, both in their forties, one dyed blond, the other brunette in low cut tops and short skirts just above their knees revealing shapely legs, had just taken their seats there, browsing at the elaborate cocktail menu.

'That's all right, isn't it?' Bob looked at Charlie, lecherous glint in his eye.

Bob was married, but it was an open secret the marriage had been on the rocks for years and both he and his wife had had numerous affairs over the years. Charlie was still reeling from Sarah's revelation of her relationship with Luigi Martello. He'd received divorce papers from her lawyer shortly afterwards and decided not to oppose it, but he was still numb. Bob knew about the impending divorce.

'Come on, you're a free man now,' he cajoled him.

Charlie stared over at the two women again. They were attractive. Desire and lust took hold of him. It'd been years since he'd been to bed with a woman; Sarah had been strictly chaste with him, even after he left prison. He wasn't sure about his performance after such a long time, but the more he ogled the women, the more aroused he was becoming. Aw to hell with it, he thought.

'You still have that pad on Miller Street?' Charlie knew that Bob had bought a "bachelor" flat in the Merchant City, a few hundred yards away from where they were. He flashed a set of keys in front of Charlie.

'Oh aye, most definitely.' Bob looked back at the women and stopped a passing waiter saying: 'The two ladies who have just sat down at the table over there, please let them know that their drinks are on me. Just put it on my tab.' Bob passed him a tenner, and the waiter went across to inform the women. They looked over and smiled, the blond shouting over 'thanks, you're a gentleman.'

Bob picked up his Black Russian. 'Come on, I don't see any wedding rings, do you?'

'No, I don't.'

Bob rose. 'Let's go.'

Charlie fetched his Magarita and followed.

He'd decided after he got away with the second act of delayed resolution of justice on Kieron McPhail that his vengeance days were over. Back then his focus would be on his business, the boys and their future careers and, most importantly, getting back together with Sarah. Months later, all that seemed to pale.

His businesses were running themselves. It'd been months since he'd had to do any real problem solving or take a major decision. All he seemed to be was a spare pair of hands for dish washing, pulling pints or serving customers food. A glorified KP-cum-waiter, sure given respect and a nod to his position as the ultimate boss, but increasingly more of a symbol needing his final signature for this or that document and nothing more.

Calum was thriving as manager at the Camlachie Arms and in just a few more years Charlie could see him in charge of the entire business, but not yet. Caleb was doing well in London and looked to have a good career in engineering in front of him. He needn't worry about the boys.

He was now seriously thinking of selling the business with the caveat, if he could get away with it, that whoever took over kept Calum on. Nobody in the trade had approached him about acquiring his operations, but he was confident if he made it clear he was considering selling, there would be suiters.

And, of course, his goal of getting back together with Sarah had crashed and their divorce was imminent. All that had seemed certain seven months ago had vanished.

He was a vigorous man in his early sixties, fit, healthy and worked out at least twice a week. But what was he to do? He ruminated on this over breakfast three days after the night out with Bob.

That night they'd chatted with the two women, Mandy and Amy, till Logos shut the back of two. Both women were single, though Mandy was recently divorced. At first Bob had led the conversation followed closely by Mandy. Charlie felt awkward at first; he hadn't chatted a woman up in years. But he soon regained his confidence and focused on Amy who reciprocated his attentions.

At Bob's suggestion they retired the short distance to his small but neat apartment nearby. There was one bedroom which Bob and Mandy quickly retired to, leaving Charlie and Amy to snog and indulge in some heavy petting on the sofa, until he felt ridiculous doing this at his age and suggested they grab a cab to his flat. Amy agreed and, after both texted messages to their respective pals, Charlie walked with her to the nearest cab rank and caught a taxi to his west end flat.

When they arrived there, he poured them both a chilled glass of Cloudy Bay Sauvignon Blanc. As she sat on the chaise longue and delicately sipped on her wine, he took a good look at her. She was an attractive brunette in her mid-thirties with a great figure. Her hair was short and bobbed which made her appear cuter.

Charlie sat beside her and she immediately took hold of him and resumed their snogging, caressing each other. After a short while, Charlie gently raised her and took her through to the bedroom, slowly unzipping and taking off her short navy dress, revealing her black bra, stockings and skimpy G string. He was incredibly aroused by her, accentuated by the black Louboutin heels she was wearing with the red soles and stilettos.

It had been ages since he had sex with Sarah, including all the years inside and he felt an incredible wave of sexual energy course through him as he took hold of Amy from behind, unhooked her bra and clasped her ample breasts in her hands, her nipples hard and erect, then eased her G string down her long, sexy legs.

As she bent before him, he could see her reflection fully in the wall mirror in front of him, revealing her lithe, toned body in all its glory including her hairless Brazilian wax which only stimulated him more as he furiously entered her from behind. He checked her face which was wreathed in pure lust and pumped her even harder; years of sexual drought now being redeemed. He came out of her, fully erect and took a packet of condoms he'd brought from the bathroom earlier.

He opened the box, took a packet out, tore it open and extended the sheath. Amy turned round, took hold of his cock and gave him the most exquisite fellatio. Waves of pleasure swept through him until he felt he was about to burst. Amy sensed this, took the sheath from him and gently put the condom on him. They went on to the bed where Charlie entered her, their rhythm lasting for ages until they climaxed in an orgasm of ecstasy.

They'd had sex two more times that night. Charlie made her breakfast the next morning, exchanged numbers with her and saw her off in a taxi.

He'd thought of phoning her but hadn't. He'd received a brief text from her later that day saying what a 'great night,' she'd had and enquiring how he was to which he'd tersely replied: 'Aye, fantastic. Catch up soon,' and heard nothing from her since.

It had been a fantastic night, the sex had been brilliant, but he didn't know if he was ready to take it any further and he still had deep, strong feelings for Sarah.

What did occupy his mind that Thursday morning over boiled eggs and toast was the plight of that young couple, the Marchetti's, trying to run their restaurant and getting picked on by a bunch of neds in the shape of the McGarvey's. That was wrong. The likes of the McGarvey's were brutal parasites who fed on hard working people like the Marchetti's who really made a city like Glasgow. And yet no-one seemed to be able to lift a finger to help them.

Charlie just couldn't get the couple's ordeal out of his head. About eleven he tidied up the flat and drove over to Dennistoun, to the row of terraces just off Duke Street, the busy main shopping street of the area, where the restaurant was sited. It was at the end of a row of businesses that included a dentist and an accountant. It was just before 12 on a Wednesday. Their opening hours displayed on the window revealed they closed Mondays and Tuesdays and reopened Wednesday lunchtime.

He walked into the deathly quiet of the restaurant bereft of customers yet. It was surprisingly large and minimalist inside with bare walls painted white and teal dotted with prints of what Charlie recognised to be the Amalfi coast, Vesuvius and the Bay of Naples. There was a bar to the left and a raised floor with tables and booths. It actually felt quite homely despite the bare walls. From a recess beside the bar, behind which Charlie guessed was where the kitchen was, a young girl appeared in the characteristic waitress's outfit of white blouse and black skirt.

'Hello, do you have a reservation?' she enquired with a wide smile and a warm voice.

'No, I don't,' Charlie replied. 'I was wondering if I could speak to the proprietor.'

She appeared a bit confused: 'Jenni or Leon?'

'Well, who's available?'

'Both. I'll just check.' She went back into the kitchen followed a minute later by a small woman, with fair hair and an equally wide smile who asked:

'Can I help you?'

He beamed a return smile. 'Aye, I was in on Saturday night, excellent food by the way. I...'

'...I thought I recognised you, thank you' she interrupted.

'And I thought I'd just pop in and see how you're doing. Sorry, I should explain, my name's Charlie Carty. I own a few pubs and restaurants in the city.'

'Yes, I've heard of you,' her eyes opened wider. 'You own the Camlachie Arms just up the road from here.'

'That's right. My son's running that now.' He couldn't help the proud parent coming out in him. 'Anyway, without being patronising or trying to tell you how to run your business, cos on the evidence of Saturday night you're doing a grand job, but I just thought I'd pop in, see if there's anything you need, anything that an old hand like me can assist you with.'

She shrugged her shoulders, still smiling. 'Thanks very much. That's very kind of you. But', she nodded towards the kitchen, 'Leon and I are doing ok. We're nearly fully booked for the rest of the week and a full house on Friday and Saturday.'

'That's brilliant to hear. But if there's anything you can think of that I might be able to help with, you know suppliers, the council, anybody, here,' he proffered her his business card, 'give me a call. I've loads of experience dealing with these sorts of people.'

He noticed as he was saying this, her wide-open stare shifted as she blinked a few times and for a fleeting second Charlie caught a glimpse of the care and worry that was probably besieging her and her husband. She clicked back into happy, unconcerned mode.

'Fine, what can I say? Absolutely. If there's anything, I'll contact you, thanks again,' she took the card from him. 'Would you like a coffee, tea?'

'No thanks, I really must be going,' he went towards the door. Just as he opened it, a group of customers were coming in. She said to him, 'really appreciate your support.'

As the customers made their way into the restaurant, he turned to her at the entrance.

'There's always people that can help you,' he said before walking back to his car.

It was three weeks before Jenni Marchetti phoned him. She said she'd like advice about 'some suppliers.' Charlie agreed to meet her at a quiet coffee shop in Finneston.

It was a Wednesday morning when he walked in. There was only a handful of customers and a lone barista behind the counter. She didn't see him at first, but he noticed how worried she looked staring at her phone on the table. Instantly, she became aware of him approaching she switched into the big smile.

They spent about thirty minutes talking about the trade and the usual gripes about rates and suppliers which allowed Charlie to broach the subject.

'And that's why you've asked me here? To talk about a supplier?'

'Aye.' She became cagier. 'Yes, there's one or two of them that are really at it with us.'

'Overcharging you?'

'Yes. And I was just wanting to know, from your experience, how you would go about dealing with that.'

He looked at her straight. 'These suppliers you're talking about. They wouldn't go by the name of McGarvey, would they?'

Her face turned white, the colour draining. She went rigid, tense.

'It's ok,' he spoke to her in his most commanding but assuring voice. 'You're amongst friends. I'm here to help.'

She stayed still for a minute, then colour came back into her cheeks, before her shoulders started shaking and great heaves of convulsive sobbing overcame her as she broke and released a flood of tears. He took hold of her, noticing the few other customers looking over at them.

'My friend has just had some dreadful news,' he announced to the shop. The other customers looked away. To the barista behind the counter, he asked: 'could I get some water please?'

'Sure,' the barista replied. He turned to Jenni,

'It's ok, nobody's looking now.'

She broke away from him. 'I'm really sorry.'

'Don't be stupid,' he chided her. She wiped her tears.

'How did you know about them?'

'The McGarvey's?'

'Yes.'

'It doesn't matter. What does is that I'm here to help.'

She continued wiping away tears and sipping the water the barista had brought.

'So, tell me what's been going on?' he asked after she'd recovered.

'About four months ago, these two guys came into the restaurant during the afternoon when we were closed and it was only Leon and me. I hate to be judgemental, but they were really rough looking, quite intimidating. They said there was a lot of vandalism in the area, windows getting broken – though I'd never seen any of that – burglaries and so on and they could help us avoid all that.

'Honestly, in my naivety I thought they were trying to sell us insurance, but it was Leon who twigged and asked them to explain how they could "protect" us. And they said they would stop local kids and gangs from damaging our place. I remember one of them, a short but heavy-set man with cropped hair and scary eyes saying in what was becoming an increasingly menacing voice, that we wouldn't want customers seeing our windows and walls covered in graffiti or us having to pay for all the broken glass. He had a horrible, horrible smile.'

She went white again at the memory of it. Charlie presumed the short muscular guy might well be Tam McGarvey himself. She resumed:

'Leon got angry as I cottoned on as well and told them to get out. But the small guy piped up -the other one stayed silent – that, and I'll always remember his exact words, "wee Giovanna was a bonny kid" and she was doing well at school, and it would be horrible if anything nasty was to happen to her, and...' She welled up and burst into tears again.

'I'm sorry,' she gulped some more water.

'Don't be daft. Who's Giovanna?'

'She's our seven-year-old daughter. She's named after Leon's mother. His family are from Naples.'

Charlie shook his head in disgust and urged her to go on.

'Leon started to lose it and went for the smaller guy, but the quiet one just produced this dreadful, sharp knife and pointed it at me. I just froze and so did Leon. Then the guy doing all the talking said they weren't, in his words, "pissing about" and they wanted five per cent of the weekly takings. There was this terrible silence for a few minutes as they just gave us this terrible stare. Then the quiet guy put the knife away and the other man said a chap called "Martin" would be at the restaurant every Friday at about eleven to pick up the payment and we'd all...' she sighed, '...we'd all do well, and little Giovanna would grow up a happy and safe child...' she stopped and her tears flowed again.

After a couple of minutes to let her recover, Charlie asked:

'How long did five per cent last?'

She gave a knowing glance. 'Four weeks and then it was ten per cent.'

'What is it now?'

'Fifty. It's killing us. We're working all the hours God sends, working our fingers to the bone just to pay them off. We've ploughed everything into this. We're getting great reviews, they're queuing out the door at weekend and we're skint and living in fear and misery and we've nowhere to go, nobody to turn to. If we call the police, I would be absolutely petrified about what could happen to...' She put her hands in the air in despair.

'It just gets worse. That guy - we know he's called McGarvey, he's told us that, he's so arrogant, he's fearless – and his mates with their women friends, have been coming in unannounced, sometimes up to ten of them, demanding a table and they're loud, shouting and swearing, frightening other customers, drinking our best wine. They even walk into the kitchen and, aw, it's just dreadful. And, of course, they don't pay. The last time they were in, that Tam McGarvey asked me direct: "how's wee Giovanna?" And I just curdled.'

'So,' she sniffed and looked directly at Charlie, 'Leon and I have decided, we're packing it in.'

'When.'

'End of the month. I hate to do this, but we're not telling staff to the last minute, we'll pay them what we own them and then we're just shutting shop.'

'Giovanna?'

'For some reason, even though I hardly know you, I trust you Mr Carty. Leon has got a job as sous chef at a place in Edinburgh. We're moving and taking Giovanna of course. Only a few people know that Mr Carty.'

'I'd rather die than break your confidence Jenni,' he said with utter conviction.

She nodded, 'I know.'

'I'm really sorry to hear this.'

'Is there anything you think you could do?'

'Does Leon know you're meeting me?'

'No.'

'Good, keep it that way. It's three weeks to the end of the month. If nothing happens, do what you and Leon intended. I can't promise you anything, but I'll see what I can do to relieve your burden. But and this is very important, don't tell anyone, including Leon, about me or what you've told me. And never contact me, ever.' He picked up his cup and sipped the remains of his now cold coffee.

'I'm going to leave you and whatever happens in the next few weeks, I'll probably never see you again unless it's in the course of normal business. You've had an absolutely shite time and you deserve a break.'

He rose, shook her hand firmly and left the coffee shop. Jenni Marchetti watched him leave wondering in hope and fear what was going to happen next.

'You're having a laugh, Charlie Carty, you've gotta be!' Ali McMahon stared incredulously at him, drawing on a fag outside the whisky bar in Glasgow city centre. They'd met at their usual table in the rear area of the pub, but the minute Charlie mentioned the McGarvey's, McMahon insisted they went outside. There was no response from Charlie. McMahon shook his head.

'Christ, you're serious, aren't you?'

Charlie was resolute. 'They're destroying that couple's business, they've even threatened their wee lassie. Nothing but parasites. Sheer fucking animals.'

'Aye, but they're organised animals, Charlie. These are not two-bit psycho losers. Nobody except for their mothers could give a toss about what happens to Kieron McPhail or Joe Jamieson. The McGarvey's are wired into the Chisholm's and the whole fucking criminal network in this city. Drugs, prostitution, rackets, money lending, reset, you name it, they're into it. Your one guy Charlie. There's was no team behind McPhail or Jamieson. You've got a whole bunch of psychos behind this crowd.'

Charlie watched as McMahon stubbed out his cigarette on the pavement, buses and cars roaring by.

'You put your finger on it, Ali,' he said to him. 'Organised. The McGarvey's are organised. And how are they organised? Through leadership. In other words, management. You run a business; I run a business. Take away its leadership and what happens? Businesses collapse, dissolve into chaos.

'The McGarvey's are a business. Take out the senior team and,' he clicked his fingers, 'they're gone.'

'Not quite, Charlie,' McMahon shook his head. 'Others take over.'

'Might do, Ali, but they'll be going for the big stuff, especially the drugs. But the couple get a break, and a good, legit business run by decent people survives.'

'But you're forgetting also, Charlie, somebody will come after you.'

Charlie shrugged. 'I'll cover my tracks like I did before.'

'Look, I'm gonny be honest with you. It's one thing making enquiries and checking up on the McPhail's and Jamieson's.

You're dealing with criminal justice, cops, social workers, debtors, creditors, whatever. It's routine. You start asking questions about the McGarvey's and you alert them. They're fucking cunning and street savvy. That's how they survive. It's a different level.'

'Ali,' he looked at McMahon levelly, 'I'm just asking for the basics. Movements, locations. Your team are professionals. They're also savvy and discreet. I'll pay you and your people very well. I know this is not routine and I'll recompense you accordingly. Just get me what I need to know, and I'll deal with the rest. There'll be no comeback on you. You know that. Now I haven't much time, just a couple of weeks. Are you gonny help me?'

Ali lit another cigarette, blew out some smoke and declared resignedly, 'for the love of God, what have I got myself into?'

ELEVEN

Britain's Got Talent had just begun when the doorbell rang.

'Who the fuck's that?' Tam McGarvey declared loudly, 'you expecting anybody?' he asked of his girlfriend. Caitlin, slumped with her feet curled up under her beside him on the sofa, flitting between watching the TV and filing her nails, replied:

'Naw,' she declared. 'It'll be wan of yer daft pals.'

He checked the app on his mobile displaying the doorbell camera footage on the front door. It looked like a biker in a leather jacket and a helmet with a package in front of him.

Walking warily into the hallway, McGarvey retrieved a large baseball bat from beside a table. In his back pocket he had a flick knife. Behind the door he shouted:

'Who is it?'

'Pizza delivery,' was the terse reply.

Feeling slightly relieved, he unlocked an array of locks and bolts and opened the door slightly with the door chain still attached. He confirmed the caller was a biker dressed entirely in black with a helmet and tinted visor which meant he couldn't see the caller's face. In his hands were two large pizza boxes with a white paper package on top.

"We did'nae order a pizza mate.'

'Whit?'

'I said, we did'nae order a pizza,' McGarvey almost growled at the delivery guy.

The fellow placed the pizza boxes and the package on

the ground in front of the door; their aroma filling the doorway and fetched a black computer tablet from inside his dark leather jacket. He touched the screen a few times, then said:

'Crombie, 127 Macintosh Avenue?'

'Naw, this is McGarvey, 127 Macintosh Place.'

'Aw Fuck!' The biker almost shouted. He placed the tablet back in his jacket and brought out his mobile.

'Shite!' he declared on looking at it.' A grim smile broke out on McGarvey; he took great pleasure in other people's discomfort. The biker continued:

'Mate, sincere apologies. I've fucked this up. It's the wrang address. But they've complained about the time it's taken, so the boss has sent another guy there. He's wanting a word with me now and I'm fucking sick of it. The tight cunt has only got two of us on tonight and the phones are going mental. Well, I've had enough.'

He picked up the two pizza boxes and the package.

'Here, pal, have two free pizzas and some drinks on me. I'm packing it in.'

McGarvey unbolted the chain delighted at the prospect of a free meal and took the delivery from the biker.

'Stick it to yer boss, eh?' a wide grin on his face.

'Fuck him.' The guy started walking away.

'Too right.'

McGarvey bolted the door and walked back to the living room.

'What's this?' Catlin asked, seeing the boxes and the package.

'Dick fucked up his order, went to the wrong address. He's

on a shaky peg wi his gaffer and he's just walked off the job and gave us a free pizza.'

He sat down and opened the pizzas. One was mushroom and ham, the other pepperoni. The package contained two 750 ml bottles of Coke and Irn Bru.

'Pepperoni and Irn Bru will dae me. You like mushroom, don't you?'

'We've just eaten an hour ago!' Caitlin protested.

'Get real, woman. It's no every night you get a free feed. Here,' he passed her the mushroom and ham pizza.

'I need to watch my figure,' she said.

'Get wired in. You hardly eat as it is. You only pecked at your supper.' He opened the pizza, took a slice and ate a bite, before opening the bottle of Irn Bru and taking a swallow.

'Brand new,' he said with satisfaction as he raised the volume on the large wall mounted TV and settled down to watch the rest of the programme.

Charlie was tempted to take off the leather jacket as it was quite warm in the car on this late August evening, but decided it was too risky. He had taken off the visor which brought him some relief. Thankfully it would be getting dark soon, making him less visible, particularly in that small new build housing estate where McGarvey lived with his girlfriend in the heart of Shettleston in the east end of Glasgow.

He was parked in a second-hand blue Toyota, which as usual, he'd bought from a used car dealer in Airdrie; he knew never to use the same people twice. Tomorrow, if all went well, he would drive to a car breaker's yard, this time in Dumbarton to dispose of the car. Tonight, he would package the biker's gear, break the visor and "instrument" he was going to use into pieces and burn them in the incinerator. He would be forensically nude.

The Toyota was in a deserted lane behind a row of Romany caravans next to a railway embankment. About fifty yards ahead, he could see the lights and raised platforms of Carntyne station. Checking his watch, he estimated he had another twenty minutes before he would drive back to the estate and McGarvey's abode.

He felt remarkably calm and stoical, set fair on what he was doing and why he was doing it. His only concern was if he was caught and trash like the McGarvey's went after his family. So, if that happened, he'd made arrangements for his savings and a large endowment to be split equally between the boys. Caleb should be safe in London, and he'd written a sealed letter to Calum, to be opened only if he should be arrested, detained, or worse, dead, that his oldest son should leave Glasgow and there was money for him to make a new life elsewhere.

Sarah should also be safe, but to be sure, he'd arranged for a significant sum to be transferred to her account, and she could relocate too if she needed to.

No, he was resolute and assured. He was on the right path. In a way, although he didn't like to indulge in fancy philosophising, this was his destiny as well as serving up good flavoursome scran to his fellow Glaswegians. But that was the past. Now he wanted to wreak havoc on scum like Tam McGarvey and his ilk.

He checked his watch. A train pulled into the station. It was getting darker. Pulling the visor back on, he drove away. It took three minutes to get to the estate, a collection of red stone, two up detached and semi-detached houses just behind the railway line. He parked the car just around the corner and out of sight of McGarvey's house which was detached. From below the seat he retrieved a large object, the "instrument", wrapped in plastic sheeting and put on a pair of blue nitrile gloves.

Leaving the car with the object he walked the short distance in the dusk to McGarvey's. It was a short avenue with the house furthest to the left. The other residences had their curtains and blinds drawn now with lights on and TV screens flickering behind them. In the distance he heard a dog barking and the chimes of an ice cream van. There was no one else around in the quite avenue.

Pausing at the door, the "instrument" in its packaging between his legs, he brought out a small, slitted card, about the size of a bank card with a protruding sharp point. Working slowly and keeping an eye out on the street and surrounding houses, he eased and slid the topmost and firmest bolt until he heard it slide and click. He stood stock still in case an alarm went off. It was not unknown for some people, particularly paranoid ones, to set their alarm the minute they locked up, even when they were in the house.

But there was no alarm. Using the card, Charlie proceeded to prise loose the five remaining locks. He turned the handle. The door opened a few inches and was then blocked by the door chain. Quickly now, as he didn't want to spend too long standing in that doorway, he brought out a pair of stainless-steel bolt cutters from inside his biker's jacket, which he'd practiced with in his flat and swiftly cut the chain; the door gave way.

Once again, His Majesty's University of Barlinnie Prison came in handy as he'd remembered vividly a "lecture" delivered by a lag, a veteran burglar, during rec time one night in the Hall, on the best way to use a slicked, greased card to open even the sturdiest locks and bolts. He silently thanked the old timer as he eased the door shut behind him. Another gem of imparted criminal wisdom Charlie remembered well from the lecture was the lag's firm instruction to:

'Check for a fucking doorbell camera and disable it right away. There's nae point getting through all they locks and your fucking coupon's all over that bloody camera.'

He closed the door and clocked the device below the small window. He wrenched it off the door and placed it in his pocket. Looking around he saw the hall was lit by a small table lamp; the only sound that of a TV. At the end of the hall was a door on the left, a set of stairs at a right angle, a kitchen ahead and a bathroom to the right. Charlie pushed the door to the left, tensing and clutching hold of the "instrument". The door opened revealing a living room with a large wall mounted flat screen TV on which a couple were belting out their rendition of Beyonce's Crazy in Love on Britain's Got Talent.

Opposite, McGarvey and his girlfriend, Caitlin, lay slumped on the settee. Caitlin, curled up like a ball, pizza carton lying on the floor, the mushroom and ham pizza largely uneaten while McGarvey's head rested on the edge of the sofa. On the coffee table in front of them lay the half empty bottles of Coke and Irn Bru. Both were gently snoring as Charlie placed the "instrument" on the floor, went over to the sofa and gently lifted Caitlin. She was light and Charlie encountered no problem carrying her out of the living room, up the stairs and into a bedroom where he lay her on the bed. Walking back down the stairs he reflected that it was at times like these he was glad he worked out regularly.

Back in the living room, the couple on the talent show had finished their act and the jury were delivering their verdicts. Charlie unsheathed the package and brought out the large baseball bat. He bent over McGarvey. Even in repose, the thug looked like a caged animal. He brought himself up to his full height and took firm hold of the handle thinking of a tearful, broken hearted and haunted Jenni Marchetti and the threats to their wee girl, Giovanna, and brought the bat down on McGarvey's skull.

His head jerked and recoiled back and forth, his eyes sprung wide open, but he didn't have time to come round as Charlie whacked his forehead with all his might, then went for his nose, mouth and jaw, blood sprouting all over the sofa, the carpet, walls and Charlie as bits of bone flew everywhere.

Once his face was a pulp, Charlie stripped him, flinging his sweatshirt, jeans, underpants and socks on the floor, before battering his body and breaking his kneecaps. Involuntary groans and gurgles emanated from McGarvey along with the sickening, crunching sounds of bones being snapped and broken.

Finally, when McGarvey was completely comatose and lying amidst a sea of his own blood, Charlie ceased and caught a breath. Behind him a comedian was trying his luck combined with some magical tricks earning some laughter and applause from the audience.

There were two mobiles on a coffee table beside the settee. One was enclosed in a pink, fur lined case which Charlie presumed was Caitlin's. The other was a black android. Charlie took off the blue synthetic gloves and replaced them with a new pair. Picking up the android he saw the fingerprint security icon and pressed the off button on the side. After a few seconds, he switched the device back on but depressed the bottom button half-a-dozen times. The screen went blank then a command asked if he wanted to disable touch recognition. He pressed "Y", and the phone came to life.

He saw the contact icon, pressed it and scrolled through the list of names until he caught the name "Mark" and texted:

"Something's come up, need to see you right away," followed by a startled looking emoji.

Charlie sent the message and placed the phone back on the table. He was grateful McGarvey used an android as the trick to get round the fingerprint security wouldn't have worked on an iPhone where the Start button was the touch recognition mechanism. He wasn't assured of that in advance, but it did allow him the chance to add an extra gothic twist to the proceedings.

McGarvey's phone pinged back. It was Mark. 'What's up Bro?!!?'

Charlie replied. 'Get your arse up here. NOW!!!'

From Ali McMahon's research, Charlie knew the relationship between the brothers was the classic gangster family situation of the older, domineering, bullying brother and the weak, deferential subordinate younger brother, confirmed within seconds when the text reply read, 'On way!'

Charlie wandered about the living room and the hall waiting for the brother, keeping the telly on which he knew would help to disarm Mark. McGarvey was completely comatose on the blood-soaked sofa, his face squashed and his legs and upper body rapidly becoming a lurid, livid purple. He wondered if perhaps he'd gone too far and McGarvey might not survive his ferocious attack. But he realised he didn't care: One less nasty wee gangster for the people of Glasgow to stomach.

He heard a car coming into the driveway and scooted halfway up the stairs beside the hall and waited. There was a rapping at the door, then he heard it being pushed open followed by a male voice bellowing,

'Tam? Caitlin? Tam?'

He could hear footfall along the hall and noiselessly went down a few stairs until he could see the back of a tall, young man enter the living room. Charlie bounded down the steps and thwacked the brother on the back of the head before he had time to react to the sight of his brother's battered, bloodied body. He collapsed and crumpled, putting an arm up to defend himself which Charlie kicked aside while he went to work on him as an ad break muffled the sound.

He wasn't as vicious with the younger sibling and let up

on the beating after he'd stripped him too, laying him on the carpet in front of the TV, but his body and face was still a mass of bruises.

Charlie sat at the end of the settee for a couple of minutes, recovering from his exertions, Tam McGarvey's bare feet beside him. The panel vote on the contestants was underway to the vocal delight or disapproval of the studio audience. The Beyonce tribute duo received poor votes which Charley thought was unfair as they'd done a good cover which he'd appreciated as he had systematically beaten Tam McGarvey.

Finally, he heaved himself up from the edge of the settee and produced a can of spray paint he also retrieved from his jacket. Walking to the far, largely bare wall of the living room, which had been painted light orange and white, he sprayed:

We are nasty pieces of shit who parasite off hardworking people. We are now going to stop before we, and all who work with us, die a long, excruciating and very painful death. Please forgive us our sins.

Satisfied with the slogan, Charlie went back to the coffee table and picked up McGarvey's mobile, clicked on contacts and highlighted nine names he recognised as McGarvey's main lieutenants from a list Ali McMahon had sent him. He sent them all a collective text:

'*Urgent!! Meet my Place. NOW!!*'

After wrapping the bat back in the plastic sheeting, he walked out of the house, closing the door, the phone still in his hand and walked back to his car while a plethora of messages came back on McGarvey's phone:

'On way.'

'What's up?'

'Be there in five.'

At the car, Charlie switched off the phone and took out the SIM card which he placed in an outside pocket of his biker's jacket. Unobserved, he swiftly opened the boot, placed the bat inside and put on a set of housepainter's navy-blue overalls over his jacket and leather trousers. and brought out a large white cotton sheet which he placed over the front seat before getting in and driving off.

He drove for about a mile before stopping in a deserted short road surrounded by tenements where he finally took off the visor, brought out the SIM card and dropped it down a street drain. On maximum alert he drove back to his flat in the west end by a circuitous route avoiding main roads; the overalls pockmarked by dried paint stains hopefully signalling to the world he was returning from a job and housepainters could be in demand, even at weekends.

It was after nine when he got home and spent the next two hours discarding his clothes, including the overalls into plastic bags, pulverising the visor, phone, bat and doorbell camera device into fragments on his trestle table and sealing them, before taking a long shower.

In his nightgown and pyjamas, he sat listening to some soothing country rock music as he savoured a Laphroaig. He felt euphoric that he'd assuredly destroyed an up-and-coming underground outfit led by a psychopath that would have wreaked even more havoc on the city, especially if they gained top dog status by taking over from the Chisholm's, whose grip on Glasgow's drug scene seemed to be diminishing by the day. And there was the Marchetti's, who now could go about running their lovely restaurant without living in fear of McGarvey.

He poured a second generous dram, a warm dayglo feeling enveloping him exorcising all the stresses and heightened overdrive of the past few hours. Charlie was particularly pleased at the neat trick he'd employed of using a powerful sleeping tablet called Zopiclone to sedate McGarvey and his girlfriend. They could be prescribed by GPs, but Charley had wanted to avoid any connection to himself and had purchased twelve in total from three separate dealers over the past two weeks. He'd bored a tiny pinprick hole in the plastic lids of each bottle, crushed the tablets and used a syringe to inject them into the Coke and Irn Bru he'd "delivered" to the couple.

He'd watched the effects of Zopiclone at night in Barlinnie when the cacophony and howling of prisoners around him dwindled as the effect of the strong drug they'd been given hit them and was inspired to use it to render McGarvey completely helpless and exposed.

Yes, he thought, that was a neat trick, a wee touch of class. He put the music up louder; it was the Eagle's Lying Eyes. How appropriate, he thought. Should he have a third wee goldie? Why not, he deserved it.

Tam McGarvey succumbed to his injuries in hospital four days after the devastating assault on him. Lurid reports of the manner of his demise, including cryptic references to some graffiti that had been sprayed on the wall at the murder locale appeared in newspaper and online reports. The reports did mention that police were conducting "rigorous" enquiries and following up leads. But there were no arrests and interest faded.

Detective Sergeant Stuart 'Stu' Hutchinson put the phone down, opened his arms wide and yawned then rubbed his eyes. That had been the twelfth call he'd made the last few hours to fellow detectives and two of his own snouts. And there'd been nothing; sweet FA. The tecs had trawled widely and there was lots of experience there. Guys and women who knew the Glasgow gangland scene extensively and his two informants, one who blagged on the Chisholm's and the other who'd won the confidence of Tam McGarvey, and they'd come back empty.

Nobody, anywhere, knew who it was who had made the calamitous move against the McGarvey's. Not a tweet anywhere in a scene, that for all its emphasis on keeping silent with terrifying consequences otherwise, in fact leaked and gossiped constantly. Nobody gossiped more than a gangster, especially after a few drinks and a cash incentive. The problem was corroborating that chatter and building up a strong case that could withstand vigorous cross-examination in court. Despite that, for all its unreliability, gossip did provide a base to start an investigation.

But here, all was blank. Zilch. Of course, the McGarvey's, like all hoodlums, had enemies, not least within their ranks. But out there Stu Hutchinson and his colleagues' wide radar net uncovered nothing. Plenty of speculation but that's all it was.

He was perplexed. He remembered the scene of the crime. It was gruesome. Blood, bone and gore everywhere. 'What a fucking kicking he's had,' he recalled Stratton, one of the younger detective constables remarking at Tam McGarvey's hospital bedside, wrapped in loads of tubes and drips and machines pinging constantly; it had been no surprise when he'd flatlined.

Mark McGarvey had come round but knew nothing except that he'd been attacked from behind; he'd caught a glimpse of a vision all in black before he'd went down. He did fleetingly say that he did see his brother and his girlfriend on the couch in the living room as if they were sleeping and the TV was on. And that was all he could tell them.

Caitlin, the girlfriend, terrified and distraught when she'd regained consciousness, could only recount, apart from the "thousands of calls" Tam had made "as usual", that they'd not left the house all that Saturday. The only thing of note she could remember of that night was the "weird" incident when a pizza delivery man had mistakenly brought pizzas to the house and gave Tam a "freebie".

This was confirmed of course with the pizza cartons in the living room. Caitlin said she'd "pecked" at the pizza, drank the Coke and then felt zonked and fell asleep.

A bevvy of lieutenants had descended on the house at the summons of "McGarvey" and came upon the sight. One of them phoned emergency and then they all fled. And the lieutenant who'd called 999 was Stu Hutchinson's snout. The DS had grilled him, but he could offer nothing. All the lieutenant's had good alibis for where they'd been before arriving at the scene. And all were loyal to McGarvey according to the snout. None had the calibre, means or insurance to move against him.

Stu turned to the snout in the Chisholm's ranks. He reported that old man Sammy kept a careful eye out on Tam McGarvey but had no reason to think he was going to move against him any time soon; they ruled with a tight fist in the east end and that's what the erstwhile Godfather wanted. Besides, the optimum time for Tam McGarvey to go against the Chisholm's was when the patriarch died and the struggle for succession was on. Otherwise, there was not a shred of evidence anywhere that the Chisholm's or anyone else in the Glasgow underworld had made any organised move on the McGarvey's.

And it had been organised, well thought out, Stu considered. This had been no ordinary whacking which almost always was a shooting attempt; that was how mobsters normally attacked each other. Highly visible and public, intended to leave a message.

This had been very different. The key was the pizza delivery evidenced by the discarded cartons in the room and Caitlin's testimony. Traces of Zopiclone were found in both their bloodstreams and been laced in the soft drinks which had been used to incapacitate them prior to the attack on McGarvey.

Did this mean an outside hitman had been brought in? Stu had made contacts with colleagues across the UK, but particularly in Liverpool, Belfast and London where the most organised crime connections with Glasgow had been forged for decades, particularly around drugs, initially focused on heroin and now cocaine and new powerful synthetic opioids, the nitazenes, which were wreaking havoc on the city's drug users.

But again, he drew a blank. And the question was why? Why, when the drug scene was currently so well-organised and under the stable command of one family, the Chisholm's, where everybody could take a cut and profit, risk everything and plunge the place into premature anarchy by taking out a leading figure like McGarvey?

Something was not right about this. Stu Hutchinson had been a policeman for over twenty-five years and worked himself up the ranks from a beat cop in Lanarkshire. He'd been dealing with gangsters for years and this was not how they operated.

There was something almost personal about this. Hitmen were employed to be dispassionate, clinical. Almost always a shot to the head. Sedating your target and then systematically breaking their bones as this guy had done to Tam McGuire wasn't the style of a professional hitman. To use the cliché, gangland hits were "business" nothing "personal."

They'd traced the pizzas, a cinch as their name was stamped on the cartons, to a takeaway called Marco's a couple of miles away in Duke Street. The owner nor his staff could identify anyone, but they'd obtained the CCTV from the shop which showed a man in black biker's gear and a visor ordering the pizzas and drinks around six-thirty on the Saturday. All they had was a shot of his back, head and sides. He'd hung around for his order and disappeared into the night.

Then there was the writing sprayed on the living room walls; that was definitely not the MO of a hit. Gangsters didn't call each other "parasites"; they thought of themselves as businessmen and whacking a rival was akin to taking over a competitor.

No, this was different, very different. Stu had to consider that some other personal motivation was at work here. That was a relief on one level as it meant his patch wasn't about to dissolve into mayhem. But on another level, it made it much harder to get a result.

He decided he and his team of three detective constables assigned to him were going to sift through all the files on known criminals in Glasgow who been assaulted over the past year and see if they could discern any pattern where their attacker had not been identified.

He picked up the phone for the squad room to tell them the good news.

TWELVE

Nothing really goes the way you planned it. This struck Charlie with a sharp pang of dismay when he drove past Marchetti's and saw a For Sale notice affixed to the entrance. He was on his way back from seeing Calum at the Camlachie Arms.

Within the past five weeks, there'd been a major development. Eric Fenwick, his old boss at the Caledon Larder, now entirely in charge of the French company Landis's many hospitality interests in the UK, had approached him and offered to buy out his entire company. The sum offered was generous and would allow Charlie to live comfortably for the rest of his life.

He was unsure what to do. Hospitality was still his lifeblood and selling the business might leave him rudderless and without a purpose in life. On the other hand, he knew he was increasingly playing a marginal role in it. Besides, life was getting rougher in the trade, competition was intense, and nobody was guaranteed to survive. Yesterday, he'd had lunch with Eric Fenwick at his old venue, Deep South, which Landis had bought off him and was now renamed the Gooseberry, which Charlie thought was a dreadful name but didn't say so to Eric.

Charlie had requested that meeting because he wanted an assurance that Landis would keep Calum on as manager of the Camlachie Arms. Eric had given him that assurance and today Charlie had dropped in unannounced on Calum and told him the "good news".

His son's reaction confounded Charlie. His dad had no business trying to pull strings for him, he told his father; he could make his own way in the trade. He'd rather Landis had advertised the job, and he would make a bid for it on his own terms.

'Stop trying to run my life for me!' Calum had insisted.

His dad was furious, and he'd stormed out of the pub and was still stewing when he'd noticed Marchetti's up for sale. 'The ungrateful sod!' he thought. He was just trying to help his boy out and that's the thanks he gets.

The For Sale sign was a welcome diversion. He was convinced after he'd destroyed the McGarvey's that the business would be safe. But here it was shuttered and for sale. What gives? He made a beeline for the Queen Mary where he found Bob Carlton. It was just after lunchtime on a Monday and Bob was able to relax over a coffee in a windowless office on the lower floor of the restaurant.

Charlie told his old trade buddy about the Landis offer and launched into a tirade about how ungrateful his son was. He heard Charlie out and then countered sharply that Charlie should be proud of his son as the boy was being adamant that he wanted to progress in the trade by his own merits and sheer hard graft as had a certain Charlie Carty, who'd made a name for himself entirely on his own.

Charlie was pulled up short. He just hadn't thought it through that ensuring a job for his son with the new owners would come across as patronising and controlling. He grimaced and closed his eyes tight.

'Fuck! I messed that up. He's as stubborn as me.'

'It's not lost, Charlie,' Bob reassured him. 'Go back to him. Apologise. Promise you'll never go behind his back like that again. I'm sure he'll come round.'

'I'm sure you're right.'

'So, you're gonny sell then?' Bob asked him. Charlie shrugged.

'I don't know yet. If Calum had said yes today, I'd have phoned Eric Fenwick right away and said "ok, make me a formal offer." But I'm not sure now.' Bob shook his head.

'It's getting tougher out there. I've been thinking about packing it in myself.' He rhymed off a few places that had or were about to cease trading which reminded Charlie:

'Talking of which, I see that Marchetti's in Duke Street is shut.'

It was Bob's turn to grimace.

'It's a fucking liberty. They must have had enough wi those gangsters and gave up.'

Charlie was genuinely bewildered but was very careful with what he said.

'I don't understand. That Tam McGarvey was attacked and killed, and I thought they'd folded. I don't get it. The couple were still being fingered for protection money?'

'Aye. The Chisholm's are back big time.'

'I thought the old boy was declining.'

'He is. But there's a new player in the family. Sammy Chisholm's grandson, Nat Chisholm...

'...Nat!'

'Short for Nathan.'

'Fuck, what happened to good old Billy or Peter?'

'Anyway,' Bob resumed, 'Nat Chisholm has really shown up his old man, Sammy Chisholm's youngest son Ian, by stepping up to the plate the last few months and seeing off an Asian outfit trying to muscle in on Chisholm outfits in the southside. The old boy was really impressed, especially with the ruthless efficiency the young guy dispatched the challengers. The upshot is he's put Nat Chisholm in charge of the McGarvey patch in the east end, including the rackets and shakedowns. He's brought the lieutenants back in line.

'The Marchetti's?'

'Aye. And if that poor couple thought Tam McGarvey was bad, they've had to think again. McGarvey was just a beginner at the psycho academy; Nat Chisholm is a total 100% fucking full on monster, but with the usual smart cunning. Word is, Sammy Chisholm sees him as the saviour for the family, able to take over when he finally goes. God help us all.'

'So, the couple just sold up.'

'Did a moonlight flit. Up and away. Some people say the guy's moved to a chef's job in Edinburgh.'

Charlie was crestfallen. All his endeavours to help the couple and save a good, independent restaurant serving great food to the community had been in vain.

'Get out, Charlie,' Bob continued. 'You don't need the hassle.'

'Aye you're right. The business has changed, hasn't it?' This was the cue for both to start talking about the past. Bob produced a bottle of vintage Bordeaux, and they spent the afternoon reminiscing until both were pleasantly smashed, and Bob ordered a taxi to take Charlie home.

The next day Charlie had a hangover. He resolved to make it up to Calum and try a different approach. Once he'd secured his son's agreement, and only then, would he contact Eric and accept Landis's offer.

Meanwhile, he was still upset and shaken about what had happened to the couple. He could still see Jenni Marchetti in the coffeeshop, her eyes filled with hope as he left her all those months ago, that someone could help her and lift the misery they were undergoing.

But he hadn't succeeded, despite the great risks he'd made. And he felt he'd let her down badly. All their hopes and opportunities thwarted. Her husband was back working in a kitchen under someone else and their confidence in investing and running their own place destroyed with nothing to show for it.

He'd scrupulously refrained from contacting her as he also had with Ali McMahon. He knew she wouldn't contact him, not least because he hadn't lived up to his word. Tam McGarvey might have gone. But Nat Chisholm had surfaced, and God knows, having heard what Bob had told him, what terrifying threats that bastard would have made to her.

He was frustrated and angry. He was reminded of Ali McMahon's words outside the whisky bar when the penny had dropped that Charlie was going to take out Tam McGarvey: "Others take over."

Yes, some bloody equaliser he was. He brooded the situation over black coffee. It seemed futile, impossible. The coffee reinvigorated him, and he remembered what else he'd said to McMahon.

'The McGarvey's are a business. Take out the senior team and they're gone.'

That was the key. His mistake was that the McGarvey's weren't the senior team; that, ultimately, was the Chisholm's. And the next logical step was to take them out, particularly the erstwhile top boy in waiting, Nat Chisholm. Yep, go one step higher.

It was madness, crazy but Charlie could feel a surge of adrenaline flow through him. He was on a mission. These parasites caused chaos and misery and inflicted terror; witness the haunted, despairing face of Jenni Marchetti. And while there was nothing he could do to make up to her, he could prevent others having to endure the same horrors.

Charlie Carty, head chef, equaliser, resolved to go after Nat Chisholm, and bring old Sammy Chisholm's tottering empire crashing. After all, he couldn't see anybody else doing it. The cops were too weak or powerless or even possibly corrupt or whatever. And the criminal justice system seemed to consist entirely of deluded liberals too soft on criminals. No, his attempt at a resolution of justice for his brother would now extend to Glasgow's leading criminal outfit. And if he died doing it – because he was determined never to go back to jail – then so be it.

He phoned and made up to Calum. Satisfied at the outturn of the call, he contacted Eric Fenwick and agreed to the sale of his business to Landis. Eric would organise the meetings with the lawyers. With the tidy sum from the sale Charlie could focus entirely on his mission. But he would need help.

Detective Constable Aruna Sharma had just been transferred to CID and assigned to Stu Hutchinson's team. She, Stratton and the other tec on the DS's team had combed through the voluminous files of assaults on criminals where no attacker had been arrested. Initially, "criminal", meant leading organised crime figures. But it was clear as daylight who their attackers were, even if the "victim" refused to name them or press charges.

They expanded their criteria to include the footmen and lieutenants but again drew a blank and extended their trawl to include fringe figures and eventually anyone with two or more convictions for assault, theft or both. There were twenty-two such cases, but with one exception it was again obvious who the attacker was, but the victim was not naming them, either through fear, or because they were most likely planning their own revenge.

The one exception was the case of Kieron McPhail who'd been attacked near the entrance to an underpass when he was completing a community sentence. Nobody had been charged, and the case remained open and unsolved. Reading through the file Aruna discovered that McPhail had inadvertently caused a stushie when he'd been given a non-custodial sentence after a random, unprovoked attack on a woman making her way to work.

The investigation focused on whether the attacker was related to the woman in any way as a revenge. But they'd come up with nothing. McPhail himself had been blindsided and hit from behind, but he did say he'd seen "an older guy" wearing a cap, possibly white, ahead of him on his mobile, with something wrapped in plastic beside him. He'd passed the man and of course was attacked.

The description was too vague, but it was clear that the "older guy" was the main suspect and that was unusual for, as the lead officer investigating noted, almost all these attacks involved young males. However, there were no further leads and the case drawled to a halt.

DC Sharma took the file to her boss.

'It's the only case in the last fifteen months where no one's in the frame. McPhail himself had no clue who might have done it, least of all an older guy. Suspicion fell on McPhail's last victim, the cleaner, but nothing emerged from that.'

'Nobody else saw the older guy?' Hutchinson asked. Aruna consulted the file.

'A postman making his rounds saw a guy he would describe as "middle-aged" walking towards the underpass wearing a white cap carrying a package of some type, but that was all.'

'And it goes nowhere from there.'

'No,' Aruna concurred. She went on:

'If it was the middle-aged guy then the object he's carrying is probably the weapon that was used and that's likely to be a club of some kind like a baseball bat or cricket bat. I looked at the injury report and McPhail was really badly done in, boss, I mean a mess.'

'And it's a fair assumption that McGarvey was savagely attacked with a bat.'

'There's something else, I noticed,' she sifted through the back of the file. 'The criminal justice social worker told one of the detectives dealing with McPhail's case that his supervisor had told him that a private detective was asking about him.'

'Was that supervisor questioned?'

She let out a sigh and shrugged: 'The supervisor went on long-term sick leave, and it was never followed up.'

'Did the social worker have any idea why a private dick was inquiring about McPhail?'

She looked blankly at the file. 'There's nothing here.'

'No mention of who the private eye was?' She shook her head.

'You wonder what the hell some folk are doing in the CID,' he muttered and went on:

'Right, it might be nothing, but you and Gerry find out who that supervisor is and get onto him.'

'Right away, Sir.'

Hutchinson got another break that afternoon when the company that made the doorbell camera from Tam McGarvey's house informed him, after a delay, that the footage from the door had been retrieved from cloud storage. This could be a major development, and Hutchinson gathered his three detectives, including Aruna and Gerry Stratton, in a basement technical room at police headquarters outside Glasgow, where a technician played the digital footage retrieved from the cloud.

It'd been a quiet day for the couple until about seven the "pizza delivery" guy appeared in his biker's outfit. It was a good picture, but the biker and the visor obscured any physical features. However, the camera had an audio feature and clearly picked up the dialogue between McGarvey and the "delivery" man.

'He's not young,' Hutchinson said immediately on hearing it. They played it back several times. 'I would say this guys in his fifties, at least.'

'That's really unusual, gaffer,' Gerry Stratton remarked. 'Most of these guys are in their twenties working in the gig economy.'

'And there's no bike,' Aruna put in. 'Check the background.' The technician froze the screen. There was a house opposite and McGarvey's car in the driveway, but no other vehicle. 'That's strange as well because these guys pick up loads of deliveries and they want to be as close to where they're delivering to as they can. But there's nothing there.'

'That's because there is no fucking bike,' Hutchinson said sharply. 'Did we get anything from CCTV coming out that estate?' he looked at Gerry Stratton.

'No, chief. We've trawled everywhere. He was good and kept well away from CCTV.'

'Yeah, he would do,' Hutchinson said resignedly. 'Any word on that supervisor?' he asked Aruna.

'He's still on sick leave.'

'Ok, we need to interview him, even if it's at his home. Get on to that right away DC Sharma.'

'Will do sir.'

They resumed watching the CCTV seeing the "delivery" guy leaving, then after an hour returning, unlocking the door proficiently with the card which caused Gerry Stratton to remark:

'He knows what he's doing.'

'Or he's learned it somewhere, inside possibly,' Hutchinson put in.

Once inside the door, the footage ended as the guy took out the device. Hutchinson requested the technician playback the footage a few times and asked for close-ups whenever the guy appeared in full view, but they couldn't get beyond the tinted visor.

'This guy's good but I don't think he's a conventional hitman, if there is such a thing. Aruna, get onto that supervisor as soon as you can. We need to know who's hired a private dick to find out about a thug like McPhail and why. It might have bugger all to do with McGarvey, but it might have some connection.'

The team dispersed leaving Hutchinson to wonder if there was any link.

'I've just had a tap on the shoulder from the CID asking me why I was wanting information about Kieron McPhail.'

Charlie stopped munching his cheeseburger. They were sitting in Charlie's car in a car park beside a MacDonald's drive thru next to the Gorbals on Glasgow's southside.

Ali McMahon had called him an hour ago on his mobile insisting they meet up immediately.

'What?' Charlie almost shouted.

'You heard. A young Asian detective constable and her sidekick.'

'What did you tell her?'

'It's customer confidentiality and privileged information and I couldn't assist her.'

'What did she say to that.'

'As I expected. She told me, If need be, they'd get a court order forcing me to disclose the name and if they found information supplied by my firm was used in pursuit of a serious crime my license could be revoked and I'm out of a job.' McMahon sighed,

'Usual shite. They've tried that on me many times. But there's a difference this time.'

'What's that?'

'I've got my own contacts in the force. I checked up on this DC Sharma. Her boss is a DS called Hutchinson.' McMahon spoke slowly. 'And he's leading up the enquiry into Tam McGarvey's sad passing.'

Charlie looked startled. 'Fuck! How did they make that connection?'

'I don't think they have yet,' the PI looked straight at Charlie. 'I think they're speculating and they're not a hundred miles off. You made a mess of Tam McGarvey. It's not a conventional whacking. They'll be pulling every informant they've got and getting nowhere. So, they'll be checking every unsolved attack.

'There's actually very few random attacks and normally a connection's found somewhere. But in McPhail's case there isn't. Nor is there with McGarvey. The MO's the same; a bat. A lot of detectives get lazy, and especially when it's the likes of McPhail, do the least they can. But this young Asian lassie's sharp and so is her boss, this Hutchinson guy.

'It's not completely unheard for PI's to be making enquiries about characters like McPhail; lawyers hire us to make precognitions; former girlfriends looking to make child support claims and so on. But it's a lead she's followed, and it's led to me.

'She asked me if the person who hired me about McPhail was, and I quote her, "a middle-aged man?"'

Charlie's eyes opened wider. McMahon went on:

'I stayed stum. We left it with her saying she might be back in touch and reminding me "not to be obstructive".'

'Jesus,' Charlie shook his head, burger left uneaten now on his lap. 'I never meant for this to happen to you.'

'They never do,' McMahon said sarcastically.

'Right,' Charlie came back firmly, 'I'll sever all connections with you. I'll...'

'...It's too late for that Charlie. If they get a court order I'm obliged to disclose. But I don't think they will. The link between McPhail and McGarvey is too thin, and they'd be forced to reveal their hand in court. No, I think they'll put a tap on my line, try and do it that way. Depends how eager they are to solve McGarvey's killing.'

'Could they be following you?' Charlie asked looking around the car park.

'They're not,' McMahon said assuredly. 'I can sniff out a tail a mile away. It's too early anyway. They'll still be considering it and need to get approval and warrants. Police are a bureaucracy. But I'm on their radar and not for the first time.'

'Again, I'm sorry.'

'Look, it's a risk. As soon as you enquire about someone, you alert them. I take that risk on behalf of the customer. I just need to take more precautions. And so do you.'

'How?'

'Do more of what you're doing. Commit nothing to paper. Strictly compartmentalise your life. Get as many burner phones as you can. If you're going to contact me, use this number,' he recited it to Charlie, 'and meet me here. Never at the office.

'Above all, when you're driving or walking, check for surveillance. Be paranoid. The same car or the same person following you, clock it or them, note it, memorise it, abort. Follow simple rules.'

'Ali,' Charlie was firm,' 'it ends here with you and me. I've given you enough trouble as it is. I'll be out your life from now on.'

'It doesn't work like that. We're linked. And I'm not sure you've stopped with McGarvey.'

Charlie stared sharply at him. It was almost as if Ali McMahon was psychic. 'What do you mean?'

'I've been in this game a long time. Most people that hire me just want trouble out their lives and people off their back. A few want justice which often blends into revenge, which the cops or the courts won't give them, and I can supply them with the info they won't get elsewhere. But it's a one-off and I never see them again.

'You're different Charlie. You want vengeance which is a form of justice. You're on a mission. It started with your brother, and it's taken over.' He looked directly at Charlie. 'I can't see you stopping, until your caught, which you will be if you're on your own.'

Charlie was perplexed. 'Where's this going?'

'Cops don't scare me. Jail doesn't frighten me, though I don't particularly want to go there. Now don't say a word after what I'm going to say; just keep quiet.

'I liked how you dealt with McGarvey. I've seen people get away with too much. You see I'm a lapsed liberal. Rehabilitation was everything for me. So called criminals were really just victims of poverty, deprivation and, what's that new buzzword, trauma.

'Yep, I was very New Testament. Understanding. Empathy. There but for the grace of God goes I. Never judge. I bought into all that. But I've changed. There are nasty, evil people out there. Sometimes there're just lazy and impulsive. But, unchecked, that easily becomes a habit and morphs into becoming pure utter wickedness and sadism.

"Now, after what I've seen in my time and my sister's attacker only getting a community sentence, I'm very much Old

Testament. Punishment, retribution and righteous vengeance. That's the key to justice. And after what happened to your brother and Jamison being allowed to walk the streets, but you left with a life sentence, I think you're Old Testament too.'

'I'll ask again. Where's this going?'

'I got really scunnered with those cops yesterday. I get it, they're doing their jobs. But they are chasing every fucking lead trying to pin down who killed that piece of psychopathic garbage, McGarvey, as if he was equal to and the same as all his victims. That pisses me off.

'No. I think you've got a way to go yet Charlie and I'm going to help you. If you want me to. And if you do, I'm here for you.'

Charlie was stunned. But felt incredibly relieved. If, despite the cops hassling him, Ali McMahon was still on side and could bring all his experience to assist him, that would be of enormous help.

'So, Charlie, Kitchen Vigilante, what were you thinking of next?'

THIRTEEN

Stuart Hutchinson and his team had agreed that going for a court order to compel Ali McMahon to disclose who'd asked him to make inquiries about Kieron McPhail was premature. The link between him and McGarvey was too tenuous, at this stage anyway. Better to do some background checks on the PI to see if anything cropped up there. And Aruna Sharma did find something.

Hutchinson was becoming more impressed with her by the day. She was sharp, patient and methodical, so he knew when she asked to see him and walked into his office with a pile of printouts that she was on to something.

'I've been doing some background on the PI, Ali McMahon,' she announced, sitting down in front of his desk, the folder with the printouts on her lap. 'He's ex-army and has had run-ins with us in the past about not sharing information, though he's never been in trouble.

'He mostly does run of the mill stuff like divorce settlements, debts, tracing people, that sort of stuff. He'd never really made the headlines, except once and I think that might be of interest to us, sir.'

'What was that?'

She brought out from the folder a hard copy of a newspaper report on the trial of a man called Charlie Carty accused of trying to kill the person convicted of killing his brother. Ali McMahon's name was revealed during the trial as the private investigator who'd provided him with information that'd helped him to track down the victim which the detectives investigating the case had uncovered but which Carty himself had never disclosed.

Hutchinson quickly read through the report. Carty was a renowned, local celebrity chef and he and his ex-wife had eaten in the Deep South when Carty had owned it, though he thought it was over-rated. Once he'd read it, he cast a glance at Aruna.

'And?' he enquired.

'Well, it's a long-shot, I suppose,' she began,' but this guy tries to kill his brother's killer. He doesn't succeed but puts him in a coma and gets sentenced to seven years.'

'And what's that got to do with Tam McGarvey?'

'Not a lot. But Carty admitted he wanted to avenge his brother's death, and it was widely thought that the attack on Kieron McPhail was a revenge attack possibly linked to a previous terrible assault he'd made on that cleaner on her way to work.

'So, Carty hires McMahon's firm to get the lowdown on his brother's killer now he's out of prison. Then McMahon is also hired by someone to make inquiries about McPhail, who lo and behold, is attacked where the only possible suspect is a,' her left forefinger pointed at her boss, 'middle-aged man.'

'What age is Charlie Carty?' he looked at the report, but Aruna answered for him,

'62.'

'And is there any link between Charlie Carty and the unemployed, street criminal, Kieron McPhail? I mean does he know or is he related to the woman that was attacked.'

Aruna retracted her forefinger.

'Er...no.'

'And I don't recall anything linking a local Glasgow celebrity chef to Tam McGarvey, do you?'

She shook her head, now looking despondent.

'But that doesn't mean we should completely dismiss it.' He was keen not to dampen her enthusiasm or diminish her confidence. He'd seen too many senior tecs in the past rubbish their subordinates' ideas and initiatives with disastrous consequences. 'Check it out further. See if we can make any tie-in to this Carty character. Thanks for bringing this to my attention DC Sharma. Good work.'

She beamed, her confidence returning, as she rose and left his office. 'Thank you, sir.'

If anybody was the authority on the McGarvey's and their activities in the east end, it was DS Logan Doyle. On the cusp of retirement, he'd spent twenty years working out of Shettleston cop shop chasing local criminals and witnessing the rise of a new breed of ruthless mobsters. Now he'd been shunted back into uniform and doing a desk job at HQ before being pensioned off. Hutchinson brought over two pints of lager to their table where Doyle sank about a third of it in one draught.

'Thirsty boy,' Hutchinson remarked.

''Aye, sure am.'

Doyle cut an expansive figure, with a well-worn grey suit, shiny red face and thin, badly combed, straggly dark hair which struggled to hide his extensive bald pate. He reminded

Hutchinson of the stock detectives he knew when he'd started out in the CID a few decades ago: hard drinking, tough, aggressive characters. The police service had changed considerably since and CID had certainly sobered up.

They were in a quiet corner of a hotel tucked away near Blythswood Square not far from Sauchiehall Street. Hutchinson used the hotel as a discreet venue to meet contacts and colleagues.

'When you finishing up?' he asked Doyle.

'Three months and I canny fucking wait to get out.'

'There's a lot feel the same way,' Hutchinson agreed.

'Ach, it's all the politics,' Doyle grunted, swallowing another large draught. 'You're hemmed in, canny dae this, canny dae that. Every cunt's got their "rights". I'm no saying there wis'nae a few bad ones among us and a few kickings getting handed out...'

'...A lot of kickings,' Hutchinson reminded him.

'Aye, there wis. But now, Christ, we're like social workers. That's what we've become, social workers.'

Hutchinson drank some of his own pint then said. 'Anyway, before we get lost in a good old day's nostalgia trip, I want to pick your brains.'

'Fire away,' Doyle had almost finished his pint, while Stu had hardly touched his.

'Did Tam McGarvey or any of his mob, his brother and so on, have any enemies that weren't part of organised crime. You know somebody who had a grudge against them?'

Doyle pondered the question for a minute. Then said:

'Where would you start? That's not the question. The question is who would dare and who would have the muscle to do it? And the answer is, very few, if any.'

'So, you've no idea who carried out that quite extraordinary attack on McGarvey?'

'I haven't a clue about that. It's not the Chisholm's I can assure you. Forget all that pish about the McGarvey's making a move against auld man Sammy. I tell you Tam McGarvey was Nat Chisholm's man all along. That's what gave McGarvey his power, he had Chisholm's licence in the east end. That's how Nat Chisholm took over so easily when McGarvey sadly departed; he was just picking up what was his.'

'What do you mean, "licence"?'

Doyle looked askance at Hutchinson. 'Seriously, Stu? How many years have you been in CID?'

'Too many, Logan. But help me. What does "licence" mean?'

Doyle looked around himself cautiously.

'It's murky out there. Sometimes we have to make deals with people to get them to provide us with information.'

'Huh, huh,' Hutchinson agreed, sipping his lager.

'Sometimes that's simply cutting a deal with the Fiscal for a reduced sentence or even letting someone walk free for providing good information. You've done that, I've done that.'

'True.'

'But sometimes it goes further than that.'

'How?' Hutchinson asked earnestly.

'Aw for fuck's sake don't be so naïve. They give you excellent material on another outfit that allows you to take them out, but in return they're allowed to operate. In other words, they get a licence.'

'I've heard of it,' Hutchinson admitted, 'but I've never seen any evidence of it.'

'Well nae cunt's gonny email about it or put it in a file. It's all unwritten, unsaid, need to know. How the hell do you think Sammy Chisholm's been able to run this city the way he has for over twenty years? Ok, we're awash wi drugs, folk are dying. But it's organised. Think how quiet it is compared to elsewhere in the country. There's nae gunbattles in the street or shootouts every week. Most importantly, Joe Public can go about their business in safety, and that keeps the politicians and the media happy.'

'Are you saying, we, the cops are keeping the Chisholm's going?'

'Money's not changing hands, if that's what you're thinking. It's a mutual understanding. The Chisholm's prevent anarchy happening. The clue's in the word "organised". They feed us info on competitors, upstarts, anybody that can upset the status quo and we let them operate within certain bounds. Aye, they'll be times when we'll haul in and jail some of their lieutenants; the McGarvey's for instance, they were due a turn. And there's nothing can be done to stop the UK wide boys, you're National Crime Agency, HMRC or the likes, coming and taking them out.

'But, overall, an accommodation is made and most of the city sleeps peacefully.'

Hutchinson shook his head. 'I'd heard some of this before, but I always put it down to pub talk or mad conspiracy theory.'

'Look, auld Sammy Chisholm's losing his grip and some senior folks in the ranks are shitting themselves that the city will dissolve into chaos with bodies in the street. Better that young Nat Chisholm takes over and keeps order, like he's doing in the east end.'

'So, Nat Chisholm's got a licence to succeed his uncle?'

'Better the devil you know. Sammy's sons are too weak. They're Fredo's.'

Hutchinson smiled. He knew the reference. "Fredo" was named after Fredo Corleone, the effete, insipid son of Vito Corleone in The Godfather.

'But, Logan, Nat Chisholm is a fucking psycho as was Tam McGarvey. They terrorise people,' Hutchinson insisted.

'I'm not saying it's right, but if you've got a couple of bad bams that keep a hundred other bad bams in order and most people are unaffected and can get on with their lives, then that's better than letting a hundred go loose, cos then nobody's safe. That's the deal. It's no perfect, but what's the alternative?'

'No bad bams.'

They sat in silence before Doyle said: 'I'm out of it anyway. Another pint?'

'No, thanks, I'm going to head up the road.' In truth, Hutchinson felt deflated at Doyle's comments. 'Just one other thing, has the name Charlie Carty ever come across your radar?'

'The chef?'

'Aye.'

'Yeah. He owns a pub in the east end, one of many he's got.

He did time for running over the guy that killed his brother a couple of years ago.'

'That's right. Well, we've found out that Charlie Carty hired a private dick called Ali McMahon to find out where the killer was staying so he could have a go at him.'

'I know McMahon, he's been around for years,' Doyle said.

'Well, we've also found that McMahon was hired by somebody unknown to get the lowdown on a vicious thug called Kieron McPhail who was attacked a couple of months ago by persons unknown.'

'So, who hired him? You think it was Carty? And why?'

'McMahon won't say. More or less told us to go to court and force him to disclose which I'm reluctant to do.'

'What's this got to do with Tam McGarvey?'

'I don't know and there might be nothing to do with it.'

Doyle finished the last of his pint. 'Do what you can with the McGarvey case. It's spooked a lot of people. Nat Chisholm's as eager to find out who topped McGarvey as we are. Maybe leave it to them, eh?'

'How do you know that?'

'What?'

'How do you know, Nat Chisholm wants to get McGarvey's killer.'

'In case he comes for him. Then we'd all be in trouble. Nothing more unsettling than a silent assassin. Right, I'm off.' He stood and tapped his finger with his nose.

'Not a word about anything that I've said. See you.'

Hutchinson watched him leave the bar feeling very

unsettled. He'd held Logan Doyle in awe as the traditional old school crime fighter. But the veteran DS's talk of Nat and Sammy Chisholm having a "licence" and his seeming knowledge of Nat Chisholm's motivations profoundly disquieted Hutchinson.

He was a straight ahead, down the line copper. Sure, there were trade-offs and compromises, and you had to give informants some slack, but giving criminals "licence" to keep the peace was on another level; it was simply corrupt on an ethical level even if money wasn't changing hands and it deeply disturbed Hutchinson. What was he up against here? He left the bar feeling he was stepping into profoundly uncertain terrain.

'Yass!' Aruna Sharma couldn't help herself shouting out. The squad open plan was empty, and she was clicking on the website for AMAC Private Investigators. She'd looked up the basic, single page, sparse site before but now studied again the brief mention of the three investigators, including Ali McMahon, that made up the AMAC investigation team. She'd been primarily interested in McMahon but now she noticed the name of one of the other PIs, Danni Hayes and wondered if that could be the same individual she'd trained with at police college and remained friendly with after they'd both graduated.

She googled the name and got a Facebook reference. She opened her Facebook page on her mobile and typed the name. Several names came up. She scrolled down and recognised the thumbnail photo as the girl she'd trained with. Like her employer's website, her FB page was scant, and her last post was a month ago. She merely mentioned she worked in "research" and made no mention she'd been a police officer. She tried accessing the Friends page, but it was private.

Aruna hadn't seen Danni Hayes for about two years, but she remembered her as quiet and a bit reserved but friendly. She'd left the force several years ago because, she admitted, the job hadn't turned out to be what she expected it to be which was the reason, Aruna knew, most people left.

She still had Danni in her contact book on her phone and texted: "blast from the past here, Danni. Aruna Sharma now DC Sharma (get me!) Fancy a catch up?'

Twenty minutes later she received the reply. 'Hi Aruna, great to hear from you. Free tomorrow for a catch up about four?'

Aruna confirmed the time and sent an email updating Hutchinson on developments.

Charlie hugged Calum tightly at the door of his flat. 'I'm here for you now, you know that,' he said to his son as they parted.

'I know, dad,' Calum replied then walked down the stairs. Charlie watched him depart, then closed the front door of his flat, leaned against it and exhaled deeply.

It had come home he thought. Calum had phoned him that afternoon sounding upset. He told him to come to the flat. There, Calum revealed that the previous afternoon two guys had walked into the Camlachie Arms asking to speak to him and saying they were from a "firm of security specialists."

His son told them they looked like mobster central casting. Both tall and menacing, one with a livid scar. Scarface did the talking and the opening demand was five percent of weekly takings to "protect" them from the surging violence, graffiti and theft that was rampant across the east end.

Calum attempted to stall, saying he would need to speak to his boss but was interrupted by Scarface saying:

'That'll be your old man, Charlie Carty, the famous chef?'

It would have been stupid to deny it, so Charlie said, 'yeah, that's him,' which prompted Scarface to remark 'say hello to your father from our boss, Nat.'

'Sure, will do,' Calum agreed.

As they left, Scarface wished Calum well, looked forward to doing business with him and his father and hoped "that lovely woman of yours, Alice, is doing well,' then left.

They'd done their homework. They always did, honing in on the most vulnerable aspects of their victim. Calum, of course, was distressed and contacted Charlie straight away. He'd tried to reassure his son; he was an old hand at this and would deal with it. And he had. He'd bought off gangsters in the past. But he knew the current crop were far more rapacious and ruthless than in the past; witness the fate of the Marchetti's. Charlie had managed to comfort his son and said he would meet the two guys when they were due to make an appearance the following week.

Calum protested it was 'too risky,' but Charlie cut him off, saying he wasn't to worry, he knew how to handle this, it was part of the trade, and it had to be dealt with. He could see his son was relieved to see his experienced father dealing with this so calmly. He also assured Calum that Alice was in no danger and not to say a word to her, which Calum had no intention of doing.

After Calum left, Charlie poured a large glass of whisky. He was blistering with anger and also bemused at the irony that his onslaught on the McGarvey's had led to Nat Chisholm directly taking over their east end fiefdom. It was nothing personal. The Chisholm's were exerting control over their domains and a popular bar/diner in the heart of the east end was an obvious target. The Chisholm's would have descended on Calum and the Camlachie Arms sooner or later

But beyond his anger, Charlie could see an opportunity to confront and take out Nat Chisholm and bring his uncle's empire of fear, misery and extortion tumbling down. He smiled to himself and reached for one of his burner phones to contact Ali McMahon on the number they'd agreed for such contacts.

Aruna Sharma couldn't conceal her delight when she walked into Hutchinson's office two days after his meeting with Logan Doyle, which still left him with an unpleasant, sullied feeling.

'You look like you've won the Lottery, young Miss Sharma,' he said to her. She beamed back at him.

'So, what's your news?' He urged her.

'Remember that email I sent you about how I knew one of the staff on Ali McMahon's team?'

'Uh huh.'

'Well, I met with her yesterday, and we went for a drink. We hadn't seen each other for ages and there was a lot of catching up to do and...'

'...you got her pissed, tut tut DC Sharma.'

'I didn't put a gun to her head!' Aruna protested coyly. 'Anyway, we got on to work and told her I was loving the CID, and she said she was enjoying her work. She was onto her fourth large glass of Pinot Grigio (I only had one) when I said to her, I was currently working on the Tam McGarvey case but getting nowhere and I could see her looking alert. I pressed on that we were just looking for a wee break when she said she might know something, but I had to keep her confidence.

'It took ages, and I had to constantly reassure her, but eventually she divulged that her boss had been making inquiries about Tam McGarvey. You know, where he lived, what his movements were.

'" Who for?" I asked her. It took another half glass to get that out of her. Ali McMahon didn't tell her directly, but it's a small office, there's only three of them and the word between her and her colleague was that it was the same client that had been making enquiries about a mugger who got beaten up himself and before that, long before Danni had joined the firm, had driven a car at a guy and nearly killed him on the basis of information that her boss had provided him.'

'Was there a name mentioned?'

'I didn't ask her directly. But she gave it to me after a while.'

'Fifth glass?'

'Yes.'

'Who?'

'She swore me to secrecy but gave it. One Charlie Carty. The chef.' Aruna almost leaned over the desk. 'He's sixty-two. That's what is now described as late middle aged.'

'Has Danni tried to get in touch since the sober light of day's hit her?'

Aruna looked sheepish. 'She's phoned and text me twelve times this morning.'

'And you've not answered her?'

'No'.

'Well, don't. She knows the drill. She's a big girl, an ex-cop and a PI. As long as you didn't ask her directly and she volunteered the information of her own accord, she and Ali McMahon are a material witness. Now write it up for the file, say that you informed me you knew the staff member and requested you to meet her informally and she revealed the information. You realise you've lost a friend.'

'She wasn't that close. But it is a bit lousy.'

'So is life. Right, let's have another chat with this private eye and then we'll have a word with Chef Carty*

'What?'

It was the second crash meeting in the Gorbals car park next to the MacDonalds' drive, in two days. The first had been when Charlie disclosed to Ali about the Chisholm's approach to Calum. Charlie had requested that. Ali had requested this one urgently.

''Say again?' Charlie asked. Ali let out a deep despondent sigh.

'One of my staff has blabbed about my inquiries re McGarvey to a cop she knows who she went to police college with. Oh, and that cop just happens to be the same cop that interviewed me about why I was asking about Kieron McPhail.'

'And she's mentioned my name?'

'Aye.'

'Then we're fucked.'

'It's not looking good, no.'

'Shite. 'What's the chances of one of your staff knowing a CID tec investigating the McGarvey case.'

'Ach, Glasgow is a village. Half the folk in my game are ex-cops. I've sacked her, but I need to take responsibility. I really thought she knew to button it always. That Sharma cop's good. I could do with her on the team, especially now I'm one down.'

Charlie was thinking furiously. The cops could pounce any time. His first thoughts were Calum. He needed to get him out of the Camlachie Arms and Glasgow pronto. He'd phone Eric Fenwick and tell him that a serious protection racket was about to hit part of his business. Landis could deal with that. After all, they would have plenty of experience of dealing with protection rackets across Europe.

But then he realised, Landis would probably run a mile. At the least they might refuse to take on the Camlachie Arms. And at worst scupper the whole deal if it came to light that the owner was on the lam for a grisly murder and a serious assault. He sank in despair in his car seat. All his plans were collapsing fast and the vary last thing he wanted, endangering his family, was about to happen. How the hell did he manage to contrive that?'

'I need to speak to Calum.' He realised he sounded desperate and tried to calm his voice. 'How long do you think before the cops come for me.'

McMahon checked his watch. 'This DS guy, Hutchinson, the female detective's boss, has asked me to "pop-in" to see him this afternoon. They'll try and shake me down and come for you after that. What's your plans? Get out of town?'

Charlie shook his head. 'I don't know.'

'If I was you, I'd do fuck all right now. Their case is actually quite weak. It's all circumstantial and coincidental. The key is don't panic – I know it's tempting – and don't alert anyone.'

'So just stay put.'

'Yes. Recover your composure, Charlie. Get that steel back in. A lot of times the cops like you to think your position's hopeless and they've got more on you than they have. That's when folk fold. Don't. Wait it out. When are Chisholm's hoods due back to see Calum?'

'End of next week.'

'Ok, let's wait to see what the CID have got to say today.'

Charlie looked over at Ali McMahon. He knew he was in the hands of the private eye.

FOURTEEN

Ali McMahon barely had time to sit on Charley's passenger seat in the Gorbals car park before Charlie barked at him:

'So, how'd it go with the cops?'

'Jesus, give me a chance to draw breath!' McMahon protested.

Charlie was agitated; he'd had a sleepless night. To add to his problems, Eric Fenwick had phoned him to say Landis wanted to know when he was going to sign the deal; they were keen to progress the takeover.

McMahon wound down the window and lit a cigarette. 'I had two of them, the DS Stuart Hutchinson and the woman DC Sharma, around me for what they called an "informal chat." They asked again who hired me to investigate Kieron McPhail and Tam McGarvey and I refused to say, citing client confidentiality and the Sharma lady cited being an accessory to serious assault and murder, about losing my licence and I still refused to say, though I knew full they knew and then the DI shows his hand by revealing it's you and how they found that out. And I just stayed calm and said I knew that, and I'd dismissed the investigator for gross misconduct and breaching client confidentiality.

'That didn't faze him, and he came back with "so is there anything you can help us with that could link him to the attacks". And I said, cagily, I was making enquiries on behalf of this client, I know nothing about how he used the information or any motive he may have had. Which, officially, is true. I don't.

'He asked me if I was still in touch with you and I just shrugged my shoulders. Then he said if you do see him, tell him we'd be keen to talk to him.'

Charlie opened his eyes wide. 'What the fuck does that mean? Come in and see us, have a cup of tea and a wee chat!'

'Naw. He's a sharp cookie. What's he saying is, we're onto him and we'd like you to talk to him.'

'Why?'

'See if I can persuade you, basically, to come clean.'

'Own up to it?'

'Aye.'

'So, I just pop in and see this DI guy and the Asian woman and that's it, confess.'

'More or less. I mean if you don't, he'll go down the usual route. Bring you in, arrest you, question you, then charge you and all the publicity that will follow. Of course, you'll get yourself a good lawyer and he'll do what he can for you and many people will see you as a hero.'

Charlie was getting annoyed with him.

'Ali, I thought you were helping me. You seem to be suggesting I give myself up. I'll get done for murder. I'll be back inside where the Chisholm's and what's left of the McGarvey's have a long reach. My family will be in constant danger. My businesses, if they're still solvent, will be sold for half their value. That's what I'm looking at.'

McMahon finished his cigarette and remained unperturbed.

'No, Charlie, I'm not suggesting you give yourself up, not at all. There might be a way out of this. But you'll need to negotiate with them. Remember, there's nothing to actually connect you to the scenes of the attacks. What's that expression you use? You're "forensically nude." Well, that's where we start.'

'You're losing me.'

He lit another cigarette. 'Let me walk you through it, but we'll get some coffees first.' They left the car, zipped up their jackets against a sudden rainsquall and walked towards a nearby coffee bar.

Stu Hutchinson was unsure how his senior colleagues would react to the proposal. He'd known them for a while and worked with them on cases, but like a few of the high-ranking serious crime people, they could be withdrawn and keep their cards to themselves.

He met them in the DI's office, a tidy, uncluttered space, so unlike his own, with a PC, and pictures on his desk of two women, one in her 50s and the other in her late 20s, and a young man about 20, which Hutchinson presumed was the DI's wife and two children. The DI, a slim man with bushy red hair named McGarrigle wearing a dark suit was sitting at a round table with another detective who Hutchinson recognised as another DS called Flannigan, a heavier man wearing a grey suit. Both were the same age as Hutchinson and veterans of policing against organised crime in the city.

He'd chosen them carefully as they'd taken on and sometimes been successful in prosecuting lieutenants of the Chisholm family, though never been successful at putting away the main family members, including old man Sammy. After carefully weighing it up, Hutchinson now dismissed Logan Doyle's talk about "licences" and "mutual accommodation" that let one team or family stay on top as it kept a sort of stasis that benefited everyone. He'd never seen any evidence of that, outside feverish alcohol fuelled talk.

Sure, the Chisholm's had been top dog for over twenty years, but that was more likely to be because it was incredibly difficult to pin hard evidence on them ensconced as they were behind sophisticated firewalls, could call upon the best lawyers and ruled by terror. The idea some of his police colleagues, particularly at the highest levels, were happy to accommodate, work with or "licence" criminal entities like the Chisholm's was repugnant to a scrupulously honest copper like Stu Hutchinson and belonged in the realm of crime fiction. No, he trusted his colleagues.

Still, as he sat down beside them, and accepted a coffee poured by McGarrigle from a pot on the table, he felt on edge but determined not to show it.

'How's things with the McGarvey case?' McGarrigle asked.

'Nobody's saying anything, no breaks, no leads,' he replied less than honestly.

'We're getting nothing as well, certainly not from the Chisholm's ranks,' Flannigan put in dourly.

'Young Nat's taking over the patch with gusto,' Hutchinson remarked.

'Which is why you're here,' McGarrigle said and that, Hutchinson knew, was the cue for him to make his pitch.

Basically, it was that Charley Carty, who he'd "stumbled

upon" in the McGarvey case, had a son who was being leaned on by two associates of Nat Chisholm at his popular bar in the east end. The father owned the pub and had suggested he took over from the son and for a few months' pay the associates but also ingratiate himself with them and invite their boss, Nat Chisholm, to use the bar for free hospitality. The idea was that Chisholm would use the bar frequently, become comfortable there and let his guard down which the cops could take advantage of by wiretapping the place. Flannigan looked doubtful and said so:

'Chisholm's very guarded, these top guys always are.'

'Yeah, but there's always a chance, he'd let his guard down. There's a private room that can hold about twenty and he might feel he can talk more freely there,' Hutchinson countered.

'How long were you thinking of wiretapping the place?' McGarrigle asked.

'I'll be upfront, and you'll be well aware of this, it could take months. But we, I mean Aruna Sharma, Gerry Stratton and I would put in the groundwork, sift through the tapes and hand any take to you. We wouldn't be asking you to spend any time on it. I know you're busy.'

'What about your McGarvey inquiries?'

'It's going nowhere,' he again said disingenuously. 'I'm down to the three of us and it might get wound up completely in the next few months. We'd still be making inquiries, and we might turn up something with the wiretaps, but it would be a more efficient use of resources and might get something on Nat Chisholm before he becomes top dog. Worth a try, eh?'

Flannigan spoke directly to McGarrigle.

'The gaffer would appreciate if he could report an active oppo on Nat Chisholm at the SMT and in front of the Chief.'

Translated, Hutchinson knew that the "gaffer" referred to the Chief Superintendent of Serious Crime who would be at the senior management team or SMT where the "Chief" or Chief Constable would be in attendance.

It was politics. They needed to be seen to be doing something where nothing else was happening with the Chisholm's. McGarrigle took the bait.

'Yeah, it would. Ok, run with it. You lead with this chef guy, write a full proposal, I'll authorise it, get you the technical assistance you need, but it's all coming from your budget. Understood?'

'Absolutely, sir, agreed.'

'And I want weekly edited highlights of the transcripts sent to me.'

'Of course.'

'Right, you two work on this,' he picked up his papers, the cue for Hutchinson and Flannigan to leave.

It had been Ali McMahon who suggested it; using Charlie's status and fame to lure Nat Chisholm to regard the Camlachie Arms as a place where he could relax free of charge and possibly confide to his lieutenants and where he might, just might, loosen up and incriminate himself and be recorded doing so. Chisholm might take to Carty and trust him. After all Carty was a bit of a legend and a hero in the east end. Not many would criticise him for seeking revenge on his brother's killer, not least amongst the gangster fraternity.

Hutchinson could have persisted in going for the chef, but it would have taken a long time to build a case and neither Carty nor McMahon would have broken easily. Above all, the prospect of ensnaring Nat Chisholm and taking him out before he ascended to the pinnacle of Glasgow's gangland would reflect well on all those taking part in it, including Detective Sergeant Stu Hutchinson. A nice way to finish his career.

It took three weeks for Nat Chisholm to appear at the Camlachie Arms. The deal with Landis had gone through. Charlie had mentioned nothing to Eric Fenwick about the Chisholm's or the cops, but Eric Fenwick had agreed to Charlie's request to manage the bar as he was "bored shitless" and to transfer Calum to another of Landis' outlets in the city centre. Eric was glad to have an experienced old hand in charge at one of their new acquisitions.

He met Stu Hutchinson twice along with Ali McMahon. On the second occasion he brought along a younger Asian detective who stayed silent throughout the meeting, but who Ali identified as Aruna Sharma. They made arrangements for two police technicians to go into the diner as alleged "contractors" improving the sound quality for singers and bands performing at the venue.

Charlie met and paid the two Chisholm hoods, including Scarface, on their second visit to the Camlachie Arms. He explained he'd taken over from his son, who'd been promoted, and he was now directly managing the bar and would look after them. He poured them a few beers and got on great with them, putting them at ease. After their third beer, they mentioned they had to get on "the boss" would be onto them.

Charlie let them know that their boss 'was welcome any time at the bar,' and Scarface said he'd pass that on.

One Friday morning, two weeks later, just before opening time, when the hoods were due and Charlie had left the doors open for them, Scarface walked in with a wiry guy of medium height with close cropped dark hair and penetrating dark eyes. He walked in straight with an icy, appraising demeanour.

'Charlie Carty?' He asked. Charlie was behind the bar loading a tray of glasses. 'Aye.'

'Nat Chisholm.'

Charlie pretended he didn't recognize the name. The guy said tersely, 'I'm these guy's boss,' with a brief tilt of his head to Scarface.

Charlie's face lit up. 'Fantastic, pleased to meet you,' he offered his hand. Almost reluctantly, Chisholm shook it.

'Like a drink?' Charlie asked.

'It's hauf-eleven. Do you think I'm an alky?' his voice was cold, latent with menace.

'Naw, of course not. Coffee? Tea?'

'I'll take a tea.'

'There's a funeral party coming in this afternoon and we're making sausage rolls. Fancy some?'

Chisholm stared at him suspiciously. 'Aye all right.'

Charlie ordered one of the bar staff to make a pot of tea and fetch some sausage rolls. Scarface declined both.

Chisholm sat on a bar stool, easing up slightly. Charlie went on:

'I was saying to your colleague here,' pointing at Scarface, 'you, some friends, your family, are welcome any time to come in to have a bite to eat on us, on me. Here,' he picked a menu lying on the bar and passed it to the mobster, 'have a look. It's fantastic food and a great selection of beers, spirits and wines.'

Chisholm barely glanced at it. 'Look, while we're waiting for the tea and the rolls why don't I show you around. There's a space at the back for private dining.'

Chisholm continued to stare right through Charlie. It was intimidating but he held his ground until Chisholm slowly got off the bar stool and Charlie took him round the venue, including the private dining room which had been set up for the funeral party, chatting continually, playing the part of mine host while Chisholm stayed silent, Scarface at his side. When they came back to the bar, the pot of tea and plate of sausage rolls were waiting.

'So, anytime you want, Mr Chisholm, just let me know in advance and the place is yours. I can arrange for...' and Charlie wittered on about the food he could prepare while Chisholm slurped his tea and devoured the sausage rolls. After eating four, he interrupted Charlie's peroration with:

'These are good.'

'Thank you.'

He ate two more, then said. 'We'll need to be going.'

'Great to meet you.'

There was a further awkward, menacing silence as the

two of them stared hard at him until Charlie realised what was required, broke into a strained smile, bent down and retrieved a white envelope from behind the bar. He was about to hand it to Chisholm, but Scarface came forward and took it from him.

Chisholm said, 'I'll be in touch,' before turning round and walking out the bar with Scarface. Some customers were coming in and Charlie retired to a small windowless office at the back where he was able to wipe the forced smile and break sweat. He was relieved to be away from Chisholm but knew he would have to deal with him a lot more over the next few weeks, if not months, a grim prospect.

But if it meant he would be instrumental in bringing down that cold, dark bastard, it was worth it. And it meant he was above board, legit, his past acts of "delayed restitutions of justice" passed over. He would be Chef Carty, The Legal Equaliser.

He broke into a smile at the thought. Things were going to plan.

It was on Scarface's fifth weekly Friday visit that he announced that his boss wanted to "hire" the private room the following Friday.

'Not a problem,' he declared, 'tell Mr Chisholm it's in hand.'

Through Ali McMahon and the burner phone he met Hutchinson and Ali at the car park that afternoon. The Asian detective wasn't there; she'd been "called away for something else", Hutchinson said.

Hutchinson was delighted at the breakthrough but cautioned that it might take a while, if it happened at all, for

Chisholm to reveal anything that could be used in court.

'He might be cold and hard, but he's a clever bastard. Never underestimate him,' Hutchinson said.

'Don't worry, I won't, Charlie said.

'Good work, Charlie,' Hutchinson congratulated him and left them. Later, back at HQ, he was summoned to Chief Superintendent Patterson's office, the "Gaffer", the regional head of CID and Serious Crime.

'How's it going Stu?' he opened good naturedly to him. Hutchinson was still full of good cheer at the day's developments.

'We've had a breakthrough, Sir. Nat Chisholm's and his cronies have taken up Carty's offer of a free dinner at his boozer and we've got the place all wired up.'

'Great, good stuff,' Patterson congratulated him.

'We not expecting revelations right away, but even if we get the odd snippet now and then, we can still build a case. Nat Chisholm's a heartbeat away from inheriting the top position.'

'Absolutely. And the McGarvey case?'

Hutchinson put his arms out. 'Not so good Sir. Treading water.'

'Well, I've got some good news for you,' the Chief Superintendent leaned forward.

'Huh huh,' Hutchinson said expectantly.

'You're getting a promotion. It's back to uniform, out of CID and organised crime, but it comes with an inspector's badge.' Patterson was beaming at him. Hutchinson was perplexed.

'Doing what Sir? I mean as an inspector.'

'Public Safety, Order and Forward Intelligence. It's a

new post. Pre-empting demonstrations and disturbances from groups like climate protestors, far right and far left demonstrators and the like. You'll be liaising with Council officials, Counter-Terrorism Command, Scottish Government, even the Security Service, the good old MI5. It'll be high profile and you'll be doing lots of media so we'll be sending you for some training, though you've got the gift of the gab so there should be no problem where that's concerned.

'Take some annual leave right away, say two weeks. Meet up with Ben Flannigan this afternoon, hand over to him and then take a wee break.'

Hutchinson was stunned.

'What about my team? Aruna? Gerry Stratton?' The McGarvey case?'

'As you said, "treading water", through no fault of your own, I hasten to add. Aruna and Gerry have been transferred to Ben. They'll work on the Chisholm surveillance with him.'

'I wasn't told about this in advance, Sir.'

Patterson was still smiling, but there was an edge to it now.

'It's part of the job. Skye one day, Dundee the next. It's the way it goes.'

'I really liked working against organised crime. I've been doing it a long time.'

Patterson's smile was beginning to fray. 'There's a lot of things we like doing and a change can be good for us.'

'Was there anything wrong with my performance? My last appraisal was very positive.'

'None whatsoever, Stu. It's a management decision.' He looked at his watch. 'Right, I've got a meeting to go to.' He stood up and Hutchinson knew no further discussion was permitted. Patterson shook hands with him.

'Get that meeting with Ben Flannigan, enjoy your break and I know you'll love public order,' and he was ushered out of the room.

He went back to his office in disbelief. A letter was on his desk confirming his new appointment, his annual leave break and details of the media training course he was to attend.

He popped his head around the squad room. Aruna wasn't at her desk, but Gerry Stratton was studiously working at his PC screen trying to avoid looking at him.

'Where's Aruna?' He asked as he approached him.

'Don't know, Sir.'

'I'm getting kicked upstairs. Did you know?'

Stratton looked like the proverbial rabbit in the headlamps.

'Congratulations, sir. I kind a heard this morning.'

You "kind a heard" did you? Cos, I didn't till just now,' he was almost glaring at the hapless Stratton until he walked back to his own office.

He shut the door and stared out of the window. What the hell had just happened? They'd just made a breakthrough with Chisholm and now he'd been unceremoniously ejected off the case. Was it a faceless, routine police bureaucratic move? Or was there something more sinister to it?

'I couldn't get them out till two. That's way past my permitted opening times, so I hoped you can have a word in the local cops' ears; don't want to lose my licence.'

Charlie was addressing the taciturn Ben Flannigan, the new detective who'd replaced Hutchinson. They were in the Gorbals carpark. Flannigan remained expressionless and just muttered flatly, 'you'll be all right.'

Charlie didn't like this guy. Where Hutchinson was warm and engaging, though Charlie knew there was an edge to him, Flannigan was cold, almost hostile, giving nothing away. He'd appeared in place of Hutchinson at a scheduled carpark meeting with DC Sharma just before the night of Nat Chisholm's "hire" and brusquely announced that DS Hutchinson had been promoted and he was now taking charge of the Chisholm surveillance and wiretap. Ali and Charlie were stunned but reckoned there was little they could do.

This was the second meeting and Charlie was recounting the events of the previous Friday night when Nat Chisholm and his entourage had descended on the bar. There must have been about twenty of them, loud and obnoxious to a man and woman and all the men sporting various shades of scars. The food was devoured, gallons of alcohol consumed, though mercifully no fights broke out.

The businessman in Charlie chafed at the amount of food and alcohol that he was serving free on a busy Friday night. To cap it all, the entire retinue stayed until the wee hours until the main man stood up from the top end of the table and declared:

'That's it, time to go.'

There were no delays or long goodbyes; at the boss's command, they rose from the table, collected coats and jackets and they were all gone within ten minutes. Charlie was impressed. Nat Chisholm exuded command and authority. He was the last to leave with his girlfriend, a slim, pretty bottle blonde. Just as they were leaving, he turned to Charlie at the door.

'That was aw right. Scran was great, eh?' he slapped the girlfriend on the backside who giggled and replied,

'Aye, it wis great.'

Chisholm was well on but could hold his drink. He resumed looking at Charlie and the levity evaporated to be replaced by that grim, menacing stare.

'Any cunt noise you up, let me know about it. Ok?'

Charlie nodded his head and said:

'Any time, Mr Chisholm, any time.'.

That stare felt like a shower of ice had been doused on him as Chisholm walked with the girl to a BMW where a driver sat waiting to take him home.

Later, a casually dressed detective looking more like a delivery driver had shown up at a pre-arranged time on the Saturday afternoon and collected the audio recordings.

'Anything from the recordings?' McMahon asked.

'Naw,' Flannigan said dismissively. 'Too early, they haven't been sifted yet, but we're not expecting much at this stage. This could take months.'

An awkward silence descended before Flannigan brusquely declared:

'I need to go. Anything happens, let me know,' before departing the vehicle followed swiftly by Sharma, who'd not said a word as usual.

'He's a fucking barrel of laughs,' Charlie said sharply to Ali.

'At least they're off our backs,' the private eye replied.

'Aye, I suppose,' Charlie agreed. Ali opened the car door.

'Come on let's get some cheeseburgers. I'm hank marven.'

Aruna Sharma was still seething that her breakthrough on Charlie Carty had never been investigated further. She was amazed and dismayed that her former boss, DS Hutchinson, had come back from a meeting on his own with Ali McMahon a couple of weeks ago and announced they were taking "a different tack" as an "opportunity" had come up that might result in a chance to ensnare the likely heir to Glasgow's leading crime family. Over her protests, Hutchinson argued all they had on Carty was circumstantial; he'd hired a PI to ask questions about McGarvey. There was nothing else and certainly nothing to persuade the Crown, or more importantly, a jury to convict. There was a bigger prize to be gained.

But when she'd gone along with Stu to that second meeting with Charlie Carty and Ali McMahon in the Gorbals carpark, she couldn't keep her eyes off the chef. His build was very similar to that of the black clad biker captured on CCTV at the pizza takeaway and then on the doorbell camera at McGarvey's house. But her biggest shock was when Carty spoke. She was convinced it was exactly the same voice as that of the biker who'd spoken to McGarvey briefly about the "mistaken" pizza delivery.

When she got back to the office she played the dialogue back from the saved recording on her PC. The voice, the tone, the inflection. It was identical to the sound of the late middle-aged man she'd sat behind in the car just forty minutes earlier. She went to her boss's office for one last attempt, but he dismissed her again.

'In the absence of anything else, his defence brief would tear it to shreds. We're going for Nat Chisholm, Aruna, focus on that.'

She liked Hutchinson. He was thorough, fair and respectful where a lot of other DS's thought women detectives should be making the tea, typing up reports or interviewing women and kids. But she really thought he'd become fixated on getting Nat Chisholm and was missing what was in front of them: that if Charlie Carty was the same man as that biker, he was almost certainly Tam McGarvey's killer.

They might not have a motivation, but the lead was good enough to pursue and not doing so really frustrated Aruna even if McGarvey was a murdering sleazebag that deserved everything he had coming. Murder was murder in Aruna's book, and they couldn't go around distinguishing between deserving and undeserving ones. Then Hutchinson got promoted, the McGarvey investigation wound down and transfer to DS Flannigan who was much more your typical CID guy with little in the way of empathy or compassion.

They were halfway back to the station. Aruna was leaning against the passenger side window as they sat at lights. Flannigan didn't do small talk, and she knew when they got back, he would disappear into his office; he wasn't a team player. Taking her head away from the window she decided to take the opportunity here in the car to ask him:

'When do you think, sir, we'll get anything from the surveillance on Nat Chisholm?'

Flannigan was dripping with contempt as he waited for the lights to change.

'It's all fucking politics. There's as much chance of Nat Chisholm shooting his mouth off in that guy's boozer as I have of getting signed up for Real Madrid. The high heidyins are just wanting to show they're doing something about Chisholm. It'll lead nowhere. Honestly, how do you think these guys last?'

Aruna was appalled.

'So, this is all just show. And those leads we have on Charlie Carty are never gonny be used.'

He turned sharply to her.

'What leads?' The lights changed.

'He'd hired McMahon to ask questions about McGarvey as he had done about Kieron McPhail, and he'd done time in prison for the attack on Joe Jamieson, his brother's killer.'

'What the fuck are you on about? Who's Kieron McPhail?' A bevy of car horns blared behind him, and he had to concentrate on driving through the lights. A few hundred yards later he pulled up on a side road.

'What are you talking about?'

She looked closely at him. He appeared genuinely surprised. She'd assumed that Hutchinson would have briefed him on this, but it now occurred to her he hadn't for whatever reason. So, she did, there and then. When she'd finished, he said to her,

'Right, when we get back, I'm going to see DI McGarrigle and you're coming with me to tell him everything you've just told me.' He restarted the car.

Aruna felt conflicted. She felt elated, vindicated even, that Flannigan was taking an interest, maybe even resuming the investigation into Carty. But also worried that she'd got her former boss into some serious trouble.

FIFTEEN

Hordes of people went by on busy Argyle Street on their way to a big concert at the Hydro, a brisk walk away. That only added to their paranoia as they sat in Charlie's car at a MacDonald's drive thru car park in Finneston, red sandstone tenements and a derelict police station on one side and a refurbished, brutalist business complex on the other.

Once Hutchinson had alerted them that afternoon and asked for a crash meeting, they decided the Gorbals car park was too risky, and they opted for here. But with the crowds swirling around them, none of them, including the experienced detective sergeant or the worldly gumshoe, could spot a tail.

'Let's make this brief,' Hutchinson cautioned them.

'What's happened?' Ali McMahon asked.

'I've been suspended,' Hutchinson replied.

'What?' Ali and Charlie responded in unison.

'Aye,' Hutchinson went on grimly. 'I've been on annual leave, and I got a text message around lunchtime today from my boss to come in as soon as possible, so I went in. I knew it was going to be bad when my boss's boss was sitting there. The upshot is that when I was handing over to DI Flannigan, I didn't tell them about the evidence I'd gathered about you Charlie.'

'What evidence?' Charlie shot back from the driver's seat.

'Cut the shite Charlie. We know you hired Ali for info on Joe Jamieson, Kieron McPhail and Tam McGarvey. We've got the doorbell footage and audio of the guy delivering the pizzas and making his way into the house and he's got your build and speaks remarkably like you. Ok, it's not a watertight case, but it's a good start.

'I'd have come for you, Charlie, make no mistake about that, but when Ali here let me know Chisholm's goons were putting the screws on you and suggested a way of setting the bastard up for a fall, it was too good a chance to pass up.

'But that young detective constable on my fast-dwindling team, Aruna Sharma, had other ideas. She's a straight down the middle, play it by the book type and she went and blabbed to Flannigan that I hadn't pursued you and the upshot is I'm suspended pending an investigation. Which means the surveillance op on Nat Chisholm - which that dour cunt, Flannigan, never had faith in anyway - will likely be abandoned.

'The upshot is they'll be coming for you two, right away, if they haven't already put a tail on you.'

'Since you're call this afternoon, I've been hyper-alert and seen nothing,' Ali said.

'I appreciate your ex-special forces, Ali, but even the best of us can lose a tail in this crowd.'

Charlie shot a glance at Ali, who ignored him. He'd no idea Ali had been in the military far less special forces which for Charlie meant SAS. It'd been Ali's idea to shift the meeting to here, lest the cops were onto them already after Stu's call that afternoon not realising there was a sold-out concert nearby.

'So, what's likely to happen?' Ali inquired.

'Most likely they'll haul you in first, Ali. Threaten you with immediate cancellation of your licence if you don't play ball, then they'll move on to our esteemed chef here.'

'And Nat Chisholm?' Charlie asked.

Hutchinson let out a deep breath.

'I doubt they'll continue with the surveillance. I realise now it was all smoke and mirrors, a decoy to pretend they were being serious about moving on him.'

'He gets a free pass to take over,' Ali put in.

'Some people in this city think it's better one guys in charge. Keeps the peace and avoids a bloodbath. Nat Chisholm gets the "licence". That's the way this is going.'

'Fuck,' Charlie said bitterly.

'Fuck, indeed,' Hutchinson agreed. He opened the door slightly. 'My career in the polis is over and you two need to look out for yourselves.' He opened the door wider, 'take care, it was good while it lasted.'

'Thanks for the heads up, it's appreciated,' Charlie said. The DS paused at the car door, nodded his head, then shut the door and merged into the crowd.

Charlie put his head against the steering wheel, despair enveloping him. 'What the hell do we do now?'

'How much dosh have you got in the bank?'

'What the fuck's that got to do with anything?'

'Because you're going to need all the money you have if you want to avoid a rap. Come on, you're loaded after you sold up to that French company. How much?'

Charlie reluctantly told him.

'That should last you a couple of years.'

'I've got two sons.'

'Who can always see their faither in prison; a great place for a man to be in his sixties. Come on. They'll be fine. A lot of folk will see you as a hero anyway.'

'What you suggesting?'

'You need to go off grid.'

'Is that your special forces training kicking in? Oh, and thanks for letting me know about that.'

'It wasn't relevant at the time.'

The crowds were thinning now and rain started falling.

'I can't believe that murdering, thieving mobster's getting away with it. They're letting him take over,' Charlie slapped the steering wheel in anger. Then he remembered. In his agitation at Ali's phone call with the news that Stu Hutchinson had suddenly resurfaced and was demanding a crash meeting, then the DS's subsequent ominous revelations, he'd completely forgotten about developments that afternoon shortly before Ali's call.

Scarface had appeared in the pub that morning. At first Charlie thought this foreshadowed Chisholm demanding a bigger cut of the takings, but the goon was there to inform him that "Mr Chisholm" was looking to have the room for himself and "a few pals" on Friday, three days hence, and if possible, could Charlie throw in some food and drink.

Charlie was excited. The more Nat Chisholm used the room, the better the chances he would loosen up and the cops could get something on him that would prevent his ascendancy to major domo of Glasgow's leading underworld family.

Of course, that hope was now obliterated by Stu Hutchinson's news and a bitter helplessness replaced it. He updated Ali whose face lit up.

'Now that's interesting, Charlie Carty, very interesting.'

Charlie appraised him closely.

'What's going through that devious mind of yours, McMahon?'

'How far are you prepared to go on this, Charlie?'

'Fuck's sake man, you're talking in riddles. We could be huckled at any time.'

'Calm down, Charlie. We need to talk. Let's go for a drink. I know a quiet place.'

The rain was becoming heavier. Charlie started the engine and turned the windscreen wipers on.

'Where to? I could murder a drink.'

Half-cut, Ali McMahon turned his computer on and typed his password. It was just gone past five in the morning and dawn was appearing through the window behind him that gave a desolate view of the office block behind him. He'd let himself in with the fob which allowed him to access the building as he occasionally had to have meetings with clients in the evenings or at weekends.

He first composed an email to Pat, his remaining assistant after he'd sacked Danni Hayes. Apologising for the short notice, he informed Pat he was closing the business with immediate effect "due to unforeseen circumstances", thanked him for his "excellent service", notified him he'd transferred six month's salary into his bank account, attached a glowing reference with the email and wished him well for the future. He checked it over a few times until he was satisfied, pissed as he was, it made some sort of sense and pressed the send button.

The timing was fortunate. There were only four active cases on the books, all being handled by Pat and coming to a natural end. Since getting in hock with Charlie Carty, Ali had effectively let his agency run down and not taken on new clients. He'd been growing increasingly disillusioned with the grubby world of private investigation for years; he'd little enthusiasm for it left and he'd be glad to get out of it.

Ali McMahon lived frugally in a one-bedroom flat in Parkhead on the east side of the city which he'd bought years ago, after he'd left the army, and long paid off. He'd accumulated substantial savings which could keep him going for a few years. His army experience had also taught him how, if needed, he could live off-grid without little or no public presence, including utilities and offline.

Apart from his agencies' sparse one page website, he'd never used social media. An only child, he had no ties, no relations and no family. Apart from a brief flirtation with a girl in the army many moons ago, he'd never had a relationship with a woman and nobody he could call a close friend. He was on his own; an inveterate loner, and if truth be told he preferred it that way.

In the past he'd lived incognito and was unafraid of doing so again for however long it took. Tomorrow, he'd travel by train to Girvan, a small Scottish seaside town on the Firth of Clyde where he would pay in cash six month's rent in advance for a cottage on farmland belonging to a former special forces comrade, who was probably the nearest person to a friend he had, though he did increasingly regard Charlie Carty in that light.

He was privy to Carty's activities for years now since the Joe Jamieson affair. He'd had a fair idea what Charlie was going to do to Kieron McPhail, though not the details and then there was the step up to a different league with Tam McGarvey. He'd admired the gory, gothic balls of that, which he'd done on his own, including the macabre twists of the sleeping pills and that neat touch of using McGarvey's own phone to lure his brother and all his goons to witness his savage humiliation. That was class.

Though counselling caution at first, he'd steadily been galvanised and re-energised by Charlie's fortitude and determination. It reminded him of his days with the regiment in Iraq when they went after bad guys without heed and eliminated terrorists relentlessly. It was Old Testament, eye for an eye, tooth for a tooth.

Back in civvy street he was immensely frustrated at what bad guys could get away with and the puny sentences meted out to them if or when they were caught. Charlie Carty saw massive injustice with what happened to his brother and the laughable "punishment" doled out to his killer. He acted, messed it up, but learned. He'd effectively destroyed a nasty bunch of hoodlums by taking out the main man and his brother.

And now when he and Charlie had come up with a way to work with law enforcement on taking down gangland boss Nat Chisholm, it was being thrown aside in favour of punishing

Charlie for the temerity of going for the bad guys and upsetting someone's corrupt and perverse idea of what would keep the peace. No, there was something fundamentally wrong about that.

They'd spent the night bevving in an old guy's bar in Shettleston where amid drunken bedlam they'd gathered in an alcove where Ali had put forward his plan to Charlie. A plan he'd only come up with virtually on the hoof after Stu Hutchinson announced that he and Charlie were in the frame for the murder of McGarvey at the expense of the takedown of Nat Chisholm.

He'd poured Charlie home in a taxi and hoped that when he awoke in the full flow of his hangover, Charlie wouldn't have second thoughts, but Ali doubted he would.

Having sent the email to his former employee, he then proceeded to systematically delete every single client file on his hard drive including the innocuous ones dealing with Charly. Despite constant efforts by service providers, he'd kept his files away from the Cloud. Once they were all deleted, he switched his PC off, unplugged it and proceeded to unscrew the terminal and take out the actual hard drive from its casing.

Placing the hard drive in a plastic shopping bag, he took one last glance around the office where he'd been based for the last fifteen years, confident he'd left nothing incriminating there, switched off the light and locked the door. He let himself out of the building by the fob which he put in an envelope and sent through the letterbox before walking in the gathering light up to Argyle Street where he'd catch an early bus to his flat.

Aruna Sharma had had a sleepless night. Word had buzzed around the squad room, which it always did in open plans, that Stu Hutchinson had been suspended. There was much speculation as to why that was, but Aruna knew well why.

She'd never seen the normally po-faced DS Flannigan become so animated as when she'd disclosed the information on Charlie Carty which Stu had failed to pass on. Her reservations about dobbing her former boss in had been temporarily forgotten when she'd listened in on some of the audio feed from the Chisholm surveillance that had been handed in late that afternoon.

Aruna had been told by Flannigan to expect to focus on the private eye, McMahon and the Chef, Carty over the next few days, but she'd not been formally taken off the McGarvey case. Listening to the feed, she heard one of Chisholm's henchmen ask Carty for Nat Chisholm and his cronies to use the private function room this coming Friday. Aruna thought her boss should be updated on this immediately, but he was dismissive.

'That's all been superseded, DC Sharma. We'll interview McMahon on Thursday. I want you to concentrate on that.'

'So, will there be anybody watching Carty's place on Friday, or listening to the tapes?'

Flannigan shook his head resolutely.

'Naw. I've already told you, waste of time and resources. I've had no formal instructions yet to stop the surveillance, but it'll be in the post. Now get to work on McMahon and prepare some good questions for when we bring him in on Thursday.'

Aruna was appalled. There would be no background police presence, nobody snapping clandestine pictures, when a known leading Glasgow criminal was associating with his henchmen and no one monitoring the feed from the surveillance. Why?

Although she had reservations about Hutchinson's tactics, she'd never questioned his motive. Flannigan was different. A grey timeserver who swung with the wind. She was now beginning to detest him. She felt really complicit in destroying her former boss, a fundamentally decent guy. For the first time in her meteoric police career, she had real doubts about what she was doing.

She got out of bed and went to the kitchen of her small one-bedroom flat in Shawlands, which she'd just recently bought with a mortgage that stretched her even though she'd put almost all of her savings she'd spent years amassing, into it.

She stretched and yawned, put the kettle on, sat down at the small breakfast bar, her boyfriend, a handyman for a local community centre and disapproved by her snobby sister and oh so middle-class parents, had built. As the kettle boiled and she looked out over the backcourts, some washing left overnight fluttering in the early morning sunlight, a feeling of immense guilt engulfed her. What the hell had she done? And how could she rectify it?

Charlie woke up with a massive hangover. His days, when he could bevvy with ease mixing the grape and the grain, endless pints of beer, whisky and cheap red wine, as he had done last night with Ali McMahon in the auld man's hangout in Shettleston, were long over. He checked the bedside alarm clock. It was past eleven.

These days, if he wasn't working at the Camlachie Arms which was rare, he rarely slept past nine. A thousand worries and concerns combined with the demands of a late middle age bladder frequently interrupted his sleep. The boose had temporarily sedated that but, awake now, his full bladder was urging relief on him which compelled him out of bed and into the loo.

Afterwards, he sat on his luxurious living room sofa contemplating last night's deliberations with Ali McMahon while swigging a bottle of water by his side.

He was in his early sixties, and he'd had quite a journey. He'd worked and made a success in the maddest profession in the world that made extraordinary demands of you. He'd risen high and survived the fallout from the collapse of the Forsyth empire, resurfaced, created his own thriving business, been the personal chef of a head of state. Not forgetting Calum and Caleb, his two amazing sons who he was so proud of. Whatever happened, they would carry on his legacy.

Then there'd been the lows: Raymond's murder, his mother's death, Sarah leaving and no reconciliation and no prospects of one as she was happily settled in a relationship with Luigi Martello. He still loved and pined for her, but the unalterable truth was, it was over, and he couldn't conceive of going out with anybody else.

He'd done time and coped with prison. He'd put Jamieson in a coma and had no regrets. He'd given the racist twat and the thug McPhail, two lifelong losers who should have been dealt with long ago by a lousy, feeble justice system, a doing they would never forget and rid the city of that parasitical, psycho McGarvey and his brother.

His attempts to go legit and work with the law on preventing the ascent of Nat Chisholm had been thwarted by wider forces he only had a glimmer of understanding, and he was angry at that, very angry.

Ali McMahon, the only person apart from his sons and his undiminished love for Sarah, that he felt close to, had come up with a solution, a Plan B. A crazy, dangerous madcap idea.

He knew the scary fragility of the hangover would hit him soon as the alcohol detoxed his system. But he also knew there was no going back. It was the culmination of his equaliser journey that had begun with the attempt on Joe Jamieson.

If the law wouldn't deal with Godfather-in-waiting, Nat Chisholm, then Ali McMahon and he, Chef Carty, would.

Ali McMahon wasn't home when DC Sharma, DC Gerry Stratton and DI Flannigan swooped on his Parkhead flat on the Thursday morning. Flannigan raced to get a search warrant, and they broke into the flat later that morning, but found nothing of any value. Flitting over to the AMAC offices they found a bemused concierge informing them the business had folded. They searched the office anyway and took computers and files, but the search was again futile.

Later that afternoon the three tecs gathered in Flannigan's office. McMahon had flown the coop, so it was imperative they detain Charlie Carty. Flannigan wanted to make the arrest early the next morning at his luxury west end flat, but Aruna Sharma made a strong case that they may as well hold back for twenty-four hours, let Carty host Nat Chisholm and his cronies for one final soiree with his associates and then detain him.

Aruna nailed it by appealing to the careerist and survivor in Flanigan.

'After all, if we closed the operation before we arrest Carty, we might lose up on getting something, unlikely though it might be, from the feed. Sort of killing two birds with one stone.'

Flannigan conceded and agreed they would arrest Carty on the Saturday morning; it was unlikely he would scarper before hosting Chisolm.

She also insisted there be background surveillance to supplement the audio. Flannigan, again, reluctantly agreed.

'All right, you and Gerry take a car, two cameras and conceal yourselves. But be fresh for Saturday morning. We're going in early for Carty.'

Back in the squad room, Aruna felt pleased with herself. It wouldn't amount to anything, the take would likely be zero, but she'd retrieved some of her self-respect knowing that there would be some police coverage of Nat Chisholm's second and probably last free night at the Camlachie Arms, courtesy of Charlie Carty.

SIXTEEN

From the top of the two steps that led to the private dining room, Charlie surveyed the wide expanse of the bar/diner from the restaurant section across to the tables and seats that made up the bar area and the customers waiting to be served at the bar itself.

It was past nine on a Friday night and it was going like a fare. The restaurant was fully booked, every table in the bar area was occupied and they were standing knee deep at the bar. In an industry bedevilled by recession and closures the Camlachie Arms was a stunning success.

Charlie had wanted it to be a community pub when he'd taken it over; accessible, affordable and popular with local people. Looking across and seeing the range of families, couples and groups of people, all good natured, in high spirits and letting their hair down at the end of the working week, Charlie considered he'd more than succeeded in that endeavour.

And that's what worried him.

He'd thought of closing the pub to the public and reserving it for Chisholm and his group. That way there would be no danger to customers and local people. Of course that would have seriously annoyed the new owners, Landis, with the loss of revenue on a busy Friday. But Charlie had clout with them, and he could have sweet talked his way round them.

No, the real problem was that it may have aroused Nat Chisholm's suspicion and innate paranoia. The businessman in him would have thought it strange that Charlie would have foregone an entire evening's takings on one of the busiest nights of the weeks to provide him with a free night. That didn't add up.

He had to make the evening appear as routine as normal. His heart had sunk earlier when, about six, a large family group of about twelve who'd booked a table, had appeared with two young children and a baby in its mother's arms. The children, despite being checked frequently by their parents, were running around, though thankfully had not gone into the private room.

Charlie breathed a deep sigh of relief when the family group requested their bill and were now collecting their coats and belongings and gathering the kids. One less thing to worry about. But there were still plenty of civilians around including two people in wheelchairs, not forgetting the bar staff and waiters: lots of opportunity for collateral damage.

He spotted Malky, Bert and Sam, the trio who had alerted him to and set him on the trail of Kieron McPhail, in with their wives drinking at a table near the bar.

Behind him he could hear the raucous sound of Chisholm's party, about ten guys, nearly all scarred, with a smattering of scantily clad molls with Chisholm clearly at the helm, exuding control, Scarface sitting beside him. Charlie, in his whites, along with his under-manager, was serving them personally. He'd had one friendly exchange with the main man at the start of the night, welcoming him and his friends once more which Chisholm returned with,

'You're a gentleman, Charlie,' then turning to his acolytes, 'top man here, runs a great fucking place here and will be serving us up some top food, so, respect,' and raised his glass to him, the cue for the rest to do as well.

Otherwise, aside from the loud banter and guzzling of large quantities of booze all was proceeding well and they weren't interfering with the other customers. They were now well on with their main course. Charlie checked his watch. Another hour. Time seemed to crawl.

He saw the large family group begin to make their way to the door and automatically snapped back into mein host mode, moving rapidly ahead of them to bid them good night.

Behind, and to the side of the bar/diner, was a car park for a set of retail units which provided great passing trade for the pub. Some of those premises were still open and the car park was reasonably full. An inconspicuous grey Skoda was parked halfway along. Inside, Aruna Sharma and Gerry Stratton sat trying to dispel the monotony which always accompanies most surveillance ops.

They'd been occupied earlier with taking discreet pictures of Chisholm's entourage arriving and entering the pub. Gerry Stratton, a veteran tec in his late thirties, recognised most of the faces and entertained the younger DC Sharma with lively stories of who was who and their previous convictions.

Gerry had noticed a red Fiat parked in front of the pub just about the time Chisholm arrived. It was late July, and the first sentiment of dusk was gathering, but the sharp-eyed tec spotted who the driver and passenger were in the Fiat.

'That's the protection unit. They'll sit there and follow

Chisholm's car home.'

'I wish we could get a protection unit when we need it,' she said to him.

Stratton laughed derisively.

'I sometimes wonder if we're in the wrong job.'

Aruna nodded. 'I know the feeling.'

Now they sat in silence listening to some background Indy music on Six Radio. It was likely the duo would only have a few hours' sleep as they were expecting Chisholm's group to leave around one or two am and they were due to hit Charlie Carty's Kirklees flat around seven tomorrow morning and take him into custody. Aruna still felt bad about Stu Hutchinson and the deflection from Nat Chisholm. But at least she'd compelled Flannigan to put a token observation on what was probably this last gathering of Chisholm's henchmen in Charlie Carty's bar before he re-entered the maws of Scotland's criminal justice system in the morning.

Now, she tried to stifle a yawn and knew the biggest struggle in the hours to come would be to fight off sleep. Stratton tried to keep them both awake by asking:

'Seen any good movies lately?'

It would be a long night.

Around nine-thirty, a dirty blue Datsun slipped into the far side of the car park at a blind spot unseen by the protection unit, whose focus was on the front of the bar, or by the two detectives in the retail car park behind.

The driver, clad in black from head to toe, brought out

a disposable Nokia mobile from his jacket, switched it on, placed it on the dashboard and waited.

Charlie's radar spotted an altercation developing between two regulars at the bar which he quickly doused by threatening them both with a thirty-day ban. It was effective as he knew it would be. They virtually lived in the bar and immediately made up and shook hands.

He moved onto the entrance as more customers, not regulars but people leaving the shops in the retail unit that were shutting, entered for a drink or a late-night snack and he spent a good twenty minutes expertly maneuvering between departing customers and finding seats for new arrivals and taking orders, deftly and swiftly executed like the seasoned old pro he was.

It was packed, but finally the pressure eased, and he went into the bustling, buzzing kitchen.

'Ok, clear the main courses, then take dessert orders from the private room.' Charlie's undermanager instructed two waiters to accompany him to carry out the task. Charlie went to the back of the kitchen to an alcove where staff hung their jackets and coats. He took a burner mobile from the pocket of a dark padded Gilet he'd worn to work and typed:

Desserts about to be ordered. Three minutes

And sent the message.

He breathed deeply, feeling nervous and tried to calm himself. He walked back through the frenetic kitchen, out into the busy bar, past the restaurant section, breathed again, and walked into the private area where the under manager and the two waiters were expertly scooping up the mainly empty plates and utensils.

'Food all right, Nat?' Charlie asked the top man as he jauntily walked past him.

'Fucking first rate, Charlie.' Heads nodded and there were murmurs of vibrant approval from around Chisholm.

'Brand new, Nat. I'll let the kitchen know,' Charlie continued into a short corridor and out of sight of the group.

The driver in the Datsun received the message on the Nokia. He put the phone back in his jacket, checked his pockets, left the car and walked towards the back end of the diner. In contrast to the blaze of lights at the front, the back was pitch black, except for lights from the small inlet windows at the kitchen; the only noise the humming of the air conditioning units and extractor fans.

The driver clambered down a short slope covered with soil and plants onto the concrete apron behind the bar. Apart from the kitchen and fire exits in the middle and far end of the building, this seemed to be all solid brick wall until the dark clad driver suddenly heard a click and a door open, it's outline indistinguishable from the brickwork around it.

He recognised the figure of Charlie Carty in the doorway who just muttered out of the corner of his mouth:

'Three seats along, left hand side of the table,' before turning round and walking back into the bar.

The black clad figure followed, Charlie darting ahead,

along a short corridor which turned into a longer passageway with lights ahead. Behind, he heard the door clanging shut and looked back, but there was no one there and he reckoned it was probably caused by a breeze.

Moving ahead, he could see the private dining room, as Charlie had described it to him. As he entered it his aim was clear, ignore the hubbub around the table and focus on the muscular but wiry guy sitting on the third seat on the left side of the table. The party in the private room all seemed relaxed, laughing and joking, talking across each other. Charlie had left the room, and he could see no other staff as he put his hand into his jacket and brought out a black Glock, G17 Luger nine-millimeter pistol.

For the dark clad figure, everything seemed to go into slow motion as he clicked the magazine ready to fire the gun. It was only seconds, but no one stirred or noticed his entrance; it was as if in the apparent safety of the diner, in the assured presence of their boss, with the protection unit outside, these experienced mobsters could drop their guard.

He aimed the pistol at his target's head and saw the tall scar faced guy beside him suddenly becoming aware of the pistol and began to react but not before the gunman fired three shots in quick succession into Nat Chisholm's head, causing blood, gore and bits of brain to splatter and everyone else in the room to be frozen into stunned, terrified inactivity.

The gunman knew this would only last a few seconds, turned and made his way back along the passageway as the crowd came round and he heard screams and the clattering of chairs as people clambered below tables. He went into the short corridor and could just make out the frame of the now closed door in the semi-darkness then to his horror realised there was no door handle. With his gloved hand he tried to press open the door but there was no leverage, then he saw the spring lock and knew to his sickening dismay the door had self-locked when the breeze had slammed it shut. He could see no key in the lock and heard footsteps rapidly coming up the corridor.

He cocked and slid the magazine again and walked back into the corridor having no option but to confront whoever was there and try and make his way out the bar another way as he was trapped here.

As he darted into the passageway he almost bumped into the tall scar faced guy who was holding a gun. Instinctively, he fired and pumped two more bullets directly at the guy causing him to collapse on the floor; it was near point blank range. Holding his gun in front of him, on hair-trigger alert, with four bullets left in the chamber, the gunman moved up to the chaos of the bright light ahead of him that was the private room.

Some new Indy band was playing a demo on the radio when Aruna, head pressed against the passenger window, heroically struggling to fend off sleep, heard the sharp crack emanate from inside the pub. Instantly alert, she looked at Stratton.

'What was that?'

'That sounds like gunfire.'

Aruna had no training or experience with guns, but Stratton had.

'Definitely gunfire,' he repeated.

Then they heard the screams.

'Bloody hell, something's going down there,' Stratton shouted.

'I'll report in,' Aruna said. She cut the music and picked up the extendable mike for the police radio and was just about to call in for armed police assistance as they were unarmed when her colleague bellowed:

'Fuck's sake, Chisholm's people are going in and they're tooled up!'

Aruna looked up to see two guys running from the red Fiat towards the entrance of the pub, one of them clearly with a gun in his hand.

'This is going to be a shitstorm,' Gerry Stratton declared as Aruna feverishly worked the controls of the radio.

Charlie was at the bar when he heard the sharp report of the gunfire from the private room.

'What was that?' Arleen, a young waitress preparing to take a tray of glasses across to a table, asked.

Charlie shrugged his shoulders, trying to keep calm, 'don't know, I'll check it out.'

Half of the bar and all of the restaurant section had heard the noise and were looking over at the open entrance to the private area, which inclined at an angle preventing them from seeing in.

'Fireworks in the private function room, Charlie? You got a license for that?' Malky asked jovially from his table in front of the bar. Charlie smiled at him as he made his way to the room only for the screaming to start and two of the women rushed out, white faced, panicking and distraught. Instantly, the atmosphere across the bar switched to tension and fear.

Charlie climbed the two steps to the room and saw Chisholm's shattered, mangled head lying back on the blood-soaked chair. He just managed to take in some of Chisholm's henchmen hiding underneath the table, some who were sitting near him, saturated in his blood, when he saw the gunman come from the passageway.

Charlie was perplexed. This wasn't part of the plan. The gunman registered this on his face and said loudly in a strained voice:

'The fucking door self-locked.' Then, equally loudly, he shouted:

'DIVE!'

Charlie ducked and felt something like a supersonic fly whizz past him, fell to the floor, heard two loud cracks in succession, then a thud before looking up and seeing the gunman aim his pistol again at the open doorway to the room. He looked over and saw a ginger haired man slumped on the floor, a large expanding pool of blood forming around him

Charlie recognised the guy on the ground as the man who'd driven Chisholm home the last time he'd had a free night in the bar. He heard the gunman shout

'There's another cunt behind him,' before edging against the wall and moving slowly to the doorway.

Charlie's attention was suddenly taken up by a movement to his left. One of Chisholm's goons, hiding below the table, shot out an arm and attempted to grab hold of the gunman's legs. Charlie sprung up, stood on the guy's arm with one foot, grabbed an empty pint glass from the table, shattered it against the edge of the table and rammed the jagged glass into the guy's left cheek. A fountain of blood spurted out, splashing Charlie's whites while the guy loosened up and gurgling noises emerged from his throat.

Charlie stood up. The women screamed while the rest of the men cowered under the table except for one guy at the far end of the table who eyed him with implacable hatred.

'You're clocked ya cunt.'

Charlie knew that meant auld man Sammy Chisholm and his successors would place a contract on him and hunt him for life. Any attempt to ride this out and claim Nat Chisholm's assassin was a hired hitman and had nothing to do with Charlie was extinguished.

With the shattered glass still in his hand, Charlie backed up behind the gunman, eyeing the henchman carefully.

'How do we get out of here? The gunman asked.

'Along the bar to the end, turn right into the kitchen and out the back.'

'That fucker's still out there,' he said, meaning the second man in Chisholm's protection unit. 'I'll divert him. Follow close behind me.'

The gunman darted from the wall and fired up into the ceiling above the restaurant section. Across the restaurant and bar, apart from a few brave souls who had darted out, people were hiding below tables, clutching hold of each other, some using their mobiles with trembling hands. The terror in the air was palpable.

'Run!' the gunman commanded, and Charlie followed him out the private room, down the steps, sidling along the bar making an arching sweep with the Glock, hopefully deterring the other guy from the protection unit who'd mingled with the customers, until they reached the end of the bar.

He spotted Malky, Bert and Sam and their wives, terror stricken below their table and fleetingly thought, 'how the hell did it come to this?' before pressing on towards the kitchen.

Just at the entrance to it, Charlie heard sirens approaching outside.

'Just what we need, the law,' the gunman spat out.

He rose up, as did Charlie. Just as Charlie and the gunman were about to barge through the swinging kitchen door a shot rang out and a bullet sped past, making the same sound as the "supersonic fly" that had whizzed past Charlie's earlier in the private room, before embedding itself in the wall.

The gunman turned round and blasted a shot in the direction of the bar area. He had no definite target, and the shot was panicked and rushed. Charlie felt like crumbling as he saw Malky on the ground, with the now familiar stream of blood gushing from his temple, his wife beside him, screaming blue murder.

Charlie was numb. They'd killed a customer; what was going on? He just wanted to lie down and stay there, but the gunman grabbed hold of him, and they barged through into the empty kitchen, staff having fled, cookers, pots and pans still sizzling, simmering and bubbling, to the back area, through the exit, fans and extractors still humming, out into the fresh night air.

Sirens and flashing blue lights seemed to be descending on them from all directions.

SEVENTEEN

'We killed a customer, a fucking regular. I'm meant to serve customers, not fucking kill them!' Charlie remonstrated loudly with the gunman at the back of the Camlachie Arms with the sound of the sirens fast approaching.

'Jesus Christ, Charlie, I didn't mean to kill him. I had to get a blast away to deter Chisholm's man. Come on. I've got one bullet. The cops are approaching. We need to scatter. I'll see you at the fallback. Now Move!'

Charlie pulled himself together as the gunman ran back up the slight slope to his Datsun.

Taking in deep breaths and attempting to calm himself, Charlie walked briskly just as the first police cars and ambulance arrived in the pub car park. He went to the retail car park, to a white Renault parked outside a now shuttered discount furniture store. He'd bought the car second hand two days ago when he and the gunman were formulating their plans, including the fallback.

He started the car, reversed, and drove out the near empty car park noticing a woman walking swiftly, almost running to a blue Skoda, parked at the opposite end. He couldn't make her out, exited the car park, turned left just as three police cars flew past him on the opposite lane and the cops blocked off the approach to the car park and the pub.

The gunman entered the Datsun, started the engine and drove out by a side entrance and traversed a roundabout just as that too was about to be closed off by the police. He lived a short distance away and knew these streets intimately. As he approached Shettleston, he slowed down and looked in his rear-view mirror. He discarded the balaclava and had already placed the Glock back in his jacket.

Checking his reflection in the rear view mirror, Ali McMahon blew out his cheeks. It'd been quite a fuck-up. The original plan had been for a quick exit out the normally unused back door and away in the Datsun leaving Charlie to try to bluff it out and stay in civvy street as he'd wanted to.

The door shutting with no key had dashed that and then the shoot out and bloodbath followed. As well as Chisholm, the target, the collateral was Scarface, the ginger-haired protection unit guy and the customer, the civilian. Yes, the civilian.

He'd killed a civilian before. In Iraq, during a search in hostile Anbar province in fledgling ISIS territory. It was a known ISIS compound, more a collection of huts, really. They'd stormed in by helicopter and he was in a room holding two guys at gunpoint on the floor when something caught his eye and a figure moved across the doorway. He instinctively opened fire and the figure fell. It was a fourteen-year-old boy, son of one of the guys on the ground. He'd been hiding from the soldiers beneath a bed in an adjoining bedroom.

Ali could still hear the mother's wailing to this day. The teenager was classified as a "combatant" and a "legitimate kill". That was Iraq. He tried to put that behind him, and he would need to do the same with the customer as he drove out to the nearby Campsie Hills where he'd get rid of the gear he'd worn for the hit and secure the Glock. Then he'd transfer to another car and drive to the cottage in Girvan where the farmer on whose land the cottage was on, if needed, would testify that he and Ali, a former comrade-in-arms, had been savouring a bottle of Glenlivet the entire evening.

'Shite!'

Mick Sinclair, otherwise referred to as "Sinky" unclutched the trigger of his Baretta 92FS handgun as he leaned against the kitchen doorway. His target, the gunman who'd assassinated his boss, had just moved as he had him in his sight and spurted up the small slope to the right out of sight.

The other, fair-haired guy in the chef's whites, who he knew to be the manager of the bar, moved up the slope in the other direction where he could clearly see a car park and a row of business units. There were only two cars parked there, a Renault in front of the row and a blue Skoda to the side of the bar. The chef was running to the Renault.

Sinky had to make a split decision. Chase the chef or try and find the gunman. He chose the chef who was in obvious cahoots with his boss's killer. Placing the Baretta in his jacket, he moved quickly through the deserted kitchen with its eerily burbling pots, into the bar, slowed his pace and mingled with the rattled customers, most of whom were fleeing out the bar. He went unrecognised as he joined the exodus out into the car park as a barrage of police vehicles, their sirens merging into one continuous cacophony, were about to descend.

Several cars were leaving the car park and Sinky swiftly jumped into the red Fiat and followed the other cars out the entrance just as the first cop cars were turning into it. Up ahead was a set of traffic lights; they were at red, and four cars were stopped ahead of him. He began to slow down when the lights turned to red and amber and he smiled as he saw the Renault scoot across the road. Sinky speeded up, hit the lights and turned left in pursuit of the Renault just in time as behind him a cop car blocked the road it's blue light flashing.

He rapidly made speed on the Renault, then braked as more police cars shot up the opposite lane. There were lights ahead, but they were at green, and he could still see the Renault. Yet more police cars and vans went past, and he knew they'd be coming from the compound at London Road Police Station which he passed on his right as he drove through the lights still at green.

Once past the lights, in a deserted area of garages, repair units and empty factories there were no more police cars, and he accelerated the Fiat and soon had the Chef's car in his sights.

Sinky had worked for Nat Chisholm since he'd been released from a juvenile prison or Young Offender's Institute (YOI's) as they were called in Scotland, eight years earlier. Waiting for him on his liberation from Polmont YOI was his best friend, Stevie McCartney with his ginger mop. Stevie couriered for one of Alex Chisholm's sons, the ruthless Nat and he enrolled Sinky on Nat's payroll.

Both Sinky and Stevie were good with their fists, had no qualms about doling out merciless beatings that included a variety of instruments, were quick learners and handy with firearms and excellent getaway drivers. They were natural recruits for Nat's close protection unit as his star ascended, and he became the favourite to succeed his granddad.

For Sinky, as for Stevie, it was an exhilarating life. Money, fast cars, women, the fear and respect from others, the power was intoxicating. Sure, there was constant danger: from the cops or the few rivals who dared to contest the Chisholm's. But that only added to the buzz.

Working for crap wages behind a bar, in a fast-food joint, or God forbid in some awful office at the behest of some suited up prick just didn't cut it. Going legit had nothing to offer him. And if he was cut down, just like Stevie had been back there in the bar, it was an acceptable risk and better than being a minion.

Stevie's killer had gotten away, for now. But the chef guy would be second best. He'd obviously something to do with Nat being shot and getting him would put him in a good place in auld man Chisholm's eyes.

Besides, killing someone closely connected to his chief's death would clear him of any involvement in the murderous and paranoiac atmosphere of revenge that would follow.

And, if the Chisholm's grip on the city did finally falter and it was widely reckoned the old boy didn't have much time left, it would be anarchy out there and a good gun-for-hire would always be in demand.

He noticed the Renault making a sharp turn left onto Dalmarnock Road that led to a bridge over the River Clyde and the nearby city boundary. He wanted to get this over fast and shot the car forward before that conniving, treacherous bastard of a chef tried to leave the city.

It was chaos in the pub car park as alarmed customers started piling out of the Camlachie Arms, many of them on their mobiles after the gunfire had subsided. Upon hearing the approaching police sirens, Aruna and Gerry climbed out of the Skoda and clambered down to the carpark to meet the approaching police convoy. The police would impose a lockdown and surround the pub before entering as there were gunmen in there. Aruna and Gerry would meet the first police responders and assist them. She knew that apart from a bevy of mobsters, including Nat Chisholm, two of his armed protection unit were in there and she could give them rough descriptions.

When they reached the car park more people were streaming out, some making for their vehicles. Gerry touched Aruna's arm

'The Fiat,' he pointed at the car.

Aruna looked over. One of the protection unit guys, unnoticed by them, had got behind the wheel and was edging the Fiat forward. Aruna could see that he would make it out the carpark before the first police cars arrived.

'Radio in!' she shouted at Gerry, 'I'll tail him. Just get me back up.'

'Don't be daft Aruna. I'll...' But she was away dashing up the short slope and making for the Skoda.

They'd already radioed in the Fiat's details on their obs duty earlier, but as soon as Aruna got back to the Skoda, she radioed she was following the Fiat, requesting backup, drove left onto the road and approached the crossroads. She could see the Fiat on this road receding rapidly southwards, but the junction at the lights was now blocked by a patrol car. She screeched to a halt. A young, uniformed cop came up to her and said to her.

'I'm sorry miss but you'll have to...'

'...I'm CID,' she interrupted him, her window wound down, her ID card in her hand. 'I'm pursuing the red Fiat that's been driven by one of the gunmen from the pub,' she said rapidly and almost breathlessly. 'Now, out of my way.'

'Ok, the policeman said, straightening up, 'but I'll need to...'

She didn't hear him as she shot the car forward, steered round the blocking squad car and drove ahead. She could see the Fiat way in the distance, then lost it as the road turned while shouting updates into the police radio and being assured by control, they were dispatching cars to assist her.

She drove past the police station, just making the lights at the crossroads, hit about eighty miles per hour, her adrenaline kicking in, followed the turn in the road and saw the Fiat turn left at the next set of lights.'

'Heading towards Rutherglen at Dalmarnock Road,' she bellowed into the radio and pressed the accelerator even harder.

A light on the dashboard was flashing and there was an ominous pinging tone as Charlie approached Dalmarnock Bridge at the Clyde. Then the Renault started rattling, shaking and slowing. He had difficulty controlling the steering wheel as it dawned on him what was happening; he had a flat tyre.

As he slowed, he noticed a car fast approaching behind him. It was dark but he recognised it as a Fiat. That triggered an alarm. The first time Charlie had hosted Nat Chisholm he and his girlfriend had been driven home in the early hours in a BMW followed closely by a red Fiat. And tonight, when Charlie took a breather and a short walk, he'd noticed that same Fiat with two guys in it stationed in the car park. He'd next seen those two guys when they'd come into the private dining room after Nat Chisholm had been shot.

He did some quick and troubling thinking. One of those two guys had been taken out by Ali. Then the second one had taken a shot at Ali as he followed behind him in the dash for the kitchen. Ali had shot back at him and mistakenly blasted Malky.

This was almost certainly that second gunman.

He couldn't outrun the Fiat with the flat tyre and he'd no doubt whoever was in the Fiat would see it as their prime duty to eliminate Charlie as an accomplice of the man who'd taken out his boss.

He brought the Renault to a shuddering halt. The fallback plan, if Ali didn't get clean away through that back door, was to drive the Renault to a side street in the town of Rutherglen just across the Clyde, dump it and transfer into another second hire car, before hiding out in a discreet B n' B he'd booked in Kilmarnock some thirty miles from Glasgow, lie low there a few days, then rejoin Ali in the hideout on the farm near Girvan.

Rutheglen was literally just across the river. There lay safety if he could just get away from this dammed gunman. The Fiat was coming up fast. He had to make a quick decision.

He brought the Renault to a spluttering halt and ran across the road still in his blood-stained chef's whites which he'd no chance to discard in his flight from the pub. There was a walkway beside the river on this side. He made it to the steps down to the path just as the Fiat pulled up behind the stalled Renault. If he could just get across that river.

Sinky got out the Fiat. He'd seen the chef, still ridiculously wearing his chef's whites, run across to the pathway. He knew he had to act swiftly. The cops would be swarming around the pub, but they would also soon have checks set up across the city including the boundary here at Dalmarnock Bridge. His priority was to gun down that chef and get out.

He ran down the pathway and saw the chef ahead of him, an obvious target. He was making a steady pace and Sinky could tell he was fit. But so was Sinky who worked out every day and jogged a good distance at least twice a week. He started running and quickly made up the distance.

The river ran still, smooth and tranquil beside the path; the night was clear and still. There was a little bend in the path which gave way to a long clear stretch. Sinky stopped, brought out his handgun, bent down on one knee, aimed at the Chef's receding but clearly visible back, cocked the gun, pressed the trigger and fired.

Charlie heard a sharp crack, then he felt a stinging sensation zip past him very like that he'd experienced back in the kitchen earlier, before he saw a spurt of dust being kicked up a short distance in front of him.

He turned round and saw the guy about thirty feet behind him, just as the path emerged from the bend, bent down with a gun in front of him. The guy was readying to fire again. Charlie looked ahead. It was at least another hundred feet before the path turned again.

He could try to zigzag and outrun the guy, but fit as he was, Charlie was in his early sixties, this guy was in his twenties. His chances were not good on the pathway. He looked at the river. It was calm. Could he swim across and make it to safety? Well, there was only one way of finding out and it was better than being a sitting target here on this isolated, lonely pathway.

Sinky saw the chef take hold of the railing of the fence astride the river. He knew he was going to take his chance swimming across the river. Sinky moved the pistol slightly in his hand towards the river, aimed – this time he knew he wouldn't miss – and fired, but not before he was pushed to the ground deflecting the shot. He heard the report of the gun as he rolled to his side and felt a sharp kick to his elbow which caused him to release the pistol.

He looked up and saw a small but powerfully built young Asian woman standing over him with a badge in her hand.

'Police. Don't move. You're under arrest,' she said resolutely.

He glanced at the gun at his side, then back up at the cop.

Could he take her, get the gun and flee? But those thoughts were dashed when he heard footsteps and saw emerging from the bend several uniformed cops, radios chattering.

He was caught and with it the fast-exciting life was over. No matter how well he might be looked after inside (and if the Chisholm's reign was over with the killing of Nat, that was no longer guaranteed) he faced a very long time locked up.

'Get that gun and I'll check the river', he heard the young plainclothes policewoman command as two policemen propelled him to his feet.

For the first time in ages, Mick Sinclair felt despair and fear grip him.

Aruna looked closely down at the river from the spot where Charlie Carty had thrown himself in. She'd heard the splash. Beside her several policemen were directing their torches at the body of water, but it was impenetrable, a sheer dark mass even in the starlight. There was no sign of a wake or a disturbance. Nothing.

As the young gunman was being led away in handcuffs back along the path to the bridge, Aruna radioed in, requesting the police helicopter with its powerful beam and infra-red detector. She looked across to the other bank. Could he have made it across? The river certainly appeared calm, but she knew that was deceptive.

More uniformed police came onto the bank, and she knew the river unit and police divers would carry out a thorough search.

Her mobile lit up, it was Gerry Stratton.

'How are you?' he asked.

'I'm fine. I got one of the gunmen just as he was about to aim at Carty who's jumped into the river. I think he might have got a shot at him, because he's in the river and there's no sign of him.'

'But you're all right?'

'Yeah, I caught up with the Fiat who was parked behind an abandoned Renault. I heard somebody running along the pathway by the river to the right and just followed as a couple of patrol cars pulled up behind me, so I knew I had backup.'

'Aye, but going after an armed gunman, Aruna...' He left the rest unfinished.

'I'm fine, Gerry,' she said calmly.

'Good to hear. I'll catch up with you soon.'

She put the mobile back in her pocket and looked down again at the dark emptiness of the river and thought of what was to come next. Would Sam Chisholm be able to hold it together despite his weak sons, the Fredo's?

Or would the city, after decades of being under the dominance of one family, succumb to a frenzy of bloodletting.

As she could hear the whirring of the approaching police helicopter, Detective Constable Aruna Sharma knew that Charlie Carty was central to the demise of Nat Chisholm.

As the bright lights of the aircraft came into view, she looked again at the river, shook her head gently and thought of what was to come.

'Oh, Charlie Carty,' she said gently to herself, 'what have you left us with?'

He winced with the pain as he hit the river. It was his right arm which had copped it. As he descended sharply into the river, streams of blood flowed by. Just as he thought he was going to hit the riverbed, the water seemed to take hold of him and brought him back up.

He tried to move his limbs and swim, but the hold of the river was overwhelming, and he couldn't move, though the pain had subsided.

You were supposed to see your whole life flash back, but that wasn't happening. Just a creeping numbness in the pitch blackness around him as the river current seemed to be pushing him back downwards again.

He was stoical. He'd had a good run, and with Ali McMahon's help, he'd taken out the heir to Glasgow's gangland empire. But that no longer mattered.

He felt a gentle, narcotising warmth envelope him in a warm embrace. All his tensions, worries and cares just seemed to float away like the air bubbles leaving his mouth.

Then a lovely image of Sarah with that dazzling smile of hers appeared. He would always love her, no matter what.

He felt sleepy and drifting but knew that wherever he was going, there would always be Sarah.

THE END